Panaché
The Spirit of Life

DR CHERYL LASSEN

First Edition
ISBN: 978-0-620-79256-1

The content of this book is a work of fiction, and any resemblance to any persons living or dead is unintentional.

www.kwartspublishers.co.za

Dedicated to

Jayme-Lee, my daughter and the love of my life.

At 6 years old, she said:

*"A good dream is a bad dream, and
A bad dream is a good dream"*

At 9 years old, she wrote:

*"If there were No children,
There would be No world,
No happiness, and
No future"*

At 14 years old, she wrote a message to
all Multiple Sclerosis patients:

*"Have Faith, and
Live life to the fullest"*

I love you Jayme-Lee

About the Book

Matilda's journey begins with the knowledge of possibilities, the taming of her mind and the control of her body. The story takes you on her journey through the unknown; of her life growing up in a humble Coloured township during apartheid and her venture through the joy, pain and laughter that was the abyss of her love life. She makes one think about the parts of us that others don't and will never see, and parts of us that others will never know. The parts of ourselves, our minds and our cares that teach, admonish, criticise, are conflicting yet simultaneously belong and exist in the same person.

Her view shows the fun part of apartheid – because that was the way that she saw and experienced it: watching White kids enjoy themselves, her attempts to act as a "Play-White," of her reclassification, her defiance of the Immorality Act, her mixed marriage, heartbreak, ridicule and pre-judgement, painting these as a set of comical challenges. Challenges that were developmental necessities of life.

Her journey takes her to the heights of achievement as a global senior executive based in Europe, travelling around the world in first-class while sipping champagne. She exposes the thoughts and the depth of her existence and essence that are invisible and intangible, yet present through experiences of love, lust, trust, delight, pain and death having no beginning and no conclusion. Matilda's soul always seeing beauty meant that many times she would travel alone, within and without her body through bewildering portals and dark tunnels to soar to unimagined heights.

The deeply complex character has fun talking to her mind and to The World at large, telling tales of the past, the present and the future, guided by a prayer, 'Grazie e Dio, Lo sai che ci sono qui. Thank You, God. I know that you know that I am here.'

About the Author

Dr Cheryl Lassen has a medical degree from the University of the Witwatersrand and a science degree with majors in Physiology and Microbiology from the University of South Africa. She has numerous scientific publications in peer-reviewed international medical journals.

Growing up during the height of apartheid in a displaced minority group, she used her awareness of experiences to challenge her thinking to overcome prejudgment and discrimination. Learning the skills of self-management has allowed her to optimise and transform these experiences into international academic achievement and personal growth.

Outside of her career, Dr Lassen is a passionate pipe organist entertaining many audiences. As an enthusiastic mountain hiker, she is provided with the means of continuous development of the body, mind and spirit.

Introduction

The journey began on a flamboyant and reckless abyss of possibilities. The bottomless pit as in the Septuagint, the unfinished creation and place of punishment. These are the waters under the earth from which springs and rivers are supplied. The separation of the waters above from those below. The waters of the firmament closely connected with the underworld of lost souls. The abyss between the righteous dead and the wicked dead. Like Abaddon, the fallen angel of the abyss, the incarnation of death.

This gulf, this chasm, this realm – creates both joy and pain. A divine deity deluding the living of celebrity, and the unveiling of things not previously known. Heaven on the face of earth or power over Hades.

Matilda kneeled before the magnificent image of the Virgin Mary, the black marble Lady of the Chapel, the Black Madonna in the Einsiedeln Abbey, and began her prayer. Matilda was covered in dust and sweat having travelled miles to reach the Black Madonna, whom she hoped would provide her with salvation. Trier, on the banks of the river Moselle, was a long way away. This oldest German city, located in the southwestern part of Germany was Matilda's extramundane haven of crudition. Matilda, aware of her appearance, kneeled before the Black Madonna and prayed, 'Grazie e Dio. Lo sai che ci sono qui. Thank You, God. I know that you know that I am here.' Matilda prayed, 'How do I get out of the hole so deep and space so boundless that cannot be measured?'

Matilda waited in stillness for the answer from the Black Madonna, and continued to pray, 'How do I get out of this bottomless pit?' The hole that has no depth seemed to get deeper still. 'How is this possible?' Matilda enquired of the Black Madonna. Matilda waited again in stillness, knowing that this would be her last prayer because walking out of the sanctuary of the Einsiedeln Abbey, there would be no more prayers to the Black Madonna. Matilda prayed again, 'Grazie e Dio. Lo sai che ci sono qui. Thank You, God. I know that you know that I am here.'

Matilda imagined that she was named after Mathilde, Abbess of Essen. Mathilde remains revered to this day, kneeling before the Virgin Mary on the "MathildenKreuz", the "Cross of Mathilde", an Ottonian processional cross. Mathilde, it is recorded, travels afar benefacting a piece of land that belonged to her mother, Ida, to the Einsiedeln Abbey[1]. Matilda, while kneeling before the Black Madonna, felt the metamorphosis of her existence, of life and love. Matilda finally prayed, 'Buongiorno Dio, sono qui. Hello World, I am here.'

There was no further prayer that could be offered. Matilda slowly rose to her feet, with erect posture she turned her head sideways, took a long deep breath in, exhaled slowly and moved graciously to the grand, old, pillared, wooden door. She turned briefly, took a last glance towards the Black Madonna and walked into the abyss of her life and love.

Part One

CHAPTER 1

2015, The Promised Land

Matilda reclined in a first-class seat on the British Airways Airbus A380, sipped on a glass of champagne and elegantly thought, 'This truly is The Promised Land.' Taking each sip slowly, while listening to the heavenly sounds in her mouth, Matilda talked to the voice in the head, 'Just listen. Take a sip and be still, so that you can hear the angels singing in your mouth. Is that the sound of heaven?' Matilda mused, 'Don't swallow too fast,' she told the voice in the head, 'listen to the sound of birds singing.' Even after Matilda had swallowed, the angelic sounds lingered, and she thought again, 'This truly is The Promised Land.' She appreciatorily realised the acquiescence of this truth. As a beautifully attractive and elegant woman, Matilda was on her way to celebrate her fiftieth birthday and thought back to that which was.

Matilda remembered her birth, like it was, kicking and screaming. 'Why are they doing this to me?' the baby smiled and laughed to herself. 'Why are you screaming baby?' the baby thought and realised that perhaps that was everyone's expectation. So, the baby grew silent for a while and smiled again. Unfortunately, her facial muscles were not yet developed sufficiently to express her smile. 'Oh, that didn't work at all baby. You need to do something different,' and wondered what all the fuss was about.

'Choo, Choo, Chooooo,' the baby heard, and remarked, 'What noises are they making? There is nothing melodious being produced by these voices.' The baby knew that she needed nutrition, but they kept putting their fingers into her mouth, which automatically started a reflex sucking sound. 'These people are so strange,' the baby thought. 'I can sense the needed breast, so why are they talking incessantly? I will now scream to get closer to the breast,' and with a high-pitched bellow permeating the air, the baby screamed and finally, there was a hush.

Firmly clenched with her lips to Ida's breast, the voices resumed their relentless chatter. The baby started to smile, 'My dear mother, Ida, she is so calm and at peace with herself. I can feel this. I will be raised to be the best I can be.' Ida had provided the first step towards teaching the gift of peace and security of the body. Matilda had learned to relax every muscle, every nerve and every joint, and be at peace knowing that she would be taken care of. Her thoughts roamed freely and took on a mind of their own, 'Perhaps that is the reason they can't stop talking with no directive outcome.'

Feeling the life inside of her body, relaxed and breathing deeply, so gentle and sublime. Ida stroked Matilda's cheek, then the back of her hand lovingly, thinking how happy they both were. That moment when two hearts and minds are joined in mutual trust and love, relaxing, breathing and letting their thoughts wander unreservedly. The baby continued to smile with the knowledge that in a few weeks' time, they would be able to see and appreciate her genuine smile.

Matilda gazed out of the window as the plane became airborne off the runway at London Heathrow Airport, and thought about, "The Promised Land", with its unlimited supply of milk, having the taste of honey. Sweetness in the mouth that sometimes turns to bitterness in the pit of the stomach. The contradiction of things that cannot be accurately predicted.

Matilda's early years were spent running around with her friends in-between the sheets and clothing that had just been hung by Ida to air-dry. The washing line was in the backyard of the small purpose-built house, with its large block-bricked walls, no ceiling, tin-roof, and open light bulbs hanging from the roof in each of the four rooms. There were no bedside lamps. Matilda smiled as she thought of an article that she had read. No bedside lamps were the sure sign of the state of poverty that she grew up in. Several sisters, brothers and destitute cousins, all piled on top of each other at night on double and triple bunk beds. Matilda knew that they didn't regard themselves as being poor as they were rich in spirit. That seemed surreally likened to a vision that recurs in the mind after reading a vivid and inspiring novel, and Matilda remembered certain scenes as they occurred.

Matilda always wore old dresses and underwear that had been handed down from the older sisters. Once a year on Christmas Day, Matilda would wear a brand-new, pretty Sunday dress, new underwear, short white socks and black school shoes to church. The white socks and shoes were bought for the following school year, as Matilda grew bigger and taller each year. There was no Christmas tree, and there were no presents from Santa, as they could barely afford the Christmas meal with Christmas crackers decorating the dining room table.

The extendable dining table could accommodate ten people cramped into the four-by-four-metre living room, which was used for dining and lounging. The same dining room table was used for their homework. Matilda was always the first to sit at the table to get the best spot for her books, and always the last to leave, studying for an exam or preparing her mind for the following days' school lessons. Her father, Oscar, always reminded her, 'Matilda, you need to go to sleep now.'

Matilda remembered the date of her birthday each year, a few weeks after Christmas, as there was no present for her. The Christmas festivities had consumed all the earnings, including the double wage and bonus, that Oscar had earned in December. Matilda was always gently told by Ida, 'Next year my dear, you will get a birthday present next year.' Matilda didn't mind that her birthday passed without a birthday cake or birthday present, and waited with joyful expectation for the following year, thinking, 'I will get a present next year, and that will make me very happy.'

Each year was the same as the last. When Matilda reached high school, she realised that she was never to have a birthday cake or birthday present. Ida gave the same response in a gentle tone that soothed her longing. Matilda had the same joyful expectation in her voice when she responded to Ida, 'That's okay, Mummy.' In her teenage years, Matilda had to choke on her tears to keep her voice optimistic, when she responded to Ida, 'That's okay, Mummy,' to not cause Ida any further pain.

Pain that Ida could escape from once a year with the two youngest, Matilda and her baby brother. Matilda asked once and never again, 'Mummy, why are we going to Boksburg?' Ida responded, and the rest of them echoed the response, 'So that Mummy's asthma can get better.'

The three of them would climb into the train at Durban station. Matilda remembered every detail of those trips each year. The sound of people talking and drinking late into the night and the smell of sweat, alcohol and tobacco. Ida held the two children close to her and tried to get them to sleep so that they would not hear the drunken conversation of the passengers on the overnight train to Johannesburg. It wasn't about Ida's asthma, because Matilda didn't see the asthma. Ida could have respite, once a year away from the infliction of emotional pain.

Matilda remembered the old "rattletrap," rattling, old rickety Ford bakkie[1] that they all piled into, to pick up Ida and her newborn baby brother from Addington Hospital, on the Durban beachfront. Her eldest sister sat in the front with her father, while the rest of them piled into the rear of the van, sitting on the hard metal floor. The next Matilda remembered, was that they were back in the bakkie, this time her eldest sister sitting in the rear with the rest of them, and Ida cradling a baby in the front seat. The old Ford with its prominent and wide front single driver and passenger seat and the rear floor being a modest painted steel. No seat belts existed back then. Theirs was not a life of a mere magic-lantern show, but one filled with love and joy.

Matilda's soul always seeing beauty meant that she sometimes had to travel alone. Matilda was on the flight from London to Johannesburg where she would meet Mae, her twenty-seven-year-old daughter. They would travel together on another British Airways flight from Johannesburg to Mauritius to celebrate her fiftieth birthday.

CHAPTER 2

"Short-term pleasure, or long-term joy"

Matilda, a few weeks before her flight to celebrate her fiftieth birthday, had dreamed of smelling angels. So, overwhelmingly divine and bewildering, the smell lingered on, with flaring nostrils to inhale more of the sweet odour, while savouring the moment. The cherubim foretaste and the seraphim aftertaste. Odour and taste that cannot be separated by the mind as it diffuses into one experience.

Still in a slumber, Matilda braced herself not to dwell on her thoughts of paying for love her whole life, sometimes with money and many times with her heart. Matilda thought, 'What was it all about and does true love really exist?' Thinking about Ida's love for her, 'Yes, true love exists.' The love Matilda thought about was the confusion of desire and intimacy. The desire for wholeness, interconnectedness and interaction based on the imagination. The desire to acquire sublime physical energy that leads to divinity, which searches for the other half to satisfy the sense of self that has the capacity for love. This "desiderio estremo", the extreme desire for affection and attention. Matilda reached for her notebook on the side of the bed and wrote:

"Inner stillness of the night seeks to find me,

A one-night stand,
A three-month stand,
A twenty-year stand,
What is a stand?
A perched attitude with no further relations"

Matilda questioned herself, 'How did I get to the state of paying for love my whole life? Is love not a gift of charity? The precious present offered and available for all to enjoy?' Matilda left her bedroom, walked barefoot on the warm wooden floor to the kitchen to make herself a cup of coffee. She filled the coffee machine with water and placed a Nespresso pod into the capsule holder. She looked intently at the three neatly framed pictures that were purchased in Rome, a long time ago. The pictures hung on the double volume wall of her luxurious apartment in Eglisau, a quintessential Swiss town along the River Rhine.

The three angels with their different poses, provide insight into their distinctive individual characters. The oldest, serious angel, strumming a sitar, had the dominant position on the wall. Her expression showing her serious concern for the two younger angels. The second angel, playful and naughty, features playing a guitar – quite a worldly, modern instrument. Her mischievous smirk conveys to all, 'I can do whatever I please'. The youngest angel at the lowest position on the wall, being a pretty blonde with rosy cheeks aglow, merrily bowing on the strings of her viola, performing to bestow pure pleasure without concern.

It was that moment when Matilda realised how obsessive a thought about something can be. A repetitive string of thoughts that cannot be halted, like a runaway train. Over and over like a repetitive wave with some breakthrough short-lived thoughts, that try to interject and dominate these repetitive thoughts. These are the melancholy repetitive thoughts with their determined intention. Matilda acknowledged the effort and effortless patterns that tamed these drifting thoughts and enjoyed being for a short while until a veil of delusion settled in her mind which grew into a state of mistrusted consciousness. The thoughts of paying for love her whole life. Matilda's illusory self thought, 'me and my story of love, lust, deceit and insanity.'

'My first love,' thought Matilda. 'I was only a 15-year-old teenager, and he was the jock of high school.' Three years her senior, who all the girls threw themselves at. Well, Matilda had her standards and waited for him to ask her out on a date to the movies. The Friday night before the date was spent on a head to toe makeover - manicuring, pedicuring, washing and styling of the runaway curly hair, exfoliating and removing all kinds of unwanted hair.

Matilda had perfectly toned legs as a result of all the sports she played, and decided on a flowing skirt, drawn up on one side — sexy, but not tarty. Matilda knew how to look and act stylish. Perfection, which he fell in love with. He told her that she was the one for him and said, 'I have stopped having sex with the other girls, Matilda.' Poor Matilda, she had no idea what was being said, until a few dates later. While walking in the park, and after much kissing, as that was all that was proposed, he broke down and confessed, 'I have to tell you something very important, Matilda.' Blissful Matilda's awareness heightened, and she waited with big bright eyes. He said, 'Last week, I had sex with your best friend, Lilly.' Matilda half-smiled, took a deep breath through flaring nostrils to keep her composure and walked to get the bus home.

It seemed as though life had stopped and that every movement she made was in ultra-slow motion. Matilda felt every stride as her left heel struck the ground while rolling through to the toe, with the motion of her right leg always coordinating with that of the left, so that one foot was always in contact with the ground. She walked along West Street towards the bus stop reserved for Coloured people in downtown Durban. Matilda remained with a half-smile on her face until she reached her four-roomed, box home in the Coloured township of Wentworth, climbed into her bunk bed in the bedroom that she shared with her sisters, and sobbed softly.

Days went by with Matilda sobbing and sleeping, sobbing and sleeping. Her sister brought her sweet tea to sip on, and Ida bathed and changed her every day, without saying a word. 'They are so polite,' thought Matilda through her sobbing until she heard her father say to her sister, almost in a whisper, 'She is dying of a broken heart, we must do something.' 'Oh, my goodness,' Matilda said to the voice in the head, 'I am not dying. I am not dying. Maybe you are, but I am definitely not dying. Wake up Matilda, wake up,' she cajoled the voice in the head.

Matilda immediately sat upright in the bed, smiled into her father and sisters' serious and concerned expressions. That was when the mania, the dilemma of the consequences of depression took over. The laughter of sanity, which in itself turns into a form of insanity. The conceptualised reality of, "I am not enough," and then has to find an identity to cling to. Feeling the pangs of conflict through her solar plexus, Matilda questioned, 'How can I be in conflict with myself? How is this possible? How do I get back to normality?'

Still not knowing the answer or way out of that dysfunctional neurosis, Matilda determined to laugh her way through it, did just that. 'Ha, ha, ha,' half crying and half laughing until the others started to laugh or perhaps half cry with relief too.

Matilda's realisation was that this was the entrance into the abyss of pleasure, compassion, forgiveness and surrender where the past had no further hold. 'I can control the voice in the head,' Matilda told the voice in the head. Matilda now knew that the possibilities of achievement were limitless. This became the labour of the Spirit of her Life. Matilda thought about freedom, about possibilities and entered the awareness of desires that served or did not serve and gently started to tidy her spirit.

The fifteen-year-old Matilda could say, 'I can cope with the chatter and clutter that goes on inside of me,' and wondered the week before her fiftieth birthday, 'How did I get into this state of paying for love my whole life?' The interpersonal dance of desire for immortality, featuring the beloved, and the need for happiness fulfilled. Matilda wanted to have fun and feel young again, not realising the most intense craving, and thought of her different types of love. The multiple kinds of love that she gave, the love that she received and the love that she desired, the extreme desire that consumed her.

'Mio Angelo,' Matilda thought, 'An angel sent by God to teach me to feel my delicate existence.' The appreciation for beauty helping the soul remember its purist form. The carnality of this desire felt within the abdomen, radiated to the rest of the body with full surrender to the intensity, promising enjoyment and pleasure.

Matilda understood why the Greeks feared Eros. Those golden, Cupidian arrows pierced directly into her heart without warning, and she could not emerge as the same person again. Romantic love that is the trouble of the heart, bringing with it tears, kisses and laments. From our loving, bringing forth the inevitable pain. Matilda would need to find her way out of this pain, and she sighed, 'Mio Angelo, My Angel.'

Philia or fond sincerity experienced in the cranium as the objective interest in logic and reason. This was Matilda's twenty-year marriage to Ed, where all things were rendered divine. It was the faithfulness to daily, simple formalities, possessing nothing but possessing everything. The depth of this understanding was beyond human reach as a necessary means to happiness. Matilda and Ed shared the same values, and their feelings of love for each other were reciprocated, mutating over time into storge.

'Agape,' Matilda considered – the unconditional and selfless love of Ida, her loving family, dearest friends who effortlessly loved her and the highest form of love, the love for humanity and the World. 'The world needs more agape,' Matilda considered. Agape, the compassionate love, altruistically given without expectation. This agape enriched Matilda's life, that her life as a fifth-decade singleton was filled with peace, kindness and joy.

Matilda, like everyone else, hankered after Eros and romantic love made popular by celebrities of old and present times. Matilda had not realised that this modern construct was only one way to love. Matilda intended for the rest of her life to access the healing and fulfilling love of philia and agape. Matilda thought about how and why she had been paying for love her whole life.

CHAPTER 3

2013, The Portal

Two years before, Matilda, smartly dressed in an Italian designer business suit, crisp white shirt and an African print scarf professionally tied in a knot around her neck, grabbed her rolling suitcase and laptop bag and walked out of her bedroom. She walked past the three angels hanging on the wall and gazed at herself in the large floor-to-ceiling mirror, framed with aged-oak, leaning against the entrance hall of her apartment in Eglisau. She smiled while observing her reflection, 'Come, angels, come gorgeous. Let's go to our success,' and walked towards the lift to meet the taxi waiting outside.

Matilda was travelling from Zurich to San Francisco via London. On the long-haul flight from Heathrow, Matilda sipped on a glass of champagne with those sparkling, heavenly bubbles that make music in the mouth, as she had taken her first-class seat on the plane. Matilda swallowed slowly, picked up her book and started to read.

She read about "the Dark Portal which was the gateway between two worlds. The portal was only large enough for individuals to pass through one at a time. In order to prepare for an invasion, the Portal was widened so that armies could pour through into the unsuspecting Kingdom. Hoping to end the threat, an attempt to close the Gateway from the other end caused the structure to be damaged and destroyed with only a tear in the fabric of reality remaining. A gap was then constructed, and watchmen placed to keep watch over the remnants of the Portal. Using a magical cloak of darkness to escape detection, the clan used the rift to return to their homeland.

Hearing these tails, the Chief planned to open a number of Portals that would lead armies to new worlds to conquer. To reopen these Portals, mystical artefacts were needed and the Portal re-opened. The Chief sent forces through the Portal to end the threat once and for all so that they could continue living as before. So, the Portal was finally opened, but the Chief did not foresee the terrible price that he would have to pay. The Portals tremendous energies and his insanity led to the destruction of his people. The clans anticipating danger on the other side, backtracked through the great, dark Portal back to their homeland agreeing to make the ultimate sacrifice by destroying the Portal from their side in order to prevent the world's destruction. They managed to survive and remain in the shattered realm to this day[1]."

'Thank goodness,' Matilda thought, 'we as the human race have rightful and moral compunction.' Matilda still had the notion that she lived in a dream world of a simulated reality. A reality of invisible, unstable and elusive portals which opened and closed without warning, having no signposts to guide you into the extraordinary opening of space and time. Matilda thought about whether we are living in a simulated reverie, depicting reality, or are our conscious minds living inside a simulation of a simulation. A hyper-reality, with the inability to distinguish between existence and a simulation of realism.

Matilda was still thinking about what would happen if we ventured outside of our biosphere through one of these Portals, when her phone beeped, and a message appeared on the screen, 'Mio Amore! How r u? I miss you. Big Kiss.' Matilda smiled and chuckled to herself and replied, 'Mio Angelo, I'm OK, I miss you too, Bigger Kiss.' Matilda thought, 'How did I get into this Portal? This trapdoor leading into the unknown.'

Well, it was time to turn her phone onto flight mode so any further messages would need to wait for another twelve hours until she arrived in San Francisco. Matilda was on her way to her career aspiration, or so she thought. Closing her eyes, she recited the St Francis prayer as the plane was already at full speed on the runway to lift-off, ascent, cruise and approach into another world. A world of hope, joy and excitement. A world of limitless possibilities. Matilda, at peace with herself and the world, a sweet smile on her lips and with eyes shut, sat back in her seat thinking about another life, like *Alice in Wonderland*[2], in a contemporaneous existence.

This time she was on a plane from Johannesburg to London, six years earlier, the two business-class seats next to hers were empty. Tears ran down her cheeks as all three of them were supposed to have been on that flight together. Tasting salty tears on her lips with her tongue, Matilda remembered that flight when her husband, Ed and their eighteen-year-old daughter, Mae were supposed to be relocating to the United Kingdom from South Africa.

They had already selected an attractive, cottagey, three-bedroom house on the outskirts of Horsham in West Sussex. The house was located in the village of Christs Hospital, known for its co-educational, independent, unique day and boarding Bluecoat High School. The school was founded during the reign of King Edward VI[3]. Matilda had been offered a global research position based in West Sussex, and they had made the decision to relocate to England.

Matilda had travelled to England a few months before for the interviews and was in possession of a permanent contract for full-time employment. Matilda and Ed made their way to the consulate office of Great Britain in Pretoria, to process the family visas for their relocation. All three applications were made, and they celebrated that evening while waiting for approval.

Ed went the following day to obtain the visa's, and Mae's had been rejected, as she was already eighteen years old. Ed was told that the immigration rule was that the dependents of the parents for a residence visa should be under eighteen years old. Mae could still travel with her parents as a visitor, and they decided that she should come on the flight with them. They packed the three suitcases each weighing about thirty kilograms. They were allowed to check-in and waited to board the flight from Johannesburg to London.

Mae, on presenting her passport for the final check at the boarding gate before boarding the aircraft, was told that she was not eligible to board the flight. The family of three stood in shock, wondering what to do. Matilda needed to start work in a few days' time, so the decision was made that Ed would remain behind with Mae. They went the following day and had the necessary entry visa approved that allowed Mae to enter the United Kingdom for a period of six months as a visitor. A strange turn of events that changed their lives forever; a portal closed without warning, and no shortcut could be found.

Matilda thought about the events that led to her accepting the unacceptable. While floating in the space of infinity, she finally came to a bump, an obstacle in the path, quite like living outside the body in someone else's. She existed within the hope and the joy of the other. Matilda knew that that was when she died to live through Angelo.

It was early Friday evening, and Matilda had arrived home after a busy day at the office. She was living in England for a few months while Ed and Mae remained in South Africa. She checked for any emails from the New Jersey office, finally logged out and closed the screen of her laptop against the keyboard. Matilda thought to herself, 'What now?'

Her colleagues were going to a bar in Brighton, the party city. Matilda ambled around the house aimlessly. The house that her husband and daughter should have been living in with her. The house was quiet, and Matilda felt a loneliness that tugged at her heart. Ed and Mae had returned to Pretoria and had no firm plans to rejoin her. Matilda felt a wave of despair come over her in the big house.

In silence, she took a long, warm and invigorating bath and said to herself, 'Why not? Go to the party city and have one drink and then you can come back home.' Matilda slowly lifted her slender body out of the bath, dried herself with a fluffy white towel off the heated rail, covered her skin in a luxurious body butter and oil, the odour of mangoes, and gracefully stepped into her dressing room.

She had converted one of the bedrooms into a dressing room to die for. Mirrors, shelves, shoe racks, bag racks and dressing rails covered with glamorous and opulent attire and accessories filled the room. She chose a tight denim Bermuda shorts and a silk top to feel at ease and confident in. Matilda, wearing high, platform, wedge sandals and dangling earrings, gazed at herself in the full-length mirror and knew that at forty-two years old she did not look a day older than thirty.

She grabbed a party bag. One that is slung across the right shoulder and hangs on the left hip. Matilda threw five hundred pounds, credit and debit cards, a lipstick and tissue into the bag and walked with lightness in the air towards her black Mercedes. She knew that she would have a good night.

On the drive along the winding West Sussex country road before getting onto the motorway, Matilda started to panic, 'Oh dear! Where are you going, Matilda? Perhaps turn back, and you can have an early evening in front of the telly. Lady with a husband and daughter back in South Africa, where the flip do you think you are going?' Matilda answered the voice in the head and increased the volume of the thumping music, 'Just to have a drink with friends.' The appropriate answer propelling her car in the direction of Brighton.

She drove along Marine Parade, with the ocean on the right, wound the window of her car down and felt the fresh sea breeze softly bruise her face. It was late spring and still twilight which made for a lovely drive. She parked the car at Churchill Square, grabbed the party bag and swung it over her right shoulder. With car keys, cards and cash dangling on her left hip, Matilda smiled at her courage to come out alone.

After much chitter and chatter with her friends in Brown's cocktail bar about the crazy week, they soon became tired of talking shop and planned the next location for the evening. A nightclub, cum-bar called the Lo-lounge in the basement of the Hilton Hotel. 'Oh goodness,' thought Matilda, 'should I head back home or join this crazy crowd?' but remained silent.

Matilda, after a couple of margaritas, found herself walking down the steep stairway that led into the Lo-Lounge. A ten-pound entrance fee was paid, arm outstretched for the ink stamp on her wrist and she confidently walked in. Slightly tipsy from the margaritas, Matilda made her way to the bar counter, plonked herself half-elegantly on a wooden barstool, crossed her gorgeous legs and wondered what came next.

A handsome, dark-haired barman in his late twenties approached her, intensely looked Matilda in the eyes and asked, 'What can I get you?' giving Matilda a full teethed, honky grin. At that precise moment, Matilda no longer existed and found herself projected into the life of Angelo. It was love at first sight with all the illumination of fireworks, orchestral symphony and magical imaging that the mind could conjure.

Angelo was the answer to all Matilda's problems, and everything else seemed insignificant. Her world had a focal point and her feelings of incompleteness, of fear, of loneliness and disconnectedness no longer existed, or so it seemed. 'I deserve to be happy,' Matilda told herself and knew with certainty at that moment that this was salvation. When she looked at the bill for her glass of white wine, she saw written in ink a telephone number, a name and a smiley face, in a popular style representing a happy humanoid.

She was saved from the emptiness and loneliness and became addicted; an addiction so habitual that she could not live without the colour of the pristine perception. Matilda's world was dappled with red roses, green pastures and plenty of sunshine. Angelo became a part of Matilda's life, or perhaps death, as she peered through the world glamorously dressed and wearing rose-tinted designer glasses. "La vie en Rose[4]".

CHAPTER 4

The pangs of apartheid

It was January 1983, when the 17-year old Matilda arrived at the entrance to Sunnyside Residence, an attractive Herbert-Baker style building for female students, on the University of the Witwatersrand campus in Johannesburg. Matilda took her suitcase and handbag out of the boot of her brother's car and contemplated the broad steps which led up to the large wooden door, with a mixture of panic and amazement. Turning around to view her surroundings, she noticed the enchanting, English-style, private garden that surrounded the women's residence. The grand building reminded Matilda of the entrance to an ancient manor house somewhere in England that she had only seen on a television screen and in magazines. Matilda was attending the pre-university semester on a full scholarship from the university, and with only a fifty rand note in her purse, she would have to make do for the next few weeks.

Her large family of about twenty-two people, crammed into the four-by-four-metre living room and adjoining kitchen at Christmas lunch, were eating Ida's Christmas pudding stuffed with five cent coins wrapped in foil. Everyone at the table jokingly gave Matilda their five cent coins to telephone home from a public phone booth, when she became homesick. Her parents tried to dissuade her from attending a university some six hundred kilometres away from her hometown in Durban because they said that they couldn't afford it.

The resourceful Matilda did not understand the phrase, "couldn't afford". She was going to find a way, a path, a portal of resources to reach her ambitions. Matilda slung her bag over her left shoulder, lifted her suitcase with her right arm, and with perfect posture, proudly walked up the short flight of steps of Sunnyside Women's Residence on the main campus of the university. She opened the large, carved, wooden entrance door to the start of her adult journey.

Matilda was told that she was to share with another student, Francis von Tonder. Matilda knew that that sounded like a White Afrikaans name and walked with dread towards the room that had been assigned to her and Francis to live in for the next few weeks.

Francis, with her spiked red hair, was already there with teddies on the bed, and the rest of her personal items decked around the room. 'I hope I have space for my things,' Matilda thought as she greeted Francis. Matilda wasn't one for small talk and started to unpack her suitcase and bag. She moved some of the teddies to make space on the dressing room table for her toiletries and placed her clothes in the wardrobe which was already packed with Francis's clothes. Matilda took a photo of her high school boyfriend and placed it on the pedestal next to the bed that she would be sleeping on.

Matilda stretched herself out on the bed with eyes looking straight ahead at the ceiling in front of her. Her mind started to drift to realms of Utopia. The end of human suffering in the lost paradise of equality and respect. The anticipation of a perfect society filled with images of a predictable future that is not yet conscious.

Francis was looking intently at Matilda and asked outright with slyness in her tone, 'What are you and your boyfriend?' The dreaded question, and Matilda took a deep breath and sighed, 'Oh, we are Coloured,' and continued to stare at the ceiling while Francis had to steady herself so that she did not fall off the corner of the bed that she was sitting on.

The evening progressed pleasantly with a trip to the canteen for dinner and to meet the other pre-university first-year students. There were two boys from Matilda's high school in Durban, but she chose to mingle with the other White students and did not want to get caught up in segregation. Matilda noticed as she walked into the canteen that the Coloured students were sitting together, and so were the few Black students talking in their African language. There were two camps of Indian students, one group Muslim and the other didn't have any outfits that associated them with the Muslim religion.

'This is not what I expected,' Matilda said to one of the White students at her table during the evening meal, but nobody wanted to comment, and that was that. Matilda vowed to herself that she would integrate with all races. Matilda went to bed that night singing softly to herself, 'Home sweet home, my heart is yearning,' and started to feel the first pangs of homesickness in the pit of her abdomen.

The following day was spent registering for the chosen subjects and attending the first few lectures. When Matilda returned to her room to freshen up before dinner, she was astonished to find all Francis's things, dolls, teddies, and the like, gone. 'That's strange,' thought Matilda with another sigh, half knowing what the reason was, she went in search of Francis.

Francis was in the library reading, and Matilda asked, 'What's happened? All your stuff is not in the room? Are you leaving?' The last question was clear to Matilda, but she pretended to ask this question to ease the uneasiness that she felt. Francis shrugged nonchalantly and said to Matilda, 'I'm sorry, but I could not share a room with a Coloured person,' and went back to reading her book. The stunned Matilda, swallowed hard, focused on her chest rising and falling with each breath and tasted the bitterness of apartheid, the first of many such events in the future. After the pre-university term, Matilda didn't see Francis again as she decided to attend a White-friendly university more suitable for an Afrikaans girl from Phalaborwa.

Apartheid was in full swing. Nelson Mandela was still imprisoned on Robben Island and the Prime Minister of the National Party, Pik Botha, was in office. Immorality, Group Areas and Prohibition of Mixed Marriages Acts, discriminatory legislation by a systematic way that was formalised in law, were enforced as part of the apartheid regime[1].

By this stage, Matilda had already transgressed many of the apartheid laws, making her the great pretender or "Play-White" as they were called. Matilda had already swum many times in the Durban, "Whites-only" beach, sat on the "Whites-only" benches in the park, travelled on the "Whites-only" bus with her sister who could also pass as White, and spent Saturdays holding hands with her teenage, White boyfriend and kissing him in public. His mother was quite relieved when he had to go to the army, as conscription was compulsory for White males over the age of eighteen years.

'Thank goodness, no criminal charges were in evidence,' thought Matilda, as this would have possibly prevented her from pleading her case in the Pretoria court for the necessary documentation to allow a Coloured person to attend a

White university. The University of the Witwatersrand was subjected to apartheid laws which prevented Matilda from registering at the university for full-time study after the pre-university semester, without the exemption documentation from the courts. Matilda was shocked to consider herself as having contravened the law and thankful that she had never been prosecuted.

Matilda remembered telling a few of her gym buddies almost four decades later, about the fun part of apartheid. After an intense physical workout at the Horsham Leisure Centre gym, they would all climb into the jacuzzi to relax. One of the guys, the long-haired musician dude who didn't work and collected benefit, asked, 'So what was it like during apartheid, Matilda?' Matilda answered, 'What a lot of fun,' laughed and continued her story.

'You see, on a Friday evening when we were still kids, and after we had bathed and dressed to go out, my father would take us to the dodgem cars at the funfair. We could only watch the White kids bumping into each other and imagine that we were in the bumping cars with them. We screamed when they screamed, and we laughed when they laughed, as they collided into each other. They allowed us to watch from a distance, but we were not allowed to come close up to the edge of the track or buy tokens to get into the bumping cars, even if we could afford it.' Matilda laughed heartily out loud and looked straight into their shocked faces with, 'Really, is that true?' written all over their faces, while staring at Matilda. Matilda replied, 'Yes, that was really true! What a lot of fun we had watching White kids ride bumping cars.'

Matilda remembered that it was joy as that was what was experienced at that time. Pain only because the thinking of the cruelty made it so. Matilda smiled to herself, 'It was a lot of fun because I remember it to be so.'

When questioned by the Professor during her application interview for medical school, the Professor asked, 'So are you not angry and upset that you were deprived because of apartheid,' to which Matilda without hesitation, confidently answered, 'Anger is a negative emotion and one that I will not entertain. Yes, we are subjected to the harshness of apartheid. It is as it is, and all I want is to achieve my life's ambition to be a doctor. I want to be a good doctor one day. My spiritual teaching is to be thankful and content with what we have under all circumstances, and to accept that somehow a path will be created for us to pass through.' The seventeen-year-old Matilda continued, 'The government is the government which I cannot change, so I focus on what I can do, and that is to fulfil my life-long dream of becoming a doctor.' Matilda spoke from the heart and was told that she scored a perfect score for her interview which guaranteed a placement at the medical school.

Matilda thought after the dodgem bumping car story and that the corrupt sense of pride during apartheid was discrimination in its extreme. Matilda would say to herself every day, 'I will always regard myself as equal to others, even if they consider otherwise.'

CHAPTER 5

2014, The Swiss mountain hike

Matilda was dreaming in her apartment in Eglisau, an extraordinary opening in space and time connecting her to distant realms. Places where the magnetic field of the earth is connected with the magnetic field of the sun, creating an uninterrupted path from the sun's atmosphere 93 million miles away, when the alarm went off. It was five o'clock on a Saturday morning. 'Oh my gosh,' Matilda told herself, 'You had better get up Matilda, or you will miss the train to Zurich.' Matilda jolted out of her bed, didn't know how the day would unfold but nevertheless kept moving while saying to herself, 'Matilda, just keep moving. Do what is in front of you.' Little did Matilda realise that she would be drawing strength from those words later that day.

It was a beautiful spring day, which Matilda remembered clearly as this was her first mountain hike after recovering from a terrible flu that February. Matilda had just returned from an exhaustive trip to the United States traversing the West and East Coast three times in a week.

This was her first big mountain hike at the start of the spring hiking season. This hike was for Charlie, her last boyfriend, or rather friend and lover. Matilda knew that was the nature of their relationship; philia with the enjoyment of intimacy. 'Okay,' Matilda thought, 'Maybe if he knows that I'm fit, he will come back to me. I hope that I can get good photos to send to him via email.' This hike would prove to Charlie that she could be the physically active companion that he wanted, and Matilda really missed him deeply. After all this time, Matilda still could not snap out of the delusion of the impossible desire to have back what she had lost.

Matilda submerged her body into a warm bath thinking about how she would cope with keeping her feet warm as she had a moderate form of Raynaud's Disease. She would need to put her tights over thermal leggings, wear ski socks and put her warm feet directly into her Timberland winter hiking boots. Matilda left her apartment dressed in a thickly-padded, bright-coloured, hiking jacket, snowshoes slung over her shoulder and backpack to match. Matilda would look glamorous even on a mountain hike in the Swiss Alps.

The Swiss Alps hiking group met at Zurich's main train station under the hanging angel. The hanging angel was a big, blue, blow-up doll with a small, pudgy face and extra-large body, clad in a colourful costume with golden wings projecting from the back of the obtuse frame. This prodigious-looking creature was suspended by a cable from the roof of the main train station building. The wings defined the hideous object as an angel. Regardless that this was not an angel, the posting for the meeting place was always, "under the hanging angel at Zurich main train station".

They had to travel the two-and-a-half-hour journey by train and bus to Klosters in Graubunden for the start of the hike which began at a pace that was way too fast for Matilda. Lagging significantly behind the rest of the group, she knew that this group were much fitter than she was, and worried that she wouldn't be able to keep up at their pace.

Brian, a gentle Spanish man, waited for her to catch-up and offered to carry her snowshoes to ease her burden.

It was a glorious, crisp, blue-sky morning and one hour into the hike, Matilda stopped briefly to listen to the sound of the river flowing over the rocks, while breathing the fresh mountain air. Matilda could see the peak of the snow-covered mountain that they would need to reach. She knew that they would have to ascend the steep incline with snowshoes, as at that height the mountain would be unsurpassable without snowshoes. At the lower levels where they were, there was no snow on the ground, and the countryside was painted with multitude shades of green hues. Matilda thought, 'I will go at my own pace and put one foot in front of the other.'

Two hours into the hike, Matilda was afraid that she would not make the next three and a half hours of the hike with the steep ascent to the Hut. Matilda told the group, 'I want to turn back. I can't do the rest of the hike.' They coaxed Matilda to keep going as the next hour was a flat part of the hiking trail. Matilda braced herself for the next hour as she continued to walk through the radiant valley between the mountain peaks.

When the steep incline commenced, Matilda had to break frequently to catch her breath and recover from her aching thighs. Her heart was pounding in her chest and her legs hurt. She told herself, 'Just keep moving and put one foot in front of the other.' She would count twenty steps and rest, twenty steps and rest. Matilda knew that at this pace, she would lag very far behind the rest of the group by at least an hour.

Fortunately for Matilda, she caught up with the group who had been trudging way ahead of her. As she came closer, she saw their dilemma and Matilda smiled. They had come across a fast-flowing waterfall that they needed to cross.

They would have been contemplating the crossing for about an hour, which gave Matilda time to catch-up. Matilda, now grinning, knew that growing up climbing over the rocks at the rock-strewn beaches in Durban and the South Coast of KwaZulu-Natal, that rocks can be tricky. She said to her fellow hikers, 'Oh, this is easy for me as I know how to walk across rocks.' She made her way through a path that she felt confident to pass, treading carefully using her walking poles to guide the depth and stability of the loose stones.

Some of the others were still stranded on the other side when Matilda crossed. She knew that she could not wait to help them, she needed to gain ground as they would soon catch-up with her. So, Matilda continued along the winding ascending path and knew that she still had another few hours of the ascent to climb with snowshoes. They soon caught up with Matilda and began fitting their snowshoes on as there was by then, a few feet of snow on the ground.

Matilda was not that familiar like the rest of them with snowshoes as this was still new to her. She would need to count ten steps and rest, ten steps and rest. She was the last one to arrive at the hut. She could see them at the top of the hut enjoying the sunshine, as they looked down at Matilda taking her ten steps and resting. Once at the top, there was insufficient time for Matilda to rest, eat and have something to drink when the group wanted to descend the mountain.

There was a risk of avalanche, and they had to go back down the same route that they had taken earlier. Matilda thought, 'It had taken six hours for me to get up here and now we need to go back down through treacherous terrain and the waterfall. Matilda, wondering if she should stay the night at the hut, put that thought aside, strapped her snowshoes over her boots and followed the rest of the group down the mountain. The descent was dangerous and slippery with plenty of snow on the ground, and Matilda landed a few times on her bottom, sliding metres down off the path.

Matilda thought, 'Oh, my goodness. What if I slide again and can't stop myself from gliding over the edge of the mountain?' Matilda knew that she needed to be more careful. Fortunately, she did come to a stop during the unexpected slides as she lost her footing and took extra care, placing one foot in front of the other using her walking poles for stability and support. Matilda had gained her rhythm, but she was still the slowest of the hiking group.

Once there was no longer any snow on the ground, Matilda with relief said, 'Grazie e Dio.' What Matilda had not realised was that the melting snow had caused part of the path to be quite slippery and she had to balance carefully with her walking poles and move very slowly through those sections of the hiking trail. Brian offered, once again, to carry Matilda's snowshoes and waited for Matilda, shouting to her, 'Come on Matilda. It's getting late, we must hurry before it gets too dark. We are lagging way behind the rest of the group.' He muttered, 'The sun will be going down soon, we need to keep moving.'

In a flash of a second, Matilda now on a narrow ridge with loose stones lost her footing and was sliding on her left side down a steep section of the mountain. Matilda landed with her left elbow lodged into the side of the slope with her left leg against the surface, supporting and preventing her body from slipping further. Her right leg had no support and was dangling from her body with her right hand struggling to grab onto the side. This was futile as the melting snow was liquid and she pulled out pieces of grass and earth with nowhere to grip.

Matilda, perched in this position on the edge of the mountain, wondered if anyone would come to find her. She refrained from looking down the steep descent towards the edge of the ridge which was a vertical plunge below. She spotted a tree growing out of the edge a few metres from where she was, and thought to herself, 'If I slip any further I should aim in the direction of the tree which may break my fall.' She thought, 'Would they send the mountain rescue?' and continued to wait.

At that point, Matilda felt the space between life and death. The open space that cannot be filled. The gap before the dissolution of life. Matilda felt that her life was suspended each moment of that wait on the mountain. Matilda's right hand was still free, and she managed to reach for her phone in her right pocket, dialled the number of a colleague that knows the mountain well to see if he could help, but there was no answer. She did not have the number of the mountain rescue either, and no one was coming back for her, so she perched there suspended on the edge of the mountain too afraid to move or try to find her way up.

As she tried to grab again and again for any grip with her right hand, there wasn't anything that could provide the support she needed to hoist herself up. Matilda heard the voice of Brian, from above, 'Matilda, Matilda, where are you?' Brian had turned back to see what had happened. He said to Matilda, 'You have to try to climb back up.' Matilda replied, 'If I can't grab anything with my right hand, I can't leave my left arm.' She knew that she could only move one limb at a time making sure that the other three limbs were secured without the risk of slipping.

Matilda instinctively started to gush with her well-manicured hands into the side of the mountain to try to get a grip. An hour had passed and Brian, still waiting, said, 'Matilda you have to climb back up here.' Brian started making ridges on the side of the mountain from his end, and Matilda did the same until she could see a possible secure way up. She started to climb, and she reached a point where her strength was failing. She grabbed with her right hand onto a ridge, took her right leg and kicked hard into the side until there was enough space for her foot to take hold. When she reached a certain height, Brian was standing directly above Matilda with an extended arm and said to her, 'Come Matilda. I am secure and will pull you up.'

Matilda thought, 'How can I trust him. He is a small man, and I weigh sixty-two kilograms. How is he going to be able to pull me up?' At that moment Matilda understood what trust meant. You have to believe in the end result and visualise a positive outcome, clear all thoughts that pop into your head, and do what is in front of you.

Matilda finally took Brian's outstretched arm, and where he got the strength to hoist Matilda up, to this day, she cannot understand. 'That is the power of Divine intervention,' Matilda knew as there was no explanation for the saintly rescue. Brian pulled Matilda up and said, 'Let us go slowly across this crest so that we can reach the other side.' Matilda concentrated on every step, placing one foot in front of the other. The sun was slowly setting, and they still had the waterfall to contend with. By the time they had reached the waterfall, the rest of the group were no longer in sight and were probably about two hours ahead of Matilda and Brian.

Matilda looked at the crossing of the waterfall and thought, 'I will not try to find the easiest route where my boots don't get wet. I will try to stay alive.' So, she took a path where the water was deep but secure. With water rising into her boots, she reached the other side with soggy, water-laden boots and soaked socks. They still had another two hours to walk, 'And I have to do this with my soggy boots,' Matilda laughed to herself slushing one soggy boot in front of the other and said out loud, 'Life is beautiful. I am still alive. I am alive. Thank you, God, I am here.'

Brian and Matilda could not find their way and at one point were knee deep in a section of the ground that was covered with snow. Matilda spotted a gravel track and said to Brian, 'Let's go along this path as this has to lead somewhere where we can find shelter.' She then spotted a red arrow on a tree a distance away and with relief knew that they had found their way again.

By the time they reached the small village to get the bus, it was after nine o'clock in the evening, and this was the last bus to take them to the train station for the train back to Zurich's main station. Matilda removed her sodden boots slowly, took off her wet socks and dried her feet with a spare t-shirt from her backpack. Brian took out a pair of clean, dry socks from his backpack and gave them to Matilda to wear. Matilda, wearing Brian's dry, warm socks, put her feet into flip-flops from her backpack and laughed at the sight she looked when gazing at her feet. At that moment, she couldn't care about her appearance as she was dry, comfortable and felt a vibrancy in her body that made her smile. With mud-stained clothes from the fall and wearing socks and flip-flops, she thought silently, 'So much for trying to look glamorous on a mountain hike, Matilda.'

It was getting quite cold that evening as they waited for the bus, and by the time they reached Zurich's main station, it was past midnight. Matilda limped, taking her sore feet, sore legs and sore body forward, boldly dragging her backpack behind her with her wet boots dangling from either end of the backpack. She went straight to the taxi-rank and paid the one hundred Swiss francs to get back home to Eglisau.

Getting into the taxi and looking out of the window at the passing traffic, Matilda thought, 'How did all this happen so quickly, and how do I cope with the knowledge of coming this close to death?' She arrived home just before one o'clock that morning and climbed straight into bed as she was too tired, couldn't stand up to take a shower and was afraid of drowning in the bathtub as her body slumped onto the bed.

Matilda had to endure the flashbacks which came streaming into her mind fast and furiously. Pictures in her mind where she was dangling at the edge of the mountain, hanging loosely at the threshold between life and death. These repeated haunting flashes did not stop and worsened every time Matilda tried to shut her eyes. Matilda tried through those unsolicited interrupting thoughts, to block out the fear that arose within her body. A fear that was still present, although having the knowledge that the danger was long past.

Matilda thought, 'If this is what post-traumatic stress is like, I have to find a way out of this craziness in my mind.' The reality was that she was safely in a warm bed, yet the fear remained in Matilda's mind. Her mind was still on the edge of the Alps, waiting to meet death. The panic heightened, accompanied by sweaty palms, a trembling body and clammy skin, with her heart racing towards the impending danger. The danger was past, leaving a reality that the mind believed to be the truth. Matilda said to the voice in the head, 'Reality is now. The past is the past. Reality is now.'

It was terrifying witnessing these pictures that were flashing fiercely and uninterruptedly through her mind. Matilda knew that she had to interject these thoughts and visions. The visions of the traumatic event being re-experienced by the mind. She had to practice what she had learned in meditation. Matilda concentrated her effort on her breathing, and breathed in and out slowly, feeling the sensation and warmth of each in and out breath, until her mind was clear and there were no more flashes of that ghastly moment. Matilda had successfully emptied her mind of unwanted thoughts. She could take control again of her mind and not vice versa.

Matilda knew that she could not live in a safety box. A bullet-proof, fire-proof, water-proof and indestructible safety box. She had to find her way out of this verge back to reality.

Matilda's eyelids grew weary, and she drifted off to sleep floating on an abyss of time, all knowing without knowing it all and woke up the next morning and greeted the world, 'Buongiorno Dio. Grazie, sono qui. Hello World. Thank you, I am here.'

CHAPTER 6

Shelley Beach family reunion

Matilda was sitting on a flight from London to San Diego and sipped on a glass filled with golden bubbles. She did not smile this time as she swallowed the magical, sparkling liquid. She was on her way to present data which was the collapse of an academic achievement after years of effort. Consoling herself, she thought, 'This is only the beginning and not the end,' as she prepared to make herself comfortable in her business-class seat for the long, twelve-hour flight ahead.

Flying back from San Diego, Matilda had two long-haul flights ahead of her. The first was to London Heathrow to catch her connecting flight to Johannesburg. Sipping yet another glass of champagne, legs outstretched and leaning back in her seat, Matilda felt like being in a time-space continuum of the past, the present and the future. She would still need to take a domestic flight from Johannesburg to King Shaka International Airport in Durban, pick up a car from Avis Car Hire, and drive to the South Coast of KwaZulu-Natal to Shelly Beach.

Matilda briefly thought about the past, where she came to a bump in the road, living outside of her body in someone else's. 'Angelo. My dear Angelo. I wonder where he is in the world?' Matilda thought. Her illusory projection of time in a space where she no longer existed without thoughts of Angelo. Thoughts of hope and joy. Having seen the portal many times, then turning away in fear. 'How am I going to get my true self back?' Matilda did not know the answer to this question as there was one problem, finding the deceptive portal of compelling reconnection.

Well, she had a few days to look forward to with her father, sisters and her younger brother and their extended families. After these two long flights and the domestic transfer, Matilda drove two-and-a-half-hours to the big family reunion at a holiday resort in Shelley Beach.

It was May 2014 and twenty years post-apartheid. Matilda remembered the last time she was in Shelley Beach in the late eighties when she was still a "Play-White". It was the only way she, her husband and daughter could rent the "Whites-only" holiday house and swim in the "Whites-only" beach with the large outdoor kiddies paddling pool. 'That was an eternity ago,' thought Matilda, and it would be interesting to see what had changed after all these years. Thinking about the cruelty and ignorance of apartheid, certain feelings stirred in Matilda. Feelings of being exiled as an outcast, as the ugly duckling that strives to continue, no matter what. A time when her soul wished to speak its truth while remaining silent to prevent being regarded with suspicion. The pretence of it all.

Matilda had a sense of relief and anticipation. Relief that the trip to San Diego had gone well. On the last evening, they danced in a nightclub in the Gaslamp district to shake off the hope of what could have been, as their bodies gyrated till the wee hours of the morning. What a night!

Now, this was a different time and place to spend with family. Matilda knew that all she could do over the next few days was to show love and be non-judgmental. This was the test to practice these two virtues. Tolerance at a high level would be required with her large and diverse family, with their contrasting personalities. Attitudes and opinions being vastly different from that of Matilda's, and she would need to demonstrate patience to these dissimilarities. Matilda intended to show love, warmth and tolerance to even the most extreme irritation or perceived irritation. These would be the thoughts to guide her over the coming days.

Climbing into the driver's seat of the Avis car after placing her luggage into the boot, Matilda remembered, 'This is South Africa, I had better not place anything on the car seats,' and placed her mobile phone into the holder on the side of the car door, and her handbag securely on the floor behind her legs. This was the safety rule to prevent smash and grab attacks from opportunists when stopping at traffic lights. She was looking forward to the love and kindness of her extended family and hugging and kissing each of them. With only good, joyful thoughts, Matilda turned the radio louder and sang along, 'What a Wonderful World[1].' A huge smile was reflected back at her from the rear-view mirror, as the cheerful Matilda followed the road ahead.

As Matilda arrived at Shelley Beach Resort and climbed out of the car, she laughed to herself as she could hear the noise coming from the swimming pool area. Coloured kids screaming and having fun. 'Oh dear,' Matilda thought, 'during apartheid this would not have been possible,' and made her way towards the loud happy sounds of the ecstatic and excitable family, picnicking on the lawn next to the pool. Kids and parents were frolicking in the swimming pool. Her family had taken over the entire pool area, with no space for any of the other residents.

They screamed and shouted at each other as if they were many miles apart, and only yelling would get their voices heard above the other shrieks. Matilda laughed again to herself, 'My family have taken over this resort. This would not have been possible during apartheid.' Matilda knew that during apartheid even if they were allowed to be at a resort like this one, she would have judged them and made sure that they were as quiet as mice, so as not to disturb the "superior" White people.

'How do you keep ten kids in a swimming pool quiet?' and Matilda laughed again. The prejudice against the way that Coloured's behave had always bothered her. When Matilda looked at it from her current perspective, they were behaving well, there were no disagreements, everyone was happy to spend time with each other and enjoying a lovely warm subtropical day. That time of the year when the humidity was lower and not as scorching hot as the middle of the summer.

As Matilda walked closer and they saw her, everyone erupted with hand-clapping, and their faces lightened up with smiles that she had arrived safely to be with them. A warm tingling passed over Matilda's body, and although exhausted from the long journey and feeling jet-lagged, not knowing what time of the day it was, she couldn't show it. Everyone was excited to talk to Matilda, to tell her their latest stories about happenings in their lives and share a hug. They were showing Matilda how the kids had grown since she last saw them.

Matilda embraced all the love and kindness that she experienced at that moment. Little did they know that Matilda had been travelling for over thirty hours flying from San Diego, via London, via Johannesburg to Durban and driving herself the over two-hour drive to be with them. Most of them had not been on a long-haul flight so had no intimation as to how the jet-lagged Matilda felt, but still, Matilda did not show or mention her tiredness to them. The imperative being, that Matilda was physically there with them, although her body clock was in a different time zone.

The "braai" meat and "boerewors" was on the charcoal grill and all the salads, bread-rolls, mieliepap and home cooked tomato-sauce, the "chakalaka," was laid out on the table[2]. They were serving themselves when someone shouted in a heavy Wentworth, Coloured accent above the others, 'Hey, Maatiiilda, I will diiiiish for you. Whaat you wunt?' Another called out to Matilda, 'Aunty Maatiiilda whaat mindrel do you wunt to driiiink?' "Mindrel", was the term for a soft drink in Durbanite English. This was part of the culture to have lots of food and enjoy each other's company. Matilda's family drank alcohol in moderation compared with many other Coloured families. There is a South African saying, "So dronk soos 'n Kleurling-onderwyser", "As drunk as a Coloured school teacher". Matilda felt it a privilege to be in a family like hers who was very respectful and showed each other so much love and kindness.

While eating a braai lamb chop, Matilda heard a few rumbles and strained to take notice of where the unique engine roar was coming from. It sounded like motorbike engines, like Harley Davidson motorbikes. Not one, not two, not ten and as the engine's distant resonance became closer and louder, the sound of hundreds of revved up Harley Davidson engines filled the air.

'What's going on?' Matilda enquired and was told that there was a Harley Davidson Rally in Shelley Beach that weekend. 'Wow,' thought Matilda, 'I wonder what a post-apartheid, Harley Davidson rally would look like?' Matilda remembered witnessing big White men with long hair and crazy biker outfits with their White girlfriends on the back seat. 'Perhaps they should have called it back then, a "Whites-only" Harley Davidson rally,' Matilda mused to herself.

Very early the next morning, on hearing the rumbling of the engines, Matilda knew that the Rally was underway. Matilda went to the main street to watch the procession, joined in the applause and shouted with the other spectators, as the bikers drove past. 'This is interesting,' thought Matilda, 'and what a transformation.' It was truly an integration she had never seen before in South Africa. An integration of White guys, Black guys, Indian guys, girls, ladies, women, and every colour and creed represented. Fat ones, thin ones, crazy looking ones, normal looking ones, business types, executive types, Rastafarians, hippies and everyone out to enjoy the Harley Davidson festival. Tents were erected in the town with all kinds of activities including beer tents, wine tasting tents, various food tents, organic products on sale and charity donation tents. People mingling in-between all the activity, enjoying the good weather and fun atmosphere. The Rally, Matilda was told was a charity event with all the proceeds to be donated to various charities across South Africa.

'Things have certainly changed,' thought Matilda as she had wondered what she would find when she reached Shelley Beach. Standing at the spectacular events in front of her, Matilda thought again about the last time she was in Shelley Beach and had to go to the "Whites-only" beach acting as if she was a White person, hoping that her hair would not get wet. 'Oh, my hair would go back home to its natural curl, and that would certainly have exposed me, right?' Matilda laughed at the absurdity of apartheid.

The next stop after watching the Rally was to venture down to the previous, "Whites-only" beach. Relaxing, listening to music and swimming, Matilda had no worries about her hair going back home when wet and returning to its natural soft curl. Matilda was a good swimmer and was able to enjoy a blissful swim in the warm Indian Ocean. The kids and young adults went to hire canoes in the river, which was also not allowed during the apartheid era and Matilda was enjoying this admiration of the fabulous effort that South Africans had made over the last two decades.

They enjoyed cocktails at the bar with a warm, friendly, welcoming service, which was a truly uplifting experience. Matilda relished the wonderful time together with her family, and as in her family, they had to have "CODESA³". CODESA actually stood for the nineteen South African groups that were represented at the Convention for a Democratic South Africa, the intense negotiations to end apartheid from 1990 to 1993 under the De Klerk government.

Okay, "CODESA" was the colloquial term Matilda's family used jokingly for a gathering of the main members of the family for a meeting to air their views under the chairmanship of the head of the household, Matilda's father, Oscar. The old man wanted his "chewldren," he would pronounce in his Transkei accent, around him and so gathered them together after breakfast on the last day of the holiday, to dispel any rift between the family members. Oscar sounding like Nelson Mandela opened CODESA with, 'Maa deeaar chewldren. Weee shood orll gert allloong. Leets torck now.'

'Okay,' Matilda thought, 'I do understand his view as he wants everyone to get along with one another.' He wanted each of them to express themselves to the others and use the opportunity to expose any rift brewing in the background of the politeness. Matilda was not aware of any disharmony, and nevertheless had a good understanding of where the meeting was heading.

During the discussion, Matilda asked one of her sisters after she had offloaded all her quandaries onto the rest of them, 'Do you think that you have a hard life?' To which her sister replied, 'Matilda, of course I have a hard life,' while looking around at the rest of the family for confirmation of this truth. Matilda paused before responding, 'Well, if you think that you have a hard life, then you have a hard life,' and paused before continuing, 'However, if you think that you have the best life in the whole world, then you will have the best life in the whole world.' Life progresses in that way which Matilda without a shadow of a doubt believed to be the case in her life. Her sister had difficulties, but at that present moment, she did not have a hard life. 'Perhaps,' Matilda thought, 'She had the belief that she had a hard life and that her life would always be difficult in the future.'

Matilda looked at her sister and said, 'Can you change that belief to imagine that your life is a good life?' Matilda's sister had a strange, mystified look on her face and frowned in disbelief. Her face said without words, 'This is not possible.' How could she go through life if it was not a hard life? Matilda was not letting this opportunity go and said, 'Well, if you believe that you have a hard life then you have a hard life. I would encourage that you change that belief.' Matilda knew that her words were falling on powdered, dry earth and there wasn't any watering that could be done to help it to grow, so Matilda had to let it be.

Matilda thought back to a time when she believed that she was ugly and fat; two untruths that only existed in her mind. Matilda knew the effort that she had to make to alter that belief. She could now appreciate and embrace the truly attractive woman that she was. Matilda wished that she could be of more help to her sister, but had to remain silent on this matter.

One of her other sisters with a high emotional tendency started to cry for no obvious reason that Matilda could understand. Matilda noticed that the others were getting irritated and reminded herself, 'This is where one has to exercise tolerance. Allow someone else's opinion or behaviour to be the way they are experiencing things.'

Matilda lightened up the discussion to neutralise the situation without deriding the tension. She thought to herself, 'I don't think that it ever goes away, but that's not the purpose of CODESA.' Matilda addressed her family, 'Everybody has their opinion and unique behaviour, so let's be tolerant and show love. That's all we need to do,' and stood up to give her crying sister a loving hug, still without any knowledge of the reason for the tearfulness. Matilda knew that there was little she could do until there was an opportunity to encourage progressive thinking. It was satisfactory for that moment to behave in a loving and non-judgmental manner.

Nevertheless, the family had fun and a joyful time together, which was the remarkable part of the family reunion holiday at the "Whites-only" Shelly Beach Resort. At the end of the few days, when everyone had to go their separate ways, they could truly embrace one another with tears in their eyes, telling each other how much they loved and cared for one another. Matilda recognised that her life was filled with love and kindness and felt agape. Matilda spoke aloud to herself, 'Grazie e Dio, Thank you, God.'

CHAPTER 7

The high school boycott

It was a cool morning in 1980, and Matilda was dressing into her high school uniform of a plain, white, long-sleeved, cotton shirt, striped tie in a knot around her neck, and maroon above-the-knee pinafore dress. Matilda was putting on her long-sleeved blazer when someone in the house turned on the radio and increased the volume. Matilda strained her ears, tilted her head with quizzical eyebrows, and tried to catch what was being broadcasted.

'University students from many universities across South Africa were boycotting. Students of all population groups across the nation were sitting on the lawns and steps of the universities and refusing to attend any lectures.' Matilda continued to pay attention to the broadcast on the radio, ' . . . and, now the high schools in many large towns were following suit.' It seemed as though high schools across the country were joining in on the boycott. Matilda didn't even really know what the word "boycott" meant. The broadcast continued, 'Black school children are out of classes and university, and college student unrest has led to many schools being shut down.' The students and pupils were making demands while the apartheid government promised reform.

The police were now also out as violence erupted with bitterness and alienation.

Matilda wondered how this would affect her as she needed to attend all her lessons during these last few years of high school to obtain top grades to achieve her ambition and dream of becoming a doctor. She had been working so hard up to that stage with straight A's in biology, physical science and mathematics, and she was sure that her grades would secure a placement into the medical school of her choice. She was already the youngest prefect in school, the class monitor and chairperson of the Science Society on top of her piano studies and performances in the National Eisteddfods.

Matilda gazed at her reflection in the mirror. She was an attractive teenager with good features and a fit body. She hated her curly, unruly hair. Nothing was going to distract Matilda as she said to herself while still looking at her reflection in the mirror, 'Yes, you will be head-girl in the final year of high school and go on to medical school.' With these thoughts, she grabbed her canvass bag of school books, took the sandwiches of chicken mayonnaise that Ida had freshly prepared and wrapped to keep in their freshness, and placed them into the heavy haversack before leaving home. She took the fifteen-minute brisk walk to a year of turmoil and uncertainty for her future.

On arriving at Fairvale High School on Tarrer Road in Wentworth, the Coloured township that bordered the Whites-only suburb of the Bluff and bordered the Indian suburb of Merebank in Durban, she found herself in the frenzy of the crowd shouting and screaming anti-apartheid slogans. 'Amandla[1],' shouted the leader of the group numerous times, with the crowd responding, 'Awethu[2],' believing that power belonged to all people in South Africa. The mob then erupted into song, 'Justice shall prevail, justice shall prevail, justice shall prevail someday. So, deep in my heart, I know that I do believe that justice shall prevail someday.' Another group were shouting, 'The truth will set us free,' and, 'Black is beautiful.' The last phrase was forbidden by apartheid. Anti-apartheid banners were swaying from left to right held high by the crowd. Matilda joined the protestors and the boycotting pupils of her high school from that day on and for many months to come.

Trying to study from her textbooks while sitting each day on the lawn of the sports field at Fairvale High School was quite distracting for Matilda. She had questions about the subjects that she was trying to study but was unable to access any teachers if she was to continue her participation in the boycott. Matilda feared for her final year ten exam results. She spoke to no one during the day and tried as hard as possible to concentrate her attention on memorising her school work and trying to figure out for herself some of the difficult mathematic equations and problems. This was certainly not optimal for an A-pass which she needed.

Some of the pupils were smoking weed in the far corner of the field, while others played football, tennis and other sports. Some were also hanging out with their girlfriends or boyfriends, making out in public. Matilda wasn't interested in any of that, as she had by then recovered from her heartache.

The boycott by the African National Congress was declared a success only a week before the end-of-year exams, and all students and pupils were encouraged to sit for their exams. Matilda only managed to achieve a B grade for mathematics which was her strongest subject. There were too many gaps in her knowledge, and she sobbed all the way home, disappointed in her performance. Matilda consoled herself, 'Well, at least there is still year eleven and twelve to get through.' She knew that she would have to make a huge effort and spend her summer holidays with her books. All due to the corrupt sense of the White man's values.

Matilda remembered reading about pride as one of the seven cardinal sins and started to search for opposite words to neutralise her feelings of anguish that had built up inside of her. She reminded herself every day, 'You have to get into medical school, Matilda.' These were the quality of Matilda's thoughts with the knowledge that she could control the voice in the head. This Matilda knew, was essential in life and stayed focused on her goal. Every day she would visualise herself in a white doctor's coat with a stethoscope dangling from her neck. Matilda prayed, slumbered, slept, chewed, ate, walked and talked, always considering a successful outcome. She would fill her mind with thoughts of equality and respect to neutralise the thoughts of worry about what apartheid may rob her of. She was not going there in her mind. She thought of hopeful expectations, finding the path to achievement and kept herself motivated by a strong, confident belief in her life-long dream.

So, as the year was coming to a close and the Christmas holidays loomed, Matilda would use the time to catch-up. She filled the gaps in her knowledge and eased into the next year of high school.

CHAPTER 8

1983, Medical school

During the pre-university semester, Matilda received the news that she had been accepted into medical school. Matilda felt an intensified sense of reprieve after the long wait for this exciting news, albeit knowing that there were many years of study ahead of her. She had to leave Sunnyside Women's Residence as there was not enough space for non-White students at the residence and ended up spending the first few months of medical school in a residence in Soweto[1], the largest black township in Johannesburg, before a place could be found for her back at Sunnyside Residence.

Matilda was back at Sunnyside Women's Residence in Braamfontein by the middle of that year. She needed to find the closest church to attend. It was seven thirty in the evening, with half a year of first-year behind her, when Matilda walked into church for the mid-week service. Greeting her at the door was the firm handshake of a lanky, tall, red-faced, blue-eyed teenager. As she took her seat in the congregation, the hymn, 'Just as God leads me I would go, I would not ask to choose my way,' was being sung. Matilda said a short prayer, 'Thank you, God, as I had no idea how I would get to service this evening.'

Earlier that evening, Matilda waited at the entrance of Wits[2] University in Braamfontein, but nobody arrived for her. A fellow senior student had been driving out of the university and saw Matilda waiting, wound down the car window and asked, 'Do you need a lift somewhere?' It turned out that he was heading in the same direction as the church on Church Street. He told Matilda that Church Street was a very long street probably a few kilometres long and that she would need to know which part of the street the church was on. Matilda had no idea where she was going, but confidently said, 'Start at the one end, and I will tell you when to stop.' Matilda assured him that she would see the emblem of the church and that they would find it. As she sat in the service that Wednesday evening, Matilda knew that she had found her divine sanctuary in the church, where she met Ed, her future husband.

It was about a year later that Ed asked Matilda on a date to play a game of squash. Once they had started dating, it was kept a secret, as Ed, being White, was afraid that his parents would object and not approve of his relationship with a Coloured girl. However, after a few months, he broke down and confessed to his mother, who to his surprise was supportive. She said to him, 'If you are happy my boy, then I am happy too.' She later told his father when he arrived home from work that day.

That evening Matilda was in a state of shock as she opened the door of her hostel room, to find Ed and his father standing outside the door. His dad immediately gave Matilda a big hug and said, 'Everything is going to be okay,' while Matilda with tears dripping onto his shoulder, said, 'Thank you, thank you.' Matilda received so much love and kindness from Ed's parents that all she could say each day was, 'Thank you, thank you, thank you.'

Matilda was living on a meagre allowance from her parents and hardly had much to eat each day, which usually consisted of baked beans on bread or Provita biscuits with peanut butter to sustain her. From then on, a hot meal was delivered every evening by Ed from the evening meal that his mother had cooked. Matilda also joined the family at the dining table for the Sunday roast lunch every week after church.

Matilda had to use her skills at being a "Play-White", as she and Ed would visit the lakes and gardens around Johannesburg, walking hand in hand in public. A happy time for them to enjoy at a stage of life, of potential attainment in complete defiance of the apartheid laws. Ed's parents would call ahead at a restaurant to make sure that they accepted the patronage of Coloureds. Matilda could not suppress the feelings of inferiority that surfaced during this display of demeanour.

Matilda remembered her first week of medical school, six months before meeting Ed. It was the peak of the summer season with temperatures way into the early thirties. Matilda dressed in a pair of shorts and cotton t-shirt, boarded the bus from the residence in Soweto for the hour drive to the main university campus in Braamfontein. The medical school was located in Parktown next to the "Whites-only" university hospital. The first year of medical school was, however, at the main university campus in Braamfontein. Matilda worried how she would cope now that she found herself, the palest person, in a student hostel for Black male and female students behind the largest hospital in the southern hemisphere in Soweto, Baragwanath Hospital. This residence was like being in prison. There was only one gate which was heavily protected by security guards, barbed wire and electric fencing surrounded the building.

Each morning the resident students would board the bus provided by the university to get them to the main Campus in Braamfontein. The long drive that, if Matilda was lucky to have a seat, provided her with a sense of relief away from the humiliation of being pressed and touched inappropriately by some of the male students. The male students would comment that they had not come that close to a non-black girl, which made Matilda squirm. Matilda tried not to think about the pushing and shoving hard against the back of her body. On those long commutes into the campus, all she focused on was her dream and studies to complete medical school.

This was a prison of the body and the mind, as the gate was shut for the weekend and Matilda could not escape as it was too dangerous to venture outside the residence. Respite came on a Sunday morning when one of the members from the church would come and fetch her for the service in Eldorado Park, a Coloured residential area twenty minutes' drive from the residence. Only students who had cars provided by their wealthy parents were able to drive out of the residence and thus escaped the confined captivity.

The six months of the prison-like existence, forcibly confined and denied freedom of movement, exposed Matilda to the harshness of apartheid that she was to experience through the eyes of her Black best friend, Dora. Dora didn't arrive back at the residence one late evening, and by the next morning, Matilda knew that something had happened. Dora had an examination and would not simply absent herself, so Matilda went to investigate. Her first place of call was the faculty office, where it was confirmed that Dora had not presented herself for the examination.

Matilda worriedly called a few of Dora's friends to find out where she could have visited the previous day. One of Dora's friends confirmed that she had taken the bus to downtown Johannesburg to have late lunch with her boyfriend. 'Oh dear,' thought Matilda, 'Dora may have been picked up by the police for being in the streets of Johannesburg after sunset,' as it was forbidden for Black persons to be in the streets after sunset. Matilda took the bus to Hillbrow Police Station, to obtain confirmation that Dora was indeed in prison. She had been picked up and put into a van that collected Black people that were still "loitering" in the city after dark. These apartheid laws were passed to control the movement of Blacks, especially in urban areas.

The police had brought Dora and her boyfriend to the Hillbrow Police Station where she was being kept in a cell. Matilda enquired, 'Can I bring her clean clothing and food to eat?' which was abruptly denied by the White officer. Matilda had to wait ten days before she saw the distraught Dora in her now bedraggled dress that she had been wearing for the past ten days. Matilda gave her friend a kind hug and took her back to the residence to have a hot shower and a warm meal.

CHAPTER 9

The mixed marriage

Matilda, kneeling in intense prayer before the shrine of Saint Andrew, the patron Saint of Scotland, in the Saint Mary's Metropolitan Cathedral in Edinburgh, smiled gently and prayed. The Scots believe that they are descendants of the Scythians on the shores of the Black Sea, now Romania and Bulgaria, and were converted to Christianity by Saint Andrew[1]. Matilda was attending a scientific meeting in Edinburgh and could not waste the opportunity to visit this marvellous Cathedral steeped in history.

Kneeling before the shrine, Matilda thought of the simple, purpose-built church in the Coloured township in Wentworth, Durban, where she and Ed were married. Flashes of her wedding day some thirty years previously dazzled before her. The church in Durban was a long way away and eons ago. Matilda thought, 'Space and time are illusory as it feels like yesterday.' The passage of time that seemed to stand still in her mind.

Matilda clad in a white, taffeta and lace wedding gown walked down the aisle on the arm of her father, to the sound of J. Clark's Trumpet Voluntary, played on the organ by her eldest sister. Ed, with cut and blow-dried hair, looked dapper in his black suit, white shirt, cumber band and bow tie. He took Matilda off her father's arm, and they strolled together down the last few steps to the front of the altar to receive their wedding blessing. The choir mainly comprised of Matilda's family, sang, 'Who shall separate us from the love of God.' Nothing would separate Matilda from the love of God, although the marriage ended twenty years later.

The only attendees from Ed's family were one of his three brothers, his mother and father. The rest of the family were too embarrassed to attend a mixed marriage wedding in a Coloured church rubbing shoulders with those that they perceived to be inferior members of the human race. Their perception of their superiority would not allow them to show compassion for their younger brother, uncle and cousin. They could not express their unconditional approval of Ed's happiness and joy. Matilda said to herself, 'What else is there to do?' as her joy would not be mired by the ignorance of others.

As for Matilda, her whole "fandamily", as they jokingly re-ferred to the large CODESA clan, were there to enjoy and celebrate with her and Ed. 'Oh, so it was still apartheid,' Matilda laughed out loud thinking back to the picture of her exit from the disadvantaged home clad in a puffy wedding dress. The majority of the Coloured community came to see the spectacle of the "White" wedding. They teased, 'Here comes the Princess, wave to us, wave to us.' The children in their flimsiest clothes ran barefoot with right hands raised above their heads, rotating their elbows left and right, in the gesture of the royal wave while running behind the 1920 Ford convertible, hired for the wedding and driven by the White man who owned the vehicle. The poor, screaming, unkempt children followed the classic Ford behind Matilda and Oscar for the one-kilometre drive to the church.

The year before the wedding, Matilda was first introduced to Ed's eldest bother's family at their home in Rustenburg, a small boere dorpie stuck in the White superiority of apartheid. She had to endure the humiliation as it was spread throughout the village that Ed was bringing his "Coloured" girlfriend to visit.

Prim and proper Matilda sat in the lounge with Ed and his parents as troops of people, led by a plump, plain-faced lady, started marching like penguins in single file from the front door, through the lounge where they sat, into the kitchen. Every fifteen minutes or so, a new penguin troop would appear, sometimes with a mix of some of the ones that had already come to take a peek earlier and wanted a second stare at the freak that Ed had brought with him.

Matilda sat in stillness and silence during this procession with a calm, dignified smile on her face, as this was to be expected. She had only agreed to the visit to please Ed's parents who sat silently with embarrassment on their faces, as the penguin procession always led by the plump, plain-faced lady continued throughout the afternoon.

More than ten years later, Matilda and Ed were visited by a young couple in Pretoria, where they lived at the time. The girl was White and the boy, Coloured. They said to Matilda and Ed, 'We want to get married and need some advice from you. How do you cope with being in a mixed marriage with all the discrimination?' Matilda and Ed freely shared the joy and pain of being in a mixed marriage.

During the course of the evening, Ed enquired into the background of the girl. She was the daughter of the plump, plain-faced leader of the penguin march to scrutinise the "freaky" Matilda, those many years previously in Rustenburg. Ed and Matilda gave each other knowing glances but said nothing so as not to create any awkwardness. Matilda and

Ed were always polite and subtle in communication and in company.

In order to be married to Ed in South Africa, Matilda had to endure even further humiliation by being racially reclassified. The Prohibition of Mixed Marriages Act, Number 55 of 1949 was an apartheid law that prohibited marriages between "Whites and non-Whites". This was one of the first apartheid pieces of legislation to be passed during the National Party's rise to power in 1948. The Group Areas Act apportioned the four racial groups, White, Black, Coloured and Indian to different residential and business sections. This meant that non-Whites could not live in the developed and affluent parts of the cities and towns which were reserved for Whites.

There was, however a provision in the law for the reclassification from one racial group to another, under certain restrictions and requirements which would need to be met. Matilda had to be reclassified from a "Coloured" to a "White", in order to be married in South Africa.

This meant a trip to the professional photographer to take front portrait and side photographs in colour, to see the shape of the nose and the colour of the skin. Matilda had to collect sworn affidavits signed at the police station from her White university friends acknowledging that she could be considered and conducted herself as that of a White person. They had to verify that her behaviour could be regarded as that of a White person. And finally, Matilda had to present herself for the dreaded interview at the Department of Home Affairs in Johannesburg, conducted by another plump, plain-faced lady. She turned out to be the mother of a colleague of Ed's and a patient that Matilda treated many years later in the university hospital that Matilda was working in.

Matilda waited for the dreaded question, 'So, kan jy Afrikaans praat? So, can you speak Afrikaans?' Matilda hoping that this would not be a stumbling block answered in her finest, Durbanite, White-twanged English, 'I can fully understand Afrikaans as Afrikaans is compulsory as a second language at school. I grew up in an English-speaking part of Durban, and although I can understand Afrikaans very well, I cannot speak Afrikaans fluently.'

It all happened so quickly from that point. Matilda was shoved into a room to have her fingerprints taken, and a new birth certificate issued that declared that the race classification, "Coloured", had been changed to "White" population group. Matilda's identity number was also changed for the numerical coding to reflect that she was a "White" person. The new identity document was to be sent in the post.

Matilda had made sure that her photo looked like a White person. She had stayed out of the sun to keep her olive skin as pale as possible and applied a heavy, pale foundation on her face. She also made a trip to a very good hairdresser who put blonde highlights in her hair and pulled very hard with a round brush during the hot-air blow-dry to straighten her hair, ensuring that there was not one strand that was left with a kink in it.

Matilda was astonished that in one day, she didn't have to Play-White any longer and if requested by the police when walking in a "Whites-only" park or a restaurant that only allowed Whites to dine, she would be permitted to enter. This happened all in one day. Matilda chuckled at the absurdity of it all and continued her pursuit of becoming a doctor.

When Matilda and Ed would interact with other White people, she was often asked, 'Oh, where do you come from?' They were too polite to ask, 'What are you?', like Francis did, as that would be too obvious as they could clearly see that Ed was White. So, the questions, 'Where do you come from?' or 'Where did you grow up?' were used instead. The follow-up question was, 'What school did you go to?' These questions were heavily loaded with the inquisitiveness to be able to put a person firmly into one of the four population classifications.

Matilda always smiled and responded in her best White-twanged English articulating every syllable, 'Oh, I grew up on the Bluff,' which was a lie, as the Bluff was the White suburb and Wentworth was the Coloured township that bordered the Bluff. But, Matilda was not going to give them the satisfaction of whispering to each other later saying, 'I told you that she was Coloured.' Matilda was not going to give them that pleasure. So, the second loaded question always followed directly after the first and Matilda would reply, 'the school on Tarrer Road.' This confused them because sections of Tarrer Road were in Wentworth and the road continued into the White section of the Bluff.

CHAPTER 10

Love of my life

Matilda felt that she blinked and was now in her fourth year of medical school. She was attending her Obstetrics and Gynaecology training at Coronation Hospital, a hospital reserved for Coloured people when she realised that she had missed her period. Matilda and Ed had been married for about six months at that stage. As Matilda walked into the Obstetrics ward to deliver her twenty-sixth Coloured baby, she had a sinking feeling and flutters in her stomach. 'I can't get pregnant now,' thought Matilda. 'I had only planned to have my children after I was qualified,' she told herself. Well, she had definitely missed her period for almost two weeks and walked towards the ultrasound room. Requesting that one of the sonographers perform an ultrasound of her abdomen, Matilda had the first look at what was beating and growing inside of her uterus. Mae was on her way into the world.

Matilda ran up the two flights of steps to the telephone that was on the wall. This was the only telephone that they were allowed to use long before the days of mobile tele-communication. Matilda was breathing heavily and out of breath when she called her husband. Ed answered the phone and Matilda said, 'I have some news to tell you.' Ed was waiting with bated breath on the other side of the phone-line as Matilda continued, 'I am pregnant Ed.' Ed screamed with delight in his voice, 'That is fantastic. When are you going to be home so that we can celebrate?' Matilda's heart sank further. He was so happy and excited, and all she felt was that her life would change forever and thought, 'How the heck am I going to cope with finishing medical school and raising a child?' Were her dreams of becoming a doctor going to materialise?

Matilda and Ed entered the smart private hospital in Parktown for their regular check-up with the gynaecologist. Ed had good medical insurance, which afforded them private medical care. The doctor took one look at Matilda and said as directly as he could, 'Stop this now Matilda. Stop this immediately. You need to start being happy and excited that you are going to be a mother.'

Matilda got such a shock that she immediately snapped right out of her melancholy and smiled at both men. Both of the men stared at her with concern written all over their faces. Matilda smiled and said, 'Of course you are right. I will stop this nonsense immediately,' and so she did. Matilda started to feel the first twinges of excitement and privilege of the gravid state that she was in. Thinking to herself, 'Strength comes from above.' She had to control her thoughts and only think of a happy time when the baby arrives. Medical school was uncertain as there was no pro-vision at that time for pregnant students.

Over six months pregnant, Matilda arrived at the med-ical school's administration office the following January, a few days late for the registration after her supplementary exams. Matilda thought that she should wait for the results of the exam before she could register. She had failed the microbiology exam at the end of her fourth year and had a re-write in January. So, here she was, a proud fifth-year medical student, and entered the administration secretary's office. Matilda was immediately blown off by the secretary, who shouted and squealed, 'You don't even belong at this university. You are merely a waste of our time and students like you are just washouts.' Matilda didn't hear the rest of it as she ran out of the office towards the toilets, crying profusely and sobbed her heart out.

With both hands on either side of the basin, tears dropped into the open basin, when another senior student came in and with concern asked, 'Can I help? What is the matter?' Matilda through her sobs told her about the ordeal with the secretary. The student smiled gently at Matilda and asked, 'So you are registering for fifth-year?' to which, Matilda nodded her head. The student asked another question, 'And you have successfully completed four years of medical school?' to which Matilda nodded again, and a small smile appeared at the corner of her lips. Matilda sprinkled some water onto her face, wiped her face with a paper towel and tried to freshen up her blotchy, tear-stained appearance. She straightened her posture and with a bump in front of her, proceeded to the administration office for her fifth-year registration.

As Matilda walked out of the huge glass automated door and felt the warm sunlight on her flushed face, she said, 'Thank you, God. You sent an angel to put things into perspective for me. Baie Dankie.' Matilda sat down on a bench outside the medical school building and remembered another time that she was in the administration secretary's office.

It was towards the end of her first-year semester when she was still living at the hostel in Soweto. A painful experience, Matilda had forgotten about, but with all the emotions reaching a peak that day, the memories came flooding back into her mind. On that occasion, she was warmly received into the secretary's office, and in-between sobs related her dilemma.

She spoke about the harassment and abuse she had to endure from the male students in the Soweto residence she lived in. She didn't fit in and felt like she was a prisoner. That was the least of her problems. Matilda had been raped by a fellow student and told nobody out of embarrassment. And now she had missed her period. She was taken to the physiology lab, and a pregnancy test was done, which confirmed that she was indeed pregnant.

Matilda questioned God, 'How can this happen to me? I am a kind and loving person and just want to be a doctor. Please God, provide guidance to me as I cannot bear this.' Matilda was asked if she wanted to press charges and this would have embarrassed Matilda's family and would tarnish her reputation, so she declined. Matilda was then instructed to go back to her residence and await further instructions.

The then eighteen-year-old Matilda walked out of the very same huge glass automated doors and pondered her fate. A life experience she could not have imagined in her wildest notion. Pain, emotionally and physically felt as a piercing sensation above the belly button that penetrated into her back and radiated to both shoulders. Matilda spoke to no one on the long bus journey from Parktown to the residence in Soweto that day.

Term exams were over, and all the students started leaving for the holidays. Matilda waited as she was told for further instructions when someone called Matilda on the telephone to tell her to pack her belongings. To pack everything and to wait at the main entrance where she was to be picked up and taken to a safe place. The warm kindness and love Matilda experienced from the two academics that collected her and loaded her life's belongings into the car were like angels from above.

She was taken to a private hospital where she needed both physical and psychiatric support. This, they ensured was provided in a private ward with such a level of care that Matilda could just pray, 'Thank you, Lord. You have once again provided for me.' There was no consideration of the cost as Matilda clearly could not afford the care that she was being provided with. Matilda received the best treatment and at the end of two weeks was able to walk out of the medical institution and taken to a private safe house to recuperate.

After a few weeks, Matilda took the bus from Johannesburg to her parents' home in Durban to spend her last few days of the holiday with her family. No one in the family knew of Matilda's plight, and Matilda had to act as if she was normal. Once again practising controlling the voice in the head, which came to Matilda's aid under these circumstances.

Matilda prayed each day that her body, her heart and her mind would heal. The deep emotional wound, Matilda ensured, was packed with moist wound dressings. The healing process starting from the base of the wound until the surface healed, leaving a large, ugly scar that Matilda covered with a plaster so as not to expose the repulsive appearance. A slow, mind-numbing process requiring patience and love.

Matilda had learned how to observe thoughts that were in her mind and feelings that she felt inside her body. Feelings that caused tingling sensations, pain and jitteriness. These feelings of unease, that seemed to only affect her while everyone around her appeared to be in control. An awfulness felt deep in the body, causing the mind to flutter from one thing to the next. On the outside, everything appeared "normal" except what was happening inside of her. Feelings she was aware of, and in stillness when taking time to peek inside the body with the mind, the unease either lingered or was alleviated.

Matilda woke up each morning with arms outstretched in bed praying, 'Lord, heal my body, heal my heart, heal my mind and heal my soul,' feeling the supremacy like an electrical current passing from her hands, down her arms and to the rest of her body. Lingering her mind on that feeling of Heavenly existence that is the life behind the physical body. Matilda ended her prayer each morning and evening with, 'Thank you, God. You have provided for me. Baie Dankie.'

CHAPTER 11

Life lessons

The beautiful and dazzling thirty-seven-year-old Matilda had boarded her flight from Johannesburg to Nice via Paris and was offered a glass of champagne as she took her business-class seat. Matilda sipped slowly on that golden, divine liquid with all the magical bubbles. As a South African executive in research, she had been invited to deliver a presentation at a global conference in Monte Carlo. Matilda was so honoured to be invited that for the few weeks prior to the trip, she worked out in the gym, exercising and toning her body every day, ate only fresh vegetables, fruit and lean protein. She was the keynote speaker, and the topic was "Research from a Developing-World Perspective".

Feeling happy and content, Matilda stared out of the window of the plane, in the early hours of the morning eating fruit and drinking black coffee for breakfast, as the plane flew over the Swiss Alps. The picturesque and indescribable beauty of the Alps with their snow-capped peaks was a wonderful gift to witness on a clear, crisp European morning. Matilda longed to one day visit this magnificent mountain range.

Matilda arrived in Monte Carlo by bus from Nice. The drive along the coast was simply astonishing as she observed the extravagant indulgence around her with the many exotic sports cars winding their way along the roads in the south of France. Her presentation was well received, and she received a lot of interest in her topic from the many parts of the world that were represented, and contacts made there would be life-changing.

Matilda experienced her first life lesson in this series. An American company consulted with Matilda to set up operations in South Africa. Matilda introduced them to the opportunity of the low costs of conducting research in South Africa, where the costs were significantly less than that in the United States. A big saving for high-quality research, and so their partnership began.

On this basis, Matilda resigned from the company that she was working for and set up a research consulting company to explore this option that she was certain would be successful. Matilda was relying on the consulting fees to support her and her family, and this was a risk that she was prepared to take.

What a life lesson. As soon as the American company was established in South Africa, and as there was no committed contract in place with Matilda, the company terminated the consulting with Matilda as they found someone for less to run their South African operation. Wow, what a blow Matilda had been dealt and she was still prepared to make a go of things.

Matilda had relied on trust without any contractual agreement in place as she had been the one to bring their business into South Africa, which they had not considered before the meeting in Monte Carlo. Matilda had to take many deep breaths because by that time she had made so many financial commitments of setup costs, a hole so deep that she would have to use all her strength and patient persistence to get out of. Slowly and determinedly Matilda started to make progress, but never quite enough to cover the overhead costs.

Onto life lesson number two. Matilda had gone into a business partnership of a fifty percent share of the research consulting company. A few months into this partnership, Matilda's business partner wanted to leave the partnership. As he had not put any money into the setting up of the company, he claimed that Matilda should pay for the months that he put his time into the setup. They settled on an amount which would be payable over the coming months.

Matilda could only hope that her business would be able to generate the required amount which she later realised was too premature to expect. Business didn't pick up sufficiently to pay her ex-business partner and so lesson number two was even direr. He sued Matilda in her personal capacity, which meant that she and her husband, Ed who were married in community of property, after seeking legal advice had to declare personal insolvency, lost every asset that they had owned and needed to start off a new base.

Their primary residence in Pretoria, the holiday home in Durban, three cars including Matilda's prized Mercedes convertible was taken from them within a short period as the court ruled against them.

Ed had a good income, so they rented a house, paid the lease on a car and life continued as usual with some adjustments. By this time Matilda had many successful outcomes with her consultancy and training programs that were being booked well in advance with a consistent influx of income. Lesson number two taught Matilda that everything is never as it appears. She wouldn't be bitter and twisted and would persevere into the future with faith and trust.

Now for the most painful of the life lessons, life lesson number three. Matilda was lecturing at a training session in research in Cape Town. During the training, Matilda received a telephone call from her father. She knew that this must be important, so excusing herself during the break, she returned her father's telephone call. Ida was hospitalised in a hospital for a week in Pietermaritzburg, about one hundred kilometres from Durban.

Matilda was informed that Ida was under the care of a physician, a name she recognised as one of the doctors that had attended one of her training sessions and well known in the medical community. Ida had suffered for many years with asthma and seemed that she was hospitalised for this reason. Matilda asked her father, 'Can I please speak to Mummy?' Ida answered, and Matilda noticed that her mother was not dyspnoeic, so Matilda asked, 'Mummy, what is wrong? Where do you have pain?' A typical question doctors are taught at medical school. Ida answered, 'In my tummy, my dear. I am sore all over but especially in my tummy.' Matilda further enquired of Ida, 'Is this new pain, Mummy. Where do you feel the pain most?' Ida replied, 'Everywhere in my tummy Matilda. The cramping pain doesn't go away, although there are times when it is worse and times that it is not so bad.' Ida continued to speak, 'I have never experienced this type of pain before.' Matilda worriedly asked, 'Has the doctor examined your abdomen, Mummy?' to which Ida responded, 'No, he only listens to my chest, my dear.'

Matilda with deep concern asked to speak directly with the doctor as she could only fly out of Cape Town the following day after the training had been completed. Matilda called the physician and was fobbed off in a harsh tone, 'Everything is okay. I know what I'm doing, and your mum is going to be okay.' Slamming the phone down in Matilda's ear abruptly interrupting the call.

Matilda remained outside the conference room, looked down at her mobile phone and knew that the workshop that she had given the group would have been completed by then. Matilda stood in shocked, frozen silence, listening and focusing on her in and out breath. Taking a few deeper breaths, she knew that she had to do something. Matilda knew immediately what she needed to do and made a call to a friend and colleague, a physician in Durban. Yes, he confirmed that he could fit her mum in-between some of his other patients. 'I will wait for your mum to arrive and will call you back as soon as I have completed my examination,' he assured Matilda.

Matilda made another call to her father and said to him in a firm, loving voice, 'Daddy, you have to sign whatever documents they give you to sign at the hospital. I know the procedure, and they will put pressure on you not to sign. Please, go ahead and sign the forms and take Mummy to the doctor in Durban. He will wait for Mummy.' Matilda pleaded, 'Unfortunately, I can only get a flight tomorrow. Please, daddy, do as I ask.' Matilda knew that her mother needed a diagnosis, a definitive diagnosis.

Three hours later, Matilda received a call from the doctor in Durban. 'Matilda,' he said, 'are you sitting down?' With those words, Matilda knew that this was serious and made her way to a quiet lounge in the hotel and sat down. He went on, 'I have bad news for you.' Matilda waited for what was coming next. 'Your mother has cancer,' he said in a gentle tone. 'I have examined her and completed an ultrasound of her abdomen. Her liver and spleen are involved as well as the lymph nodes. Your mum has a small cancerous lump on the skin of her neck,' while Matilda was taking all he said in, in frozen silence.

She was numbed by this stage. He continued, 'We can do a biopsy to assess what cancer it is and recommend the appropriate treatment.' Matilda in a whisper replied, 'Thank you so much. I really appreciate that you could fit my mum in today. Please send her home, and I will be with her tomorrow. Let me first discuss this with her and I will get back to you.' Matilda went to complete the lecture that she was delivering in a surreal state, not mentioning any of the bad news she had just received to anyone.

Getting to the bedroom that her mum was resting in the following day, Matilda gave her mum a big hug and kiss. Matilda asked her mum, 'Mummy, do you know what is wrong with you?' Ida replied, 'Please tell nobody that. I don't want any fuss.' This was typical of Ida. No fuss when she was just diagnosed with terminal cancer and could only think of everyone else. Ida never once mentioned the "cancer" word. Matilda had to ask Ida, 'Mummy, we can get a proper diagnosis to see what type it is, but this will mean chemotherapy, radiotherapy or both.' Not sure if Ida understood, Matilda waited for her mum's reply. Ida smiled peacefully at her, and it felt like the day Matilda was born. The same peacefulness Matilda felt when latching onto Ida's breast, when they were both at peace with each other and the world. This peace that surpasses human understanding was felt between mother and daughter.

Ida replied, still never using the "cancer" word, 'I have lived a good life, Matilda. I have raised all of you children, and now I am ready.' Ida continued, 'It is not necessary for any further tests as I understand that this is in my whole body and know what that means.' Matilda had asked Ida a few times with the same response and therefore left the bedroom where her mum lay to address the family in the adjoining lounge, where they had gathered waiting for Matilda to speak to them. Matilda gently said, 'Mummy has terminal cancer. It is spread all over her body and she does not want any further tests or any cancer treatment.' Matilda now in more of a firm tone said, 'We need to respect our mother's wishes. Please, family, we should respect Mummy's wishes.'

There was a silence that was deep and serene in the room. Tears now flowed freely with much hugging and support provided for each other. 'So much love is in this room,' Matilda thought. A harmonious peace and this topic was never opened again. Cheering each other on before going in to see Ida, their tears were dried and smiles placed on each of their faces, so that they could greet their mother, wife, mother-in-law, grandmother, aunt and grandaunt with the love and joy that they felt for her and each other.

Matilda considered the gamut of events, all in the continuum of one year with portals arbitrarily opening and closing, and no way of anticipating these transformational systems. A vortex of uncertainty.

CHAPTER 12

Mother's Day

Ten years after Ida's death, Matilda lay sleeping in her king-sized, memory-foam bed on the first floor of her new house in the hamlet on the outskirts of Horsham, breathed her morning in and out and gently smiled while opening one eye at a time. She heard a commotion downstairs and thought, 'What the hell is going on down there?' Matilda stirred in her bed, not quite ready to get out of bed. Getting out of bed for the past year and a half had become a slow process for Matilda. 'I wonder what the racket is about downstairs,' and listened to the sounds while trying to raise her body into a sitting position on the bed.

'They will kill each other if I don't get down there soon,' Matilda still trying to get her body to function thought, 'Oh dear.' Charlie was trying to get his sister to stop trying to get the filter coffee machine going, as Matilda was the only one who knew the trick to prevent the coffee from spilling all over the table and onto the floor causing a mess. 'Get out of bed,' Matilda told herself, 'Get out of bed before there are casualties down there.' Matilda was hosting the Mother's Day lunch in England for the Hart family. Violet, Charlie's mum, being the mother to be honoured that day.

Matilda knew that she needed to get downstairs soon. Sue had stayed overnight and Charlie, Matilda's boyfriend, 'Oh no Matilda he is only your friend and lover. No boyfriend was ever mentioned. Don't think about that now Matilda,' Matilda considered that she had to get up. Matilda, taking one step at a time, slowly walked down the stairs of her house and entered the farm-style, modern kitchen sensing the tension between the two grown-up siblings.

Charlie and Sue were simmering at a high vibration. Matilda calmed the situation with her peaceful presence, and smiled at brother and sister while preparing the filter coffee machine, switched it on and waited for the calming aroma to infiltrate the room. Matilda wanted to go to church that morning, but something didn't feel right, and she thought to herself, 'Oh, come on Matilda. There is no way that you can leave these two alone in the house. There would certainly be bloodshed and victims sprawled on the floor.' Matilda gave a small chuckle to herself and decided to stay and take care of these two bickering adult siblings.

The simmering reached boiling point about an hour later and Matilda found herself sandwiched between the howling Charlie and furious Sue until they were screaming simultaneously at each other inaudibly. Nothing that was said was comprehensible until Sue grabbed her bag and walked out of the house towards her car. Matilda pleaded to them both, 'This is your mum's day guys. Let's make this a pleasant and enjoyable Mother's Day for Violet.' Well, that didn't deter Sue as she stormed out of the house, slamming her car door, while still screaming, 'I'm not coming back to lunch.'

Matilda had no idea how this escalated and went into her room to pray. She continued in a prayerful spirit while preparing the roast lamb and roast chicken, and the rest of the traditional Sunday roast lunch of steamed vegetables, roast potatoes, parsnips, pork stuffing, Yorkshire puddings and home-made gravy. Matilda used her thoughts to direct the rest of the day and said over in her mind, 'This will be a lovely and enjoyable day for Violet and the rest of the Hart family.' Matilda would ensure that this was so, as Violet deserved the very best from everyone. And, indeed, this was the case as they all sat at the mango-wood dining table enjoying a wonderful roast dinner and getting along splendidly. Sue, now with a glass of wine in her hand, looked happy and proposed a toast to Violet and Matilda, the two mothers at the table.

Sue and Violet had brought Matilda a plant each which Matilda took as a symbol of their love for her. The plants, despite having to spend many days without direct care from Matilda due to her travels around the world, continued to thrive and survived in their special place in Matilda's kitchen of that charming house in England for many years, long after Charlie had gone on his way to another relationship.

CHAPTER 13

The break-up

Matilda was left with deep and longing sadness for the next few years getting through each day singing to the lyrics of Michael Bublé's song, 'It's a beautiful day and I can't stop myself from smiling, If I'm drinking, then I'm buying.' So, with a few glasses of wine, the pain was tolerable for short intoxicated periods. Ending the song with, 'Oh, baby, every day that you're gone away, It's a beautiful day.'

A month before the Mother's Day saga, Charlie had found a position in a town some two hours' drive from Horsham. Matilda was commuting to Zurich each week on a Monday morning and returning on a Thursday very late in the evening. When she arrived at the house in the hamlet out-side Horsham, she would light the fire to warm up the cold, empty house, pour herself a glass of red wine and watch the golden glow of the wood burning. For a few months, they tried to plan weekends, which became harder for Matilda as she sometimes needed to fly out to a destination somewhere in the world on a Sunday afternoon. This would shorten the weekend, reducing the time that they could enjoy being to-gether. They both sensed a strain in the relationship.

One weekend during that summer after Mother's Day had passed, Charlie arrived in his car to spend the weekend with Matilda. She looked at him and knew, 'He wants to be with someone else.' Matilda's heart sank, and she tried not to cry in front of him, spending time in the bathroom balling her eyes out, as she sensed the end of the relationship.

Matilda intuitively felt, without any exchange of words on the topic, that something would change dramatically. She had to face a truth that was difficult to bear. They made love for the last time, and Matilda said calmly to Charlie, 'I suppose you want to be with someone else? I am sad but will cope. Thank you for being such a wonderful friend, and I will miss you.'

Matilda felt her heart break in many pieces which would take time to heal and so she gave herself the time to mend. A healing process that instead of suturing only the superficial layers closed, made a pact with herself that she would cut open the surface that had healed quickly, leaving the deeper tissue unhealed.

As Matilda felt the broken tissue below the healed surface, she took a sharp scalpel and deliberately exposed the unhealthy tissue beneath. Matilda packed the gaping wound every day with a fresh dressing to provide the wound with the ideal conditions to heal completely. The antimicrobial wound dressing would kill off any microbes that tried to grow, slowing down the healing process. Every day, Matilda removed the wound dressing and prepared a new, fresh dressing, packed it into the wound and protected the wound with a secure bandage.

Sleeping at night was a challenge as the pain and discomfort prevented Matilda from assuming her comfortable sleeping posture. With perseverance, each day was used to allow cells close to each other to glue together until the tissue healed and all that was left was the surface of the wound to close. A slow, tedious process and one Matilda was certain would bring her to a state of surrender to what is, with healing of her body, mind, heart and soul.

Weekends were spent at the Leisure Centre in Horsham, having a vigorous gym workout, swimming a few laps in the indoor pool and sitting for lengthy periods in the jacuzzi, steam room and sauna, singing softly to herself, 'It's a beautiful day,' trusting that this was the case.

Weekends turned into weeks, months and years slowly passed, as she released her emotional pain, surrendering to what was. She had lost herself, as she lived her life first through Angelo, and then through that of Charlie. Matilda felt and stayed with the excruciating pain, watched it until slowly the pain subsided and could not hide and lay dormant to surface at some future time. Matilda was not running away from this pain and into the extended arms of someone promising salvation which was only illusory.

Wanting to live a deeply fulfilling life, Matilda was going to persevere through to the bitter end. She was on her path to the means of finding true freedom, a space of beauty, rich in joy and blissful happiness. Happy with herself and the world, smiling, laughing and dancing every day, not needing to live her life through that of another again, relishing inner graciousness and sweet peace.

CHAPTER 14

Dr Jekyll and Mr Hyde[1]

Singleton Matilda was on a plane for her weekly commute from London Heathrow to Zurich Airport and remembered a biblical story. "The Jews never had anything to do with the Samaritans as it was forbidden for a Jew to go to Samaria. The Samaritan's were of mixed race – half Jew and half Gentile by intermarriage. This form of racism was rejected by Jesus, and instead of going through a popular Jewish town, He went straight into the heart of the forbidden territory. The Jews, despising the Samaritans, often avoided Samaria by crossing the Jordan and travelled on its Eastern side."

Matilda's weekly commute between the two cities of London and Zurich was the life Matilda had to endure. With only limited work permission to work in Switzerland, Matilda had to maintain two homes. The quaint house in the hamlet outside of Horsham that she and Charlie spent weekends in, but he was long gone now, and an apartment in Eglisau in the north of Switzerland along the River Rhine. It was easier when there was Charlie to go back to in England, and Matilda spent many weekends there on her own finding solace at the Leisure Centre in Horsham and attending church on a Sunday.

Matilda thought about Jesus's rejection of racism and felt this deeply. Her South African passport had many restrictions in both countries. Each week on the commute back to Heathrow, Matilda had to stand in the long queues for non-European Union passport holders and each week was required to complete a landing card. Every week for over a year, Matilda had to endure this, week in and week out. Matilda reassured herself on that flight, 'Sometimes, no Matilda, all the time,' she thought. 'God, some call The Universe,' Matilda didn't mind what term was used even if some people said 'Nature.' Matilda thought to herself, 'God directs us or uses circumstances to compel us to go where we ordinarily would not desire to go. God's purpose,' Matilda thought, 'must override our comfort. Don't question and just do what is in front of you,' as the plane touched down safely at Zurich Airport to another week of hugely satisfying and enjoyable work.

Matilda was glad that she had a job and could contribute by putting all her effort into achieving the corporate goals of the company she worked for. She thought back to a period a few years before she met Charlie.

It was Christmas Day in 2010, and Matilda was sitting all alone eating Christmas lunch in her apartment that she and Angelo had recently moved into at the centre of Horsham. The table was set for one, decorated with Christmas crackers, candles and tinsel. She had prepared turkey with pork stuffing, a special recipe she had learned more than two decades previously from a Scottish colleague and close friend. She had cooked a gammon glazed with a home-made apricot sauce, roast potatoes and steamed vegetables. She couldn't stop crying, and every time she tried to pull herself together, the sobbing worsened. Determined to still enjoy her deliciously cooked Christmas lunch, Matilda persevered through the meal.

She had not realised that things could go downhill so rapidly. She could not snap out of this negative spiral. It was almost four years into an emotionally volatile relationship with Angelo, the love of her life. She didn't want to get to this point of having to make a diagnosis of Angelo's erratic behaviour and felt that she had to start her analysis.

There was a pattern of mood and emotional lability and instability, fluctuating with or without specific or significant triggers. At first, this behaviour confused Matilda because she knew that this was not depression or any of the other psychiatric conditions that she was familiar with. During her psychiatric training at medical school, Matilda was very interested in these disorders and so remembered information on the various mental disorders. Matilda knew the depression diagnostic criteria, and this was not depression.

Angelo often said to Matilda as he recognised that his behaviour was not normal, 'You are the doctor, darling. So, tell me what is wrong with me?' He would usually mention this when he recovered from a bout of banging his head against the wall in a fit of rage. On one occasion, he repeatedly punched his fists so hard against his head that he ended up with two swollen blue eyes as if he had been in a fight in the pub.

Matilda often responded, 'I am your partner, hon, not your doctor,' and would leave it at that until the next fit of rage. She encouraged him, 'Go and see your doctor or a counsellor.' However, the time had come for Matilda to confirm a diagnosis and she was going to do this on her own. Scurrying through various diagnostic criteria, she found what she was looking for.

Her worst nightmare was that here was the love of her life with a borderline personality disorder, or BPD. Perhaps "emotionally unstable disorder" would be a more appropriate term. It was the fluctuation from extreme closeness and love, a form of idealisation, the part Matilda had been thriving on for the past four years, to extreme dislike and anger without any overt triggers, the part Matilda had much difficulty understanding.

Matilda said to herself once she had arrived at the conclusion of her diagnosis, 'Now that you know this. What can be done about it?' Later that evening when Angelo had returned from his Christmas Day lunch that had been spent with his family, Matilda noticed that Angelo was in a good mood, so all was good for that evening. Matilda started nicknaming the two personalities of Angelo Dr Jekyll and Mr Hyde. So, this Christmas evening she was spending with the kind and loving Angelo.

They were planning on buying tickets to the London Sky Bar to celebrate New Year's Eve to see the London fireworks from the comfort of the black-tie, posh event at the top floor of the Millbank Tower. Matilda was excited when she booked and paid for the five hundred pound tickets. A fortune, but she so wanted to experience the London fireworks without bracing the bitter cold and the crowds. She wanted to experience this in style dressed up in an evening cocktail dress.

Angelo looked very handsome in a suit and tie and their evening in the London Sky Bar started in a good, happy mood and ended in disaster as Dr Jekyll turned into Mr Hyde in front of Matilda and the other diners at the bar. Angelo ended up in a huff, dismal looking facial expression, talked to no one and drank one double Jack Daniels on the rocks after the other. This left Matilda celebrating the entry into the New Year with a glass of champagne and dancing on her own to the house music pumped out by the DJ.

Angelo remained slumped in a corner looking sorry for himself until he drank too much and was dozing off to sleep in a sitting position. Matilda had no choice and went to sit next to him to wait for him to wake up. The security officer came and asked him to wake up and leave the bar, which they then did. They walked to London's Victoria Station in the bitter cold as there were no available taxis at that early hour of the morning. Matilda needed to quickly change her high-heeled shoes to ones that she could walk in, put on her ankle length furry coat and gloves to survive the freezing weather and followed Angelo to the train station for the train to Horsham.

The embarrassing ride on the train from Victoria Station was one Matilda won't forget. Every time she tried to sit next to Angelo, he pushed her away and went to sit somewhere else. Matilda had to follow him, bracing herself for the humiliation, as she was trying to prevent him from eating the sushi he had bought at the train station. 'Sushi, for Pete's sake,' thought Matilda, 'He will throw up all over the carriage if he eats sushi when he is so drunk.' Matilda eventually sighed with relief as he was too drunk to eat the sushi and slumped his head on her shoulder and slept the rest of the way to Horsham.

The following two days were spent nursing the New Year's Party hangover, this time with the affectionate Angelo. Matilda instinctively knew that this negative energy was dangerous and couldn't shake off the uneasy feeling, suspecting and anticipating adversity.

CHAPTER 15

Bewilderment

By the next day, she had come down with a high fever, joint pain and full-blown influenza symptoms. This lasted for the next ten days, which she spent in bed, hardly being able to speak or take a shower. She had influenza, the worst she had ever imagined having in the past. The kind and loving Angelo took care of Matilda and even though he worked a long way away and would stay close to his work during the week, drove the two hours in the traffic each evening to make sure that she was okay.

Two weeks later, when the fever had subsided, Matilda knew that something was not quite right with her. The fever, nasal congestion, headache and coughing were a distant memory, but she still had muscle pain, joint pain and extreme fatigue that she was experiencing for the first time in her life. She dragged herself to work, and every time she tried to read something on the computer screen or in print, the words danced in front of her and seemed to run off the page. Her boss insisted that she review scientific documents that were due and assist with data review, which she couldn't do as her vision was blurred, the letters appeared distorted, and she couldn't concentrate on anything.

The world seemed upside down and her general practitioner was also puzzled by these symptoms. Her relationship with her boss was strained as she tried to cope, but was unable to contribute to any meaningful work to achieve the tight deadlines. Matilda would arrive home in the evening completely exhausted, flop straight into bed until one evening as she tried to get up and go to the toilet, her legs felt like heavy poles that didn't seem to function and gave way under her. Angelo helped her get onto the toilet and then back into bed.

Matilda had no idea what was happening to her. As a doctor, she tried to assimilate the combination of symptoms into some kind of pattern, but was even more baffled as the days passed until she experienced the first push-crash cycle. On that day, she felt a little better and needed some provisions from the grocery store which was only about a two-hundred-metre walk from her apartment. She took a slow stroll, bought what she needed, returned home and cooked a lovely meal. Angelo and Matilda had a pleasant and enjoyable evening, which was very similar to a regular evening they had enjoyed over the past few years.

When she awoke the next morning, Matilda experienced burning muscle pain in both her legs as if she had run a marathon. She was unable to get her legs to function and lay there in bed staring at the ceiling. Matilda knew that there was something seriously wrong, but she did not have a diagnosis. The only energy she had each day was to take a bath, as she could not even stand in the shower, and make herself a cup of tea. The pain and cramps in her legs worsened the second day and persisted for about six days.

By the end of the first push-crash cycle, Matilda woke up, felt as right as rain and thought, 'Perhaps that is now over, and I can get up and do all the things that I needed to do this past week.' She started cleaning the house, washed her hair which was a big job to blow-dry the unruly curls, prepared the evening meal and waited for Angelo to get back from work. She felt back to her old self again and was planning to go back to work the following day. She didn't want her career to be affected.

Then came the second push-crash cycle, which seemed worse than the one before, and no amount of analgesia was relieving this muscle and joint pain. Matilda spent days hobbling from the bed to the couch in the lounge and back. This was a struggle as Matilda was not one for staying in bed and could only move at a slow pace, holding onto the sides of the walls and furniture. She would make her bed and stagger to the couch, lay there gazing at the ceiling, waiting for time to pass. This cycle lasted for a few weeks. By the fifth push-crash cycle, Matilda's mobility worsened, and she had no way of finding out how to prevent these cycles. She made an appointment with the doctor and had to use a walking stick which Angelo had bought for her, to get from her apartment to the taxi for her doctor's appointment. Using a walking stick and moving at a snail's pace, Matilda felt as though she was an octogenarian.

Still puzzled by what was going on with her body, Matilda's doctor suggested to run multiple blood tests and said to her, 'You may have myalgic encephalomyelitis/chronic fatigue syndrome, ME/CFS but it's only two months since your symptoms started. We are not allowed to confirm the diagnosis according to the diagnostic criteria until you have had these symptoms for six months.' Matilda thought, 'What a confusing diagnosis and how ridiculous is this. Why do I have to suffer for another four months before they will make a diagnosis?' Matilda thought to herself, 'I need to get home to rest now, and I won't have any stamina left to do anything today. Once I get a small gap where I feel slightly better and able to read, I will google this ME/CFS.'

Matilda thought, 'They certainly didn't teach us that at medical school.'

The effort to get to the doctor's appointment the previous day set Matilda back even further. She now had blurred vision, the ringing in her ears worsened and reading or watching TV was impossible, her ataxia and the sensation that she was going to topple over worsened. The pictures on the TV screen were distorted, and Matilda developed sound and light sensitivity. When she tried to have a sip of wine, she was so violently ill that she avoided all chemicals altogether and any food containing preservatives would make her feel quite ill and woozy. All she could do was lay on the couch or on the bed waiting for time to drift by.

Matilda knew that she would have to wait another two weeks before her symptoms subsided sufficiently to be able to read. When the day came where she recovered slightly from that push-crash cycle, Matilda felt, 'Yeah! I can do something else than simply gaze at the ceiling today.' Over the next few days, Matilda was able to read for a maximum of one hour each day using this time to search the internet for anything that she could find on ME/CFS.

Matilda made an appointment with the neurologist as her neurological symptoms were not subsiding. The neurologist diagnosed post-viral syndrome and told Matilda to rest as this would take a few months to recover. That was a blow for Matilda as her career was progressing well, and she didn't have a few months to recover. 'Syndrome, syndrome,' thought Matilda quizzically, 'That is when us doctors diagnose strange patterns of symptoms that don't quite fit together.' The medical definition for a group of symptoms consistently occurring together, 'and most of the time don't know what's really going on and have no specific treatment.' Matilda thought, 'This is not an appropriate diagnosis.' Finally, with persuasion, Matilda convinced her general practitioner that waiting six months was not necessary and the referral to a Specialist was made and the diagnosis, ME/CFS, confirmed.

Matilda still didn't know what this ME/CFS meant or what the prognosis was. This diagnosis was even more confusing than the post-viral syndrome that the neurologist had proposed. "Chronic fatigue," Matilda knew was erroneous, 'I do not even feel tired. I want to get on and do things, but my body holds me back. My legs don't work like they used to, my arms can't lift any objects, I feel unwell, and these symptoms that are exacerbated by even the mildest of exercise doesn't make sense to me.'

'Well,' Matilda said to Angelo, 'Medical science has let me down as they know that this illness occurs, but they have no medication to prescribe.' Determined to fully recover her health, Matilda looked up the National Institute of Health and Care Excellence, NICE, Clinical guidelines. The guidelines recommended cognitive behaviour therapy, or CBT, which Matilda discarded as she did not have depression. Granted, that sometimes she would feel helpless and shed a few tears, she was not depressed. The other recommendation was graded exercise, so Matilda thought, 'If they recommend exercise, then I must exercise.'

'So,' Matilda reckoned with herself, 'as soon as I feel like I can walk again, I will take a walk and try to walk each day, and if the guidelines mention that I will get better this way, then they must be right.' By month five following the first symptoms, Matilda woke up bright and early considering that she felt fine. 'Today is the day,' Matilda said to herself, 'Today, I will start the graded exercise and take my first walk. I feel fine enough to leave the walking stick behind.'

Matilda walked out of the apartment wearing exercise tights, a t-shirt and trainers. Her route took her along the road towards the Norman Parish Church of St Mary the

Virgin, built about 1247, the oldest building in Horsham, and in continuous use for almost eight centuries. Matilda felt a sense of warmth and spiritual contentment, as she passed by the gravestones in the churchyard. She strolled past the tombs and memorials of the deceased Horsham townspeople, who provided their enrichment to the church.

Turning away from St Mary's Church, Matilda entered the farm gate where cattle were grazing and continued in the direction towards the nature reserve, the green belts preserved for nature. It wasn't a long loop, and Matilda had gauged that the walk at a slow, steady pace would take about forty minutes. A two-mile walk was sufficient for the start of her graded exercise program.

As Matilda walked through the woodlands, she thought about her older brother who was dying of cancer, and she knew that she would only have weeks before they would call her with the news of his passing. Angelo's BPD was under control for these past few months with very little fluctuation of emotions, which made life easier and bearable. This was always the happy, blissful period in-between it's fluctuating extreme.

Two miles and forty minutes later, Matilda was back in her home and felt the best she had felt in a very long time. She believed that her ME/CFS was cured and that she would go on as normal, and wondered if she fabricated all the outrageous symptoms. She prepared a lovely meal of roast chicken and steamed vegetables, set the table, had a refreshing shower, freshened up her make-up and played on her electronic piano while waiting for Angelo to get home from work.

What a lovely romantic evening with candles lit at the dinner table and enjoyment of the way that life should be. Relaxing on the couch watching a wildlife documentary, Matilda placed her legs on Angelo's lap, and he gently stroked her knee with warm passion and love, giving Matilda a desirous kiss on her lips. He lingered on her right cheek and whispered gently into her ear, 'I love you darling,' to which Matilda replied, 'I love you too, hon. I am so happy.'

CHAPTER 16

Pacing

'Crash, bang, boom,' Matilda heard her body howl at her when she woke up the following morning. Angelo had already left for work, and she could only move her legs ever so slightly. They felt like two solid, heavy, dysfunctional appendages attached to her body causing her excruciating muscle and joint pain. Severe pain that she had never experienced before, with all the ME symptoms returning to have a festivity in her body.

She couldn't open her eyes completely because of severe light sensitivity. She reached in the drawer next to her bed for a set of earplugs as every sound reverberated through her whole body like electric shocks that had no direction or purpose. Matilda imagined this as an uninsulated electrical current given free rein throughout her body. Her head ached, her joints ached, and she felt violently ill and nauseous, as though she had the flu without the fever.

Matilda started to cry as the phone rang next to her which sounded like a harsh alarm. Matilda thought, 'I have to try to reach for the phone and answer.' She placed the phone on the pillow and rested her head on the receiver. She tried to speak, but only whispers were coming out of her mouth as if she didn't have a voice and was slowly moving her lips.

She heard, 'Matilda, Matilda, are you there. Are you okay?' It was her sister who lived in Australia. She went on, 'Matilda, do you need me to come out to help you?' Matilda replied softly and slowly taking her time to think of each word as her mind was not sharply focused, 'I am so sick today because I overdid it yesterday. I only walked for just over half an hour and now this will take a long time for me to recover.' Her kind sister lovingly said, 'Oh dear Matilda, Oh dear Matilda. You are not one to stay in bed and you thought you were fine yesterday. Please don't exert yourself. We will have to figure something out.' Matilda ended the conversation saying, 'Don't worry, Angelo has gone to work, but he will be back later. I can cope until then.'

All Matilda could do on that day, was to roll out of her bed and crawl to the toilet when she felt that her bladder was about to burst. Not able to shower, she felt sad lying there with eyes covered with eyeshades, providing protection from the harsh daylight. With eyes covered and earplugs in her ears, Matilda thought, 'This is what it is like for a person who cannot see and cannot hear.' It was unendurable darkness and quietness with thoughts roaming freely in her mind, following a range of itineraries. Thoughts flitting from one place and event to the next, whether past, present or future.

Pleasant memories or not so pleasant memories and the imagination of good and not so good. Matilda watched the activity in her mind as there was nothing else to do. It was no use thinking about not having taken a shower, as that was not going to happen that day. 'Why ponder on what I can't change and have no control over,' thought Matilda and waited what seemed like an eternity.

Angelo came home in not such a good mood and sat on the bed next to Matilda and said, 'I'm not geared up for this darling. I can't have a girlfriend that is so ill. Tell your family to come and take care of you. I can't do this anymore,' and left to go watch a program on TV. Matilda had to put the earplugs immediately back into her ears, as the TV sounded like a violent storm at sea, with waves crashing into each other. She gently sobbed, and with tears moistening the pillow, she tried to muffle the sound so that Angelo could not hear her and surge into a state of unendurable rage. 'I couldn't bear that today,' sobbed Matilda softly.

'So, NICE was not so nice. Why did they recommend exercise?' considered poor Matilda. Matilda figured out that her symptoms were linked to exertion, but could not analyse or draw distinct conclusions from the pattern and complexity of the range of symptoms that she was experiencing. Angelo was back in the bedroom, and Matilda took the earplugs out for a minute. He said, 'I have been on the phone with your family in South Africa. Your sister will come and take care of you for a few weeks.' Matilda answered, 'But I don't need a few weeks. This is now month five, and my doctor says this will take a few months. Who is going to look after me for months, hon?'

There was no reply, and Matilda put the earplugs back in her ears, used the eye-shade to cover her eyes as she reached for the sedative antihistamine and swallowed the tablet with a glass of water. She hoped that sleep would come soon and tomorrow would be another day to cope with.

Matilda thought, 'I have already lost months of not being at work and trying everything possible to get well and now what do I do?' Without clear answers, Matilda started to cry again. A sad cry of despair, and thought, 'Medical science has let me down.' Nobody seemed to have the solution, so now I will need to wait another indefinite period before I can have the capacity to read about this illness and try to discover the remedies for myself.

A few weeks later, Matilda was able to do basic things although still house-bound. Matilda could manage about three activities per day. Shower and dress, then rest in bed for three hours. Have a meal, usually consisting of soup that was easy to eat and digest, and rest for three hours, spend thirty minutes on her computer searching for answers and rest for the remainder of the evening. Three activities per day with each day having the same pattern and as each week progressed, some symptoms slowly subsided.

Matilda determined to find answers found this on a ME/CFS website. Eureka! This made sense for the first time from teasing through all the jargon on the internet and confusion of myalgic encephalomyelitis, what causes it, how to treat it with the confusion of chronic fatigue syndrome and the babble online that went on and on without clear answers. 'How do I recover from this debilitating and devastating illness that is robbing me of my life, my career and my happiness?'

Matilda wanted simple and straight-forward answers with solutions that she could follow religiously with the hope of a full recovery. By this stage Matilda's neurologist and physician seemed to be losing hope and said to her, 'Oh, this may take more than a year for recovery, and some patients never recover at all.' Matilda would not entertain such thinking and each day tried to make sense of the therapeutic process and guidance that the website recommended. This would be a long-haul journey, and one Matilda was determined to travel, to regain her health. Matilda knew that if she as a doctor was so perplexed, imagine the fate of other patients. The recommendation was months, not days, not weeks, but months to a steady improvement and possible recovery.

Matilda continued to do her three activities per day and waited, three activities per day and waited. Her sister took the long flight to London from Durban, via Dubai, to assist Matilda with her recovery. After a few weeks, she would take Matilda outside for one activity per week. Only one activity per week. Perhaps a ride to the Horsham Park to sit on a bench or a slow walk to St Mary's Church. These weekly activities were still too much, and push-crash cycles fluctuated, each time not as severe as the last but nevertheless, still push-crash cycles.

This was not of any use, and Matilda had to revert to her allowance of only three activities per day and no weekly activity. Two weeks before her sister was to return to Durban, Matilda asked her to pack up her belongings and put everything into storage in Horsham. Boxes were bought, newspapers collected for the glassware, and the packing began. Matilda needed to go somewhere where she could lie in bed with her eyeshades, earplugs, do three activities per day, take the supplements, diet and medication that was recommended and have nothing else to be concerned about, other than her health and well-being.

Mae was adamant that Matilda should come to South Africa to stay with one of her sisters in Pretoria. Matilda knew that would not work, as their house was too noisy with teenagers and there were steps to climb which Matilda clearly was not able to contend. That was not a solution, and Matilda asked her sister and her husband in Australia if she could come and work on her recovery in their home. They gladly offered and Matilda travelled to Sydney via Singapore from London. Matilda booked herself a business-class seat, knew that she would need to reduce her activities to two per day for the few weeks before the long flight and sedate herself to make the journey endurable.

CHAPTER 17

The tunnel

Angelo helped with the final cleaning and returning of the keys and drove Matilda to Terminal Five at Heathrow Airport and handed her over for wheelchair assistance to an airport attendant. British Airways would take care of her for the rest of the journey, which they did. They allowed Matilda to stay on her flatbed in business-class from the time the plane was at cruising altitude and helped her into a sitting position minutes before the landing. Matilda timed her sedation so that she was fully awake for the landing. Sleeping with eye-shields, earplugs and wearing sunglasses while being pushed in a wheelchair, Matilda survived the two long-haul flights and arrived at Kingsford-Smith International Airport in Sydney. Matilda, proud and fashionable, had Angelo pack comfortable, yet stylish trousers and a silk top and had a small bag with her make-up and hair products to ensure that she looked well-groomed for her arrival in Sydney.

She was assisted by the ground staff at the airport in Sydney and into the care of her sister and brother-in-law to spend as long as she needed in their guest bedroom in their new house in The Ponds, a suburb on the outskirts of that big city. Angelo wanted to accompany Matilda, and even with a deep longing to have him by her side, Matilda knew that this was her journey to take alone.

The journey out of the endless abysmal crater. Matilda had no sight of the depth or the surface and felt stuck somewhere between these two ends. Many days were spent in gloomy stillness where Matilda imagined that she was in an endless, dark and quiet tunnel. Matilda lay supine in the bed with an outstretched, stiff neck on a comfy pillow, to cope with the severe pain of muscle spasms especially in her neck. Matilda waited, and waited, and waited in dark quietness to see if any light would shine at the end of the tunnel.

A wheelchair was bought, and Matilda was pushed to limit her level of exertion when needing to go to the pharmacy and health shop for her nutritional supplements and medical supplies. On one occasion, she walked slowly from the entrance of the shopping mall to the pharmacy thinking that, that may be okay. Even that short distance was not tolerated by her body. Another push-crash cycle caused another setback which lasted a few weeks with the number of activities per day needing to be drastically reduced.

Religiously following the ME/CFS website's advice, Matilda limited her activities, paced herself each day, took the supplements, made changes to her diet and rested each day in dark stillness. The stillness brought a new quality to Matilda's life, and she learned to observe her mind during those long months in dim solitude. Matilda practised breathing meditation to clear the mind, the body-scan mindfulness meditation to heal the body and did a few simple stretches, an activity that was added to her three activities after three months of being in the dark, quiet room in The Ponds.

Living in her mind for many months, Matilda remembered flying first-class in one of the most sophisticated aircraft sipping on exclusive vintage champagne with bubbles that magnified through her body with every sip and smiled to herself with tears in her eyes. Tears welled up and rolled onto her cheeks as she remembered looking out of the window of the plane early one morning before arriving into Heathrow Airport, expecting a sign to guide and provide her with the reassurance that she needed to sooth her despair. She saw a circular rainbow above the clouds, the shadow of the plane in the centre of the rainbow and the rainbow floating at the same speed as the plane. Tears had soaked the pillow that she lay her stiff, painful neck on, while she thought of the time in the future when she would get her life back.

Matilda had these months to pause and reflect on the loneliness that she felt during periods of Angelo's BPD tantrums. Matilda after much pleading on his part refused for him to come to Australia to visit her. Matilda thought, 'My physical immune system and other organ systems are clearly defective, and now I can use this time for physical healing and to strengthen my spiritual immune system.' Matilda said a short prayer, 'Grazie e Dio, sono qui. Thank you, God, I am here.'

Those long, dark and quiet days, weeks and months aroused thoughts of old wounds that surfaced in the mind allowing for a slow, steady healing to occur. A complete and sympathetic restoration of the historic spiritual home built in the mid-sixties. Matilda could feel the sensation of this slow, steady healing as she lay in bed without the eye-shields and after a few months, no longer needed ear plugs and visualised what it would be like to be healthy and vibrant again.

One day during these long dark days, there was a sudden flash of light, and Matilda laughed, 'A light. I see a flickering light. It comes and goes, but I see a light.' Then gradually, the flickering light turned into a steady light which became brighter and nearer. Matilda, now chuckling to herself with eyes closed, 'I can see the light at the end of the tunnel,' and said loudly to herself, 'I now know that I will climb up mountains!'

Matilda lay in bed and visualised walking through the woodlands in West Sussex. She could see the tall trees in the forest standing on attention with open gaps among the branches beaming strong rays of sunlight that penetrated into her heart and her soul.

Matilda still needed a wheelchair and now was up to five activities per day with no push-crash cycles. She held this vision permanently in her mind every day until the tunnel disappeared. She was transported by an imaginary elevator to the surface. This was the lift of faith and hope.

Matilda was in the lounge of her sister's home when the song "Feliz Navidad!" started playing on the radio. Matilda jumped up and started dancing in ecstasy as her brother-in-law walked into the lounge from work. Matilda shouted, 'Look, Look,' waltzed Matilda, 'I can stand without falling over. I can dance,' and continued dancing and singing, 'Feliz Navidad,' with rapturous swinging of the hips and twirling her body with arms outstretched. They both burst into laughter as they danced together until they collapsed in a heap of joy on the sofas.

That moment of bliss when a baby takes its first steps and the mother cannot wait for the father to return to show him the wonder. Matilda could not wait for her sister to return home from work to show her that she could stand unaided, she could walk, and she could dance. Later all three of them were shaking their hips and twirling energetically to the Christmas song signing, 'Feliz Navidad. I want to wish you a Merry Christmas from the bottom of my heart.' It would be Christmas soon and almost a year had passed from the start of Matilda's journey to vitality and happiness.

At that moment Matilda was floating on a sea of faith, hope and love, and now needed to make plans to return to England after Christmas. Plans to return to her life, work that she loved so much and woke up every day saying, 'Hello World, I am here.'

Part Two

CHAPTER 18

Hello World, back in England

Matilda was back in England that January of 2012 and figured that she should join a local social club to cope with the loneliness. She took up the invitation to go to the Sunday evening comedy club at Horsham Theatre, arranged by a guy named Charlie. Here was Matilda, all dressed up in skinny black jeans, high-heeled ankle boots and a tight sweater to show off her frame. She chose a black, stylish, hooded winter jacket, a cream knitted scarf and black leather gloves to finish the look. The Horsham Social Group met before the show at the Black Jug, a pub opposite the theatre where she met Charlie for the first time.

As soon as he spotted Matilda entering the pub, he came up to greet her with a broad smile and indicated which table they were seated at. Matilda blushed and had to escape quickly to the bar counter, fanning her face with her right hand as she flushed with excitement. She ordered a large glass of Sauvignon Blanc, tried to calm herself down and couldn't stop thinking, 'Oh, my goodness, he is nice.' Matilda blushed, 'Oh my gosh. He is a good-looking guy!' This was an instant attraction with a rush of blood to the head. Matilda thought, 'One needs more blood in the head to keep a clear mind at times like these. Nature surely has good reasons for its effects.'

Life after returning to England was lonely without the support of Angelo. She had found an annexe above the double garage of a farmhouse down a long-gravelled country road a few miles from Horsham. Most of her furniture was still in storage in Horsham as the one-bedroom tiny annexe was too small to fit all her furnishings, books and clothing. Nevertheless, Matilda was coping as she still needed to pace herself with limited activities each day, as she was slowly regaining her health.

Matilda was working for a few hours per day for two days a week to slowly get back into a regular work routine. She had no choice as she was still far from being able to do the activities of a fully able-bodied person. This evening of the comedy club would be a trial to evaluate whether she could cope with a few hours out in the evening without any ME symptoms. She met the rest of the socialites, all who seemed to be in a similar predicament, having recently moved back to the area or relocated from other parts of the United Kingdom. The comedy show was enjoyable with a bit too many swear words. During the interval, Charlie immediately dominated the conversation with Matilda which she was pleased about, recognising that the attraction was mutual. Matilda smiled to herself thinking, 'He is probably mid-thirties, but I'm young looking too! I wonder if he will still be interested?'

Matilda woke up on the morning of her forty-seventh birthday and started her daily, "Hello World" recordings, on her Audio Memos app on her iPad. Matilda began the first recording, 'Hello World, I have just listened to David Guetta's song, "The World is Mine"! Today is my birthday, and I'm snowed in. Fancy being snowed in on one's birthday?'

Heavy snow had fallen the previous night, and it was still snowing which made it impossible for Matilda to drive her Mercedes E350 coupe out of the gravelled farm road. The rear-wheeled drive vehicle was covered with snow, the tires barely visible and would take days before she could drive her car again.

Matilda had planned a walk in the woodlands behind the farm with Charlie, but due to the snow, the walk was postponed. 'World, I was supposed to go out for a walk, so will need to take a walk down to the local pub and have a drink, and at least I would have celebrated my fabulous birthday.' With a crackly and almost a slight sob, Matilda went on, 'I have to dig very deep today to stay in good spirits.' Matilda had to cheer herself up, 'You can cope on your own if you think about being happy and joyful, enjoy how beautiful it is in the winter wonderland outside and count your blessings,' now Matilda was sniffing in tears. 'Don't take yourself seriously Matilda and listen again to "The World is Mine", and dance around the annexe. That should cheer you up.' Matilda captured what was going on in her mind and ended her first daily recording with, 'Okay World. I can have my breakfast now.'

The following day Matilda woke up in good spirits and said, 'Hello World. This is such fun talking to you. I'm so glad I survived yesterday and eventually walked in the fresh snow to the local pub, The Dragon. I had some dinner and a glass of wine with my colleague, and at least celebrated my birthday. The walk was great exercise. The walk back was simply dazzling, as the bright moonlight reflected off the fresh white snow and even the torch that I had taken, was not needed, because there was so much bright moonlight on that clear star-glittered evening.' Matilda returned after the pub dinner feeling invigorated, full of energy, refreshed and was ready to have a good night's sleep.

The following morning, Matilda spoke to the World while drinking her coffee in bed, 'All was good for my wonderful birthday, World. Now I intend to get up and make myself look beautiful,' Matilda laughed at herself, 'I feel energised and have a good day at work planned. A good, happy, joyful and peaceful day where I can be an inspiration to others. That is my intention for today,' Matilda said out loud into her recording.

A few days later, Matilda was talking to the World as there was nobody else to listen to her. 'Hello, World. There are some flurries this morning, and I still can't get my car out of the snow. I tried yesterday to dig the car out with a spade, and after a few pointless attempts, had to give that up. I hope that the neighbours didn't see the chump I was making of myself, which must have seemed quite senseless,' and snickered to herself with visions of the posh Matilda in high-heeled boots trying to shovel snow from under the car tires.

She felt okay about being back at work but was concerned about the big meeting that Thursday, that would determine whether they would keep her employed. Matilda knew that this was sickness discrimination and accepted the future whatever it was to bring. Matilda spoke into her iPad while reading her daily spiritual message, "He leadeth me beside the still waters[1]". 'Every day I start with a clean slate, shaking off yesterday, considering that my actions are in harmony with what lives in my soul. And when your actions are not in harmony with your soul, then you don't feel good.' Matilda's voice mellowed, 'World, I can't rely on entertainment to distract me. It's up to me to have good intentions, so today, my intention is to look and feel beautiful, both inside and out and to wear a smile on my face. I hope that the weather is okay later because Charlie is going to take me for a walk in the woodlands behind the local pub.'

Matilda sniffed, 'Ah, I'm so fortunate to have met him. He has become a good friend.'

Lying in bed that morning flat on her back with arms outstretched, Matilda felt a sensation of glowing light radiating through every part of her body as every cell in her body renewed and healed. It was as though the glow penetrated deeply into and beyond her form. Matilda had often wondered about spiritual healing and finally comprehended a power, an energy source that could not be understood with the mind. Matilda smiled to herself, 'You start to feel better, and you know that you can tap into that wealth of healing energy,' Matilda supposed to herself and the World, 'I am going to heal. I go to my success.'

The following day, Matilda and Charlie were taking a stroll in the woodlands behind The Dragon, when Matilda shouted with delight, 'Oh my goodness!' She stopped dead in her tracks and breathed the fresh country air deeply. 'What is the Matter?' enquired Charlie, who looked alarmed by the sudden outburst. Matilda was awestruck and could not even get the words out of her mouth. She felt a glowing sensation engulf the essence of her being.

Matilda watched the sun's rays as they piercingly penetrated through gaps in the tall forest trees. The rays that shone directly onto her face and her body penetrated into her heart and touched her soul. She quietly said, 'Grazie, Grazie e Dio. Grazie.' Charlie looked perplexed and waited with patience for Matilda to speak. Matilda told him about visualising every day for many months while she lay in the dark and quiet room in Sydney, the very splendour that was before them, at that instant. The picture imprinted in her mind had kept her focused on regaining her vitality.

'He understands,' thought Matilda with a smile as they continued walking as the slanted, golden sun rays shone through the woods, scattering onto the ground of the West

Sussex countryside. A blissfully, unique and emotional moment of surrender and thankfulness.

The next morning, Matilda said, 'Hello Word, it's a lovely morning and today I hope that I can get my car out of the snow and not look ridiculous doing so. I'm putting a social smiley face after that statement. I had a lovely day yesterday, went to watch "War Horse?" the movie, and had a bite to eat with Charlie, which was enjoyable. I came home early and went straight to a restful sleep of twelve hours. I know that I still need a lot of rest as I regain my health.'

A few days later, Gioachino Rossini's opera, *The Barber of Seville* came to an emotional end at the Royal Opera House in Covent Garden. Matilda put her gloved hand through Charlie's bent elbow as they walked to the London underground to get to Victoria train station for the Southern Service train to Horsham. As the train approached Horsham, Matilda and Charlie were standing very close together and smiled looking directly into each other's eyes. Charlie had warm, deep blue eyes and an affable, loving and gentle smile of knowing. Their lips moved closer until they were gently touching each other's, while still remaining smiling at one another. The long sweet kiss was their first in the series of the wonderful time they enjoyed each other for the following year and a half.

Matilda needed to get over Angelo and thought, 'I wonder if this will help? Could getting intimate with Charlie help me get over Angelo?' She sorely missed Dr Jekyll and was glad that she was no longer in contact with Mr Hyde.

Matilda thought, 'Okay, I will give this a try. We are both single consenting adults.' Matilda was not in any conflict with herself about this decision as both her head and her heart were aligned.

CHAPTER 19

Hello World, ladybirds

A week after Matilda's birthday it was still snowing in West Sussex, and she couldn't get her car out of the snow. She woke up with a strange bubbliness as she read her daily message which was to "lay aside this ardour of mind that exhausts the body and leads you to commit errors[1]". Matilda questioned herself, 'What does ardour mean?'

Matilda spoke to the World, 'So, World, to lay aside ardour of my mind is to slow down, not be intense and take things as they come. I would have to practice this as I'm feeling all bubbly from the kiss last night. Ah! I want to dance around the tiny annexe all day.' The significance was a caution for Matilda to remain calm, hold up and go about her day peaceably and quietly. This was a good challenge for her as excitement needs to be tempered sometimes.

Matilda had to practice what she had learned about being mindful, being aware of everything around, inside and outside of her body. Matilda felt this excitement just above her bellybutton. She felt the need for calmness, the act of behaving in a way that was in discord with what was actually going on inside of her.

She started her morning with a couple of deep breaths, a fifteen-minute meditation, some yoga stretches and said a prayer. Matilda thought about the big meeting the previous day that confirmed her potential redundancy. Knowing that she needed a better offer to cope financially, she contended to leave things to "The World" to sort out and continued to read her book and planned to unpack some winter clothes that were still in storage.

The following day Matilda spoke to the World. 'Hello, World. There were flurries again last night. It will be cold today, but the sun is out featuring clear blue skies. It is my no make-up, no looking beautiful day, to wear comfy clothing, walk barefoot, rest, pot around the annexe, do some yoga and enjoy the fine, crisp winter's day.'

There were warm, sharp, penetrating sun rays bursting through the windows into the loft annexe. Matilda opened a window to enjoy the crisp air and sat legs outstretched on the rustic leather couch when on that freezing winter's day, dozens of ladybirds came flying in through the window and shared the annexe with her.

There were friendly ladybirds all over Matilda's arms and shoulders bringing with them purity and happiness. Matilda spoke to the World, 'This is so pretty, and I will now have a quiet, chilled out and relaxing day with these affectionate ladybirds that have brought me blessings of prosperity.' Matilda knew that the ladybirds were her good omen and would carry her illness away with their wings. Matilda intended to take deep breaths, relax, take a walk in the woods, read and listen to chill-out music.

Sunday arrived, and Matilda woke up and said, 'Hello World, I'm preparing myself for church this morning. The ground is still covered with snow, but my car is safely in a location to drive out of the driveway. No looking senseless today. I had a quiet day yesterday, felt a bit lonely and had to get through that feeling but had the ladybirds for company. Thank you for sending them to me, World. I'm feeling a lot better and healthier today. My hope is that everything works out well and every day is filled with kindness and trust.'

Matilda's message for the following day was, "love thy neighbour as thyself?". 'Loving myself means a day of rest today,' Matilda conceded, took a poetry book off her bookshelf, made herself comfortable on the sofa with the companionship of the ladybirds, and laughed to herself, 'It's Matilda's free day, ladybirds,' determined to put Angelo behind her and not think about her redundancy.

CHAPTER 20

Hello World, emotional pandemonium

18 February 2012

'Hello, World. I'm feeling very peaceful today and thinking about what to do for the rest of the day,' Matilda's voice was low-toned, contemplative and peaceful. 'I have to spend the entire day on my own. I'm trying something new and turned off my mobile phone to prevent myself from reaching for the phone every five minutes in the hope that Angelo was going to send me a message or Mae was going to call. This interferes with my disposition. And, I will do the same with my email.'

Matilda was living on hope that Angelo would call or send a message. After waiting with heightened anticipation and the day filled with thoughts of expectation, Matilda switched her phone off to practice controlling that despondent feeling of fervour. Matilda said, 'Okay World, I don't want to feel like that today.'

Matilda went through the day with no telephone and no email, pretending that she was on a long-haul flight sipping champagne. Time to let her thoughts drift, 'I'm going to be on an imaginary plane today addressing the conflict in my mind. On the one hand, I know that the relationship with Angelo is not working and on the other hand, I am still holding onto the illusion of hope.'

Angelo's fluctuation from being loving, gentle and kind one minute to the other extreme of anger and rejection made the separation of the temperament from the person, unbearable. Matilda imagined, taking a huge sharpened razor to slash the emotional bond to make room for her spontaneous spirit to soar.

'I need to sever the connection so that it cannot be re-paired and over time dwindles until it is hanging by threads. I feel the pain through my entire body. I usually feel the pain in my left arm that cuts into the bone.' Matilda was living on hope that those few moments, or the few times that she was really in a state of blissful pleasure, could overshadow all the pessimism surrounding the relationship. The peaks and troughs didn't fit with her natural flow.

'My message for today mentions that through affliction a better person emerges, to make your soul pristine and perfect. I have to face up to the reality of this relationship, World. Let us see how the rest of the day progresses. I will try to have positive thoughts and think about happy endings.'

Matilda considered the symphony of the journey of life. We want to get to the finale, yet the pleasure of the nuances of the dissonance and harmony magnify the voyage. The masterpiece will reach its climax at a point.

CHAPTER 21

Hello World, "dronk verdriet"

21 February 2012

'Good morning World, Matilda said into her iPad,' bemused that if anyone saw or heard her, they would immediately call to have the relevant authorities escort her to the Institute for Crackers.

She woke up that morning with appreciation and a feeling of vibrancy, which was a good thing after the previous night of "dronk verdriet – drunken grief". 'World, I spent some time, no most of the evening, last night feeling sorry for myself,' Matilda chortles to herself and the World. 'Ah! Letting all my sentiments spurt onto the floor causing a messy puddle. All due to me facing redundancy at work, the fear of not having a job and the fear of change. I'm afraid of having to relocate back to South Africa as I am still on a work visa. I am afraid of going out to seek employment. All this was a source of distress for me yesterday. How ludicrous is that World? It all got a bit overwhelming, which is okay. It was okay to feel apprehensive, and I let it all out in a fit of tears, misery and absurd behaviour.'

After Matilda's usual glass of wine and a small port, she couldn't stop herself even with all her qualms about the preservation of her liver. Her liver didn't have any say in the matter, as she gulped one glass of wine after the other and threw heaps of popcorn and crisps into her mouth. It all became overwhelmingly meaningless, and she couldn't control the ruminations that existed inside of her. She longed for a numbing of her senses, thinking about all she had been through the past year, and what she was being coerced into.

She had always imagined after relocating to the UK, and after accepting that Ed and Mae were not going to join her, that once she was settled, she would remain working for the next few decades with the same company until she retired. She would reside in a big detached house in Horsham and live happily ever after with Angelo. Well, this was certainly not the case as she contemplated a future of unemployment and without the love of her life.

By the time she had finished one bottle of wine, and the music was at full blast to her pelting of Nora Jones', "I'll be your baby tonight", she was sozzled and started crying. With a tear-streaked face, Matilda was obtaining inspiration from karaoke-style tunes played from her mobile phone through the blue-toothed Bose speaker.

Standing up on the couch, one arm outstretched as if on a stage, with the other clasping a wine glass, she wiggled her body while singing her heart out. All was doom and gloom, and her life had no meaning, as all the pain of the past surfaced to haunt her and annihilate her spirit. So, with her liver in a state of astonishment, she ignored the moans thinking, 'What does my liver matter at this point?'

'Okay World, I'm sorry for my prolific behaviour last night, but everything feels brighter today. I didn't have a good sleep as my mind was too active. That's okay too, as some nights you have good sleep and some nights you do not. I tried using positive affirmations. You know, the Americans are high on positive affirmations, so I thought that this would help me during the insomnia, but that was demanding, and I finally gave up.

I met with Human Resources, who offered me a junior position which I have gracefully declined. I thought quietly during that meeting, "I go to my success," while continuing to listen to their banter of sound waves, that went in one ear and came out the other. I don't even remember what they were exactly proposing and needed to turn the volume down and had to finally switch off, as the sounds became more muffled. That was a little bit of a surprise for me to deal with.

There is enough money to be able to buy Mae a house and a car and have her university fees and allowance paid for the rest of the year. Finally got a call from her yesterday and she was quite chatty. She is desperate to move out of where she is staying at the moment, and I have to help her do that.

This is a period in my life that I need to take one day at a time and see how things pan out. When the time is right, everything works out the way that it should.' Matilda shook her body vigorously, threw both hands up in the air flinging bygones over her head to land in the nether, and said, 'That's all in the past now!' and laughed heartily.

CHAPTER 22

Hello World, the buzzing bee

24 February 2012

'Hello World', Matilda said with a lofty tone in her voice. 'Charlie and I went to see Don Giovanni[1] at the London Opera House last night, and that was incredibly uplifting. And once more, like a fool, I fell in love with the Casanova, the villain, the bad man that we all yearn to be with. I only got back at midnight last night and have to work today.

This weekend I will be alone here and will give myself time to think things through. It is interesting that my message for today is that it doesn't matter if there is injustice in the world, that we should always strive to have joy and peace even if we are faced with slights. My intention is to be joyful, peaceful, friendly with everybody and have a great day. Ha, that's going to be a challenge!

All's good as I'm getting healthier every day. I have the odd pain here and there and the fatigue that sets in after a long day which is improving. The tinnitus doesn't seem to be subsiding which produces the sound of a swarm of humming insects in a tropical forest. It disturbs me at night and keeps me awake, but it is tolerable, as I imagine that I'm on an island in paradise. That's a nice way to think about it, World, as I would get frustrated and that won't help me at all.

I'm going to make a full recovery from this ME. I can't see the ME anymore. I think it is hiding under the ladybird's wings and they are going to fly away to some faraway place giving my body relief.'

27 February 2012

'Hello, World. It is Monday morning, and I need to start getting ready for work today. I start working full-time, and regular routine starts today which is an adjustment to get used to. The audible sounds of the HR mentioned that I need to work through the last months of my redundancy notice period. I didn't question them knowing that we were functioning on different frequencies and disputing my case would be pointless. World, I managed to temper the other voices in my head that were objecting.

I had a quiet, peaceful weekend on my own. At times, it gets challenging being on my own, but the loneliness doesn't last too long, and I get through it. I find things to occupy myself with and use this time to appreciate my life. I enjoy the things that I can enjoy on my own, such as the kind of music I want to listen to, read my favourite books, read poetry, practice on the e-piano or surf the internet, without the BPD to interfere with me, thank goodness.

On Friday evening, I realised what I really want. I want to have a deep, meaningful relationship filled with love and kindness. I will daydream about the mysterious man who is going to share my life. So, off to do my exercises, yoga and then to work. When I return, I will continue to daydream, while I prepare a delicious, nourishing meal. I have that to look forward to, hey World.'

4 March 2012

'Hello, World. I'm thinking about a weekend that Angelo and I had last year in Winchester. That weekend also ended in tragedy and BPD commotion. It was a sunny day, and after visiting the cathedral, we found a friendly beer garden overlooking the river, decorated with hanging baskets of colourful flowers and rustic wooden tables and benches. A sociable bee kept buzzing by and finally decided to settle on Angelo's lunch. As he tried to flick the bee away with the back of his hand, he tumbled all his food onto the floor.

I could not help myself and burst out laughing which he didn't appreciate. In a huff, he refused to order another meal and didn't speak to me for the rest of the evening and the following day. All I could think about was the fright on his face, and his eyes almost popping out of their sockets, when the bee arrived to check out his lunch. I'm still laughing World. I can't help laughing every time I think about that saga. Okay World, so that's the past dramatisation of the BPD.

What was the relevance of that story? Oh yes, my message for today is from the inspirational book that I bought at the Winchester Cathedral that day, which I read every day. Today's text is that the souls are at peace and "they live in blest eternity[2]". Last night I was completely overwhelmed with feelings of loneliness again. I tried to ask Ida why I was feeling lonely because her soul is in blessed eternity, but there wasn't really an answer. That is a good thing, as what could really be a response to a question like that, hey World?

Then, when I woke up, it was not loneliness, it was the joy of solitude, there to provide me with the enjoyment of things that make me happy without any spectacle. There is joy in being alone, being with your soul and having joy in separateness. Okay, World, I know it all sounds very strange, but that is the way I am coping with it, okay?'

6 March 2012

'Hello, World. I had a bit of anxiety when Angelo called saying that he wanted to come and fetch his stuff today. I would like some closure on that so that I can move on with my life. I don't know where I'm moving on to, but that seemed like a nice phrase to say, that I hear a lot on American television. The present provides me with certain challenges and then I read, "in quietness and confidence will be your strength[3]". The two key words for me today are "quietness" and "confidence", to do everything in a quiet and calm spirit. I can smile now after that night of "dronk verdriet",' Matilda said imagining a laugh-out-loud emoticon.

'World, I will try to not lose my inward peace for anything whatsoever even if my whole world seems upset. My intention for today is to be quiet and to be confident, and that will lessen any anxiety that may arise through the course of the day. Let the day unfold in its own way which I'm so grateful and appreciative of. Those are good intentions for today. I hope you agree World?'

10 March 2012

'Hello, World. I heard the news yesterday that I'm definitely being made redundant,' Matilda spoke into her recording in a soft whisper. 'Matilda, why are you whispering?' and she hears the other voice reply, 'I have to cope again with rejection. I have to dig deep to not lose my happiness and peace.' Matilda's voice of intention says, 'Oh, are you feeling sorry for yourself again Matilda?' Matilda settles with, 'Okay World. It has been a perplexing week and I'm looking forward to a nice weekend at the Spa. Always have something enjoyable to look forward to after bad news, hey World. At least I got that one right!'

CHAPTER 23

Hello World. A smile tells a story

12 March 2012

'Hello, World. I had such a lovely few days at the Spa Hotel this weekend enjoying full, glorious sunshine walking in the splendid Northamptonshire, countryside. I couldn't have asked for anything nicer than spending a few magnificent days with Charlie.

The spa is famous for its intensity of scorching and freezing alternating debaucheries. Dissipations that contradict yet are complementary. The extremes of warm and cold experiences that provide different sensations to stimulate the senses.

World, my favourite is pouring an ice bucket over my head after exiting the sauna or entering the ice cave following time in the crystal steam room. The hydrotherapy pool massages pressure points on the body quickening the circulation. Pure luxury in the heart of Northamptonshire. Okay, I sound as though they are paying me to advertise to you, World.'

Matilda was glad that Charlie was not averse to the experience and seemed to be enjoying all of the occurrences that weekend, leaving with a smile and a glow in the cheeks. Matilda and Charlie finally consummating their alliance.

Matilda continued to talk, 'Hey World. I received notification of the fabulous bonus which is going towards getting Mae a house. My message for today is, and Matilda started singing while gliding around the room with arms outstretched, "The Lord Bless you and keep you, The Lord make His face to shine upon you and give you peace". I have the full blessings of full sunshine with clear blue skies, and after these few days in the Spa, I have a relaxed and peaceful disposition which has been absolutely fabulous. Mae is getting her life sorted too. She is busy with university, focused and sounds happy which makes me smile.'

13 March 2012

'Hello World,' Matilda talks into her iPad while sipping on her tea. 'It looks a bit drizzly today, and I should get up and go to work. Now that I'm going through this redundancy notice period, I need to get through every day with a smile on my face. My daily strength today is about the beauty that lives in the soul. I need to let the beauty shine and manifest itself in meekness. It was lovely last night as Mae needed help with an assignment and I was able to assist her with that. This allows us a sense of nearness and expression of unconditional love.

To practice unconditional love towards myself is accepting myself just the way I am: a special person. That beauty needs to radiate in a non-judgmental manner with loving acceptance.'

Matilda was developing in self-awareness and the expression of unconditional love. Matilda remarked, 'World, I'm grateful for that understanding. I need to get ready for work now and see how the day unfolds in all its beauty. Okay World, all is good.'

14 March 2012

'Hello, World. Oh, it was a difficult day yesterday, and I'm trying to cope with feelings of rejection and disappointment acknowledging that in a few weeks' time I will have to move on from my current place of employment and make a change. I still don't know where I'm moving on to so I will see if the Americans on YouTube have any answers on how to cope.

I got through most of the day in high spirits, with a smile on my face and feeling positive. And then it hit me that it is the end of a chapter and I started mourning the loss and shed a few tears. Don't worry World, I didn't have the "dronk verdriet" again this time.

When I googled, "how to raise your self-esteem after redundancy," it popped out that I should spend time putting my resume together, which is supposed to boost my self-worth.

I feel a bit tearful and want to shed all these tears so that they can be replaced with assertiveness and confidence. These last few days have been quite lovely, walking in the countryside, going to the theatre and experiencing wonderful things to appreciate and enjoy in my life.

I opened the first page of my resume on my laptop but didn't write a single word. The voice in the head said, "Matilda, first end the sorrow of loss, and the feelings of disappointment and rejection will be replaced with optimism". Do you agree with the voice in the head, World? Because sometimes the voice in the head says strange things to me. I will put those thoughts aside now and update my curriculum vitae to boost my confidence. I'm lying in bed with my nice warm cup of tea and breakfast, and there is no rush, I suppose.

I'm not in the highest of spirits as I can't just be bubbly all day and smile when there are circumstances and life-changing situations to cope with. Okay, World?' Matilda questions and seeks The World's approval with a deep sigh.

CHAPTER 24

Hello World, contemplating the future

16 March 2012

'Hello, World. It is the warmest day of the year, and it is my baby's birthday. Mae is now twenty-four years old. How did the time alter things so quickly? Mae was complaining that she found two grey hairs and I told her that the joy of ageing is when you find grey hairs that are not only on your head but on other more discreet parts of your body. I failed to mention the other pleasures, like brushing further down your lower set of teeth with your toothbrush, as the gums start to recede with age, exposing more enamel.

I didn't realise that until my dentist pointed it out to me. He was just as shocked because he couldn't wrap his head around my age from the state of my teeth, and the age I appeared on the outside. I laughed and said to him, "Oh, so now I am middle-aged," to which he said, "Please, don't mention the middle of age, Matilda. That certainly doesn't suit you". We both smiled and laughed, although I was struggling with the cotton-wool balls between my gums and lips, which was quite an abysmal sight. I think he has a mirror on the ceiling so that you can see how outrageous you look, to scare you so that you return to pay for your next six-monthly bill. He also has to pay for university fees too, I expect.

Oh precious, Mae sounds happy and has a good day planned and then dinner with friends to celebrate her birthday. Wish I could be there but I can't, and as long as she is happy, I'm okay. I sent her some money as a birthday present today. She likes money, but you knew that already, didn't you World?

Okay, I have pined the loss of my job, and I'm now over with all the lamenting and feeling sorry for myself. I don't think of my last employment as a thing of the present but as a thing of the past. A big smile is back on my face, like a smiley humanoid, which has been helped by the entertainment of the consummating with Charlie.

My subconscious fears are about change, and I need to address these fears. I will enjoy whatever the day is going to provide for me. It is this day and that is all I have as I celebrate my Mae's birthday today. All's good World, and I need to get on with my day.'

17 March 2012

'Hello, World. I was thinking about how I would like to spend the weekend considering five qualities: compassion, kindness and patience. Patience is a challenging one, as I always want to move things along too quickly. It is just taking each moment as is comes. The fourth one is humility, which means removing or putting the ego aside. I tend to walk with my ego preceding any movement that my body makes and thus prevents me from experiencing beauty, especially the beauty in others. I'm trying to think what the fifth one is.

Oh yes, gentleness. I keep forgetting that one which seems deliberate for me to forget. Gentleness is a tough one to practice as I'm a kind of vigorous person. Gentleness is taking it calmly and slowly, touching and experiencing things and having a soft nature. I think that is what gentleness is. Those are the five things that I will think about this weekend.

I have done my yoga and exercises; I feel invigorated and tomorrow will go out for a long walk. I may even take the train into London.'

18 March 2012

'Hello, World. Today is Mother's Day in the UK. I thought about Ida, in heaven. You know, the Americans call heaven "the spirit world". We called it heaven when we were small and went to church. Do I have to change calling it heaven, World, and go along with the American terminology? Ida was always such a wonderful person, and I have fond memories to cherish. It is a nice thought, thinking that she is happy in heaven.

My intention today is to practice forgiveness and compassion, to love, to be pitiful and courteous, just like Ida. She taught me that we can't change the bad things that happen in our lives, but what we do have control over is to give happiness, be kind, be loving and to have compassion. I can only try, and I think she will be proud of me for trying.

My intention is to accept things that were in the past are in the past and move onto enjoyable and successful things in the future. Well, this will be another week to try to put the past behind me and look forward to a nice Easter weekend. Okay, World.'

19 March 2012

'Oh, Hello World. The sun is shining brightly today. It is such a splendid day, and I'm sitting here in bed drinking my cup of earl-grey tea that Angelo and I bought in Sri Lanka a while ago, but the tea is still good.

I feel so well and am getting better and better each day. Although I look okay on the outside, it really is what is going on inside. Okay World, I will keep smiling as you know there are other associated explanations for the smiling like a social-media big smiley.'

21 March 2012

'Oh, Hello World. It will be a beautiful weekend and so tempted to drive to Wales on my own. I don't mind, or there may be something else closer that I can do this weekend. The weather is so divine, and it would be a shame to miss this opportunity. You know, World, when the weather is fine in the UK, you have to revere in every second of sunshine, as one never knows when the brightness may disappear for another few weeks.

When I woke up this morning, I said my prayers, asking for everything that I need. My message for today,' Matilda chuckles and reads, "Lord I know not what I ought to ask of Thee[1]".

'That was exactly the way I felt this morning when I read, "Thou only knowest what we need, Thou lovest me better than I know to love myself. Oh, Father give to thy child that which he himself knows not how to ask. I dare not ask even for crosses or consolations; I simply present myself before Thee. I open my heart to Thee; behold of my needs that I know not myself. Smite or heal; I adore all Thy purposes without knowing them. Teach me to pray. Pray Thyself in me[2]".'

'I will live the day in prayer and accept whatever comes my way with gratitude. Okay World,' and Matilda smiled to herself.

CHAPTER 25

Hello World, beauty in every day

24 March 2012

'Hello, World. I had a lovely dinner last night and drove this morning to Corfe Castle, with its thousand-year-old fortification that stands in its grandeur above the village. I then made my way to the coastal town of Swanage, in Dorset. It is so charming and glad I made the trip. I'm in Swanage watching the ocean, while the sun is setting on this appealing sandy beach along the promenade with its colourful beach huts. I have been in the UK for five years, and this is my first visit. I have Charlie to thank for suggesting this. It's late afternoon and I'm really enjoying the weekend, feeling as pleased as punch. Okay, World.'

25 March 2012

'Hello, World. Oh, it's Sunday, and it was a remarkable day yesterday. I woke up in this peaceful, historic manor house that has been converted into a hotel in Corfe Castle. The manor house reminded me of Sunnyside Residence at my university many years ago, during apartheid. I had not been in a manor house of this splendour, until yesterday. No chatter, no clutter, traditional and very tranquil. The dinner I had last night was graciously provided with impeccable English service. I felt equality here, and nobody asked me if I was a "Coloured". I don't think that they were whispering behind my back, "I wonder if she is a Coloured?" I had to smirk when I thought about Francis' reaction when she realised that she was to share a room with a "Coloured" person. Those apartheid memories I cannot forget.

Anyway World, I arrived for dinner and was escorted to the grand lounge for pre-dinner drinks, serviced with olives and nuts next to the fireplace. While having my glass of sherry, the menu was brought for my perusal. The dinner table was set appropriately for three courses before being escorted to my table. Oh, starched, white tablecloths and beautifully folded serviettes with food that was exceptionally memorably delicious.

I can still taste the seared scallops on pork belly with apple sauce that I had as a starter. For the main – rainbow trout accompanied by a New Zealand Sauvignon Blanc, my favourite region and varietal. Even though I dined alone, it was special and entertaining with every gulp and mouthful. I wished that every other person in the world could experience this.

Breakfast was also specially plated with so much taste, attention to detail and wonderful service. Ah, I don't want to drive back to Horsham and spend the afternoon on my own, so I'm going for a walk with Charlie, his sister and his mum, both of whom I will meet for the first time. I wonder if they will ask me, "What are you?" but I don't think so. I have prepared a response though, "I am an interplanetary freak". That would shut anybody up that asks me that question in the future, especially South Africans.'

Panaché The Spirit of Life

Later that evening Matilda spoke to The World. 'Hello, World. I drove the two hours back to Horsham and had to sing along to Whitney Houston's, "I will always love you", to keep my nerves under control, as I was going to meet Charlie's mum, Violet, and his sister, Sue, for the first time.'

Wondering what to wear, Matilda chose a long halter-neck, rose-printed summers dress that was tight on the waist, flowed to full-length and had straps that pulled her cleavage into a rounded mould. They would be impressed with the sexy, stylish and trendy doctor that he was dating. Matilda tells The World, 'Oh, I'm not sure if we are dating or we are not dating. Perhaps we are friends that enjoy each other's company and consummate. I don't know what to make of it all, really!' as Matilda arrived at the pub. The beer garden was overflowing with families enjoying Sunday roast lunch in the warm English sun.

Matilda parked and climbed out of her Mercedes to the glances of a few of the patrons. She made sure that every physical movement of her body was controlled and poised, that whoever saw her would be impressed at the glamour, style and casualness of the lady climbing out of her luxury car. A slight smile on her lips, Matilda had to make an impression seeing that it was her first introduction to some of the members of the Hart family. 'Oh dear,' poor Matilda nervously commented to herself, 'I wonder if this means that we have a real relationship, but I'm not so sure,' and let the thought evaporate into the ether.

Matilda strolled into the pub and went first to the main indoor section of the pub to see if she could find Charlie. 'Oh, dear me,' she said to herself as she spotted the three of them sitting outside on the shady veranda on that warm spring afternoon, already eating their Sunday roast lunch. Matilda declined to order a meal as they were well underway with theirs, and she was anyway too nervous to eat in front of them. She ordered a glass of white wine to dispel the apprehension that she felt.

On the outside, she looked cool in the colourful silky summer dress, calmness written all over her smiling face while she spoke of the delightful trip to Corfe Castle and Swanage, but certainly was not collected. Her thoughts were running a mock inside of her head. She couldn't stop thinking that when she was greeted by Charlie, instead of planting a loving, luscious kiss on her lips gave Matilda a friendly hug. Matilda was still thinking about the agape hug when she greeted Violet with a firm handshake. Violet didn't seem to be the hugging type, so Matilda restrained herself there. Sue came forward and gave Matilda a full body, clingy hug which gave Matilda the impression that Sue was a deeply passionate and warm person. Matilda later found out that Sue had passion parallel to that of an expressive Sicilian.

Matilda's dress, make-up and style had the projected effect when Sue remarked, 'Well,' she said, 'This is a first, as we didn't expect such a fashionable friend of Charlie's.' Her words were said with admiration. Charlie sat there grinning at both of them, exposing both top and bottom sets of clenched teeth. They surveyed Matilda sitting with her legs crossed, lengthy summer dress drawn up slightly to get a bit of sunlight to reflect on the golden, sun-kissed skin of her lower legs, while drinking her glass of Chenin Blanc and answering their questions furtively.

Sue, pleasantly commented and winked, 'I suppose you won't be coming for a walk in that dress?' to which Matilda nodded, returned the wink and smiled saying, 'I have a change of clothing in the car for the walk.' Matilda knew that her next outfit for the walk should be equally fashionable and chose a white knee-length denim tights and a bright pink tank top bought at Zara Women, and selected a pair of white and pink Nike trainers. Matilda sensed that her extraordinaire was not what they had expected.

Charlie was the northern Irish adventurer, Bear Grylls' fan and wanted to camp, trek and own a rugged Land Rover and here was this contrast, Matilda in their presence. The incongruity was certainly not what they had expected. Matilda was determined to put her best foot forward on a day such as that, so continued with the walk, engaging in pleasant conversation and was grateful for the warm, dry weather as her white and pink trainers would have looked a sight if there was mud and puddles along the footpath they had chosen to loop around. All she wanted was Violet and Sue's approval, and to get along with them, although she couldn't stop thinking about the agape hug.

Charlie's mum thanked Matilda for helping Charlie during this challenging period of his life as he was recovering from heartbreak after the break-up with his ex-girlfriend. She had broken up with him a few months earlier during the previous winter on their ski holiday in France.

Well, there was now Matilda to ease the discomfort. Matilda noticed that Charlie didn't touch her at all throughout the lunch and the afternoon walk and wondered what was going on. They had spent many nights intimately together by then, and that should have already been acknowledged by the family.

This was so confusing, but Matilda convinced herself that although she didn't understand any of what was going on, she had to keep walking, making conversation and to smile her way through the afternoon along the brooks and ravines. She would be comfortable in any situation. She was still in a state of confusion about Charlie's lack of tenderness when they went back to his parents' house after the walk to have Sunday afternoon tea.

Charlie had moved in with his parents after the break-up and losing his job. So here was the son and brother whose hurt seemed to be tapering by the association with Matilda. They were happy about this.

Matilda was introduced to the chickens and the horses. They had home-baked sponge cake for tea, and this reminded Matilda of Ida's home-made cake on a Sunday afternoon. There was always something baked for Sunday afternoon tea, even in the humble home that she was raised in. They sat out in the garden enjoying the sunshine, drinking tea and eating cake.

Matilda continued to speak to The World later that evening. 'Driving down to Corfe Castle and exploring the old ruins of the Castle gave me time to reflect. You are faced with life as it was many centuries ago and for me, it is about my life right now in this place. I hope I do not sound pensive World? I sound as if I have a big question mark in my head about Charlie's lack of closeness in front of his family. I'm sounding like I'm giving things a lot of thought and I should rather let it be. I'm going to say a really deep prayer now and get into bed. Okay World, Goodnight.'

28 March 2012

'Hello, World. I had an interesting day yesterday. I don't really feel motivated as I work out the last few days of my notice period at work. Mae called and chatted for an hour. She is living on her own and gets a bit lonely. I asked her to come to Mauritius and Knysna with me for the holiday which would be fabulous, but I think she would like the money, as you know she likes money. My message for today is not to let our past experiences dictate and affect how we experience things in the future. Okay World, I will see how I progress with that.'

29 March 2012

'Hello, World. I received a belligerent and awful message from Angelo that hurt me. I suppose that was what the message had intended, for me to get hurt and I was terribly hurt. He has so much pain, my dear Angelo, the love of my life. My intention is to heal the hurt now and be gentle on myself. I thought that I would wake up and wouldn't be weepy, but I'm still upset. The hurt exposed all the emotional upheaval of my work situation, where in six weeks' time I will be unemployed. The rejection overflowed and is still overflowing and what makes it harder, is being so far away from Mae, and it's not just that, it's having to cope with everything here in the UK on my own. Apologies World, I'm feeling sorry for myself, once again. Oh, dear me!

I'm starting to feel physically healthier and improving very rapidly, but I still have a few ME symptoms. There is always the fear that I would get sick again and I have to deal with that fear, a fear of the future wondering what is in store for me. I received a touching message that has enriched me today, "There shall no evil befall thee[1]". I have to bear whatever happens to me nobly, so, should be okay, hey World?'

CHAPTER 26

Hello World, uncertainty abounds

1 April 2012

'Hello, World. It is Sunday morning, and I'm feeling quite peaceful and restful today. I went for an interview in Cambridge on Friday which went pretty well. Charlie came with me and we spent the evening and the day in that lovely romantic city. Watching the sunset while drinking champagne from the rooftop bar of the hotel which was poignant, with all the historic buildings nearby. All sorts to smile about and happenings that enrich one's life.

My message, "Surely goodness and mercy shall follow me all the days of my life[1]," provided me with the acknowledgement of Heavenly Presence. Thank you, World, I needed that. Yesterday was a lovely day spent punting along the River Cam, exploring all the colleges of the prestigious university and going to visit Kings College Chapel, the highlight of the day. It was a privilege to be there and being able to explore the legendary city with more than agape hugs. There were no members of the Hart family in the immediate proximity so you can read between the lines.

It's a peaceful day today thinking about my message, "And Thou shalt guide me with Thy council, and afterwards receive me to glory²". Okay, World'.

3 April 2012

Matilda woke up and with a lilt in her voice said, 'Hello World,' as she laughs at herself giggling like a schoolgirl. 'I need to say what my intention for today is. My intention for today is to increase my self-knowledge. Self-knowledge is about knowing yourself better but do we really know ourselves? I'm not too sure about the answer to that question. I will change it to be more self-aware of how I'm feeling every moment of the day.

I don't have any challenges to think about today. Thank goodness for this day of reprieve. All I can do is practice being aware in every moment. When I'm taking my bath, getting dressed or driving my car. Not to let my mind wander too much because we can't prevent the mind from wandering, as that's what the mind does. I was watching my mind, and it ventures along so many different meanderings. I need to bring my mind back to awareness of how I'm feeling at every moment.'

Matilda questioned herself, 'How are you feeling, Matilda? Where has your mind wandered to?' Matilda laughs again, 'I don't know who I am. I am Matilda. I think I'm Matilda. I don't think I know who I am. I know where I am. That's what I know World, and I know that the birds are singing, the sky is blue, and it should be a happy and jolly day because I still can't tell who I am. Okay, World. That's it.'

4 April 2012

'Hello, World. I must offload on you this morning. I felt like dispelling gag yesterday after I had a conversation with a colleague at work. I really felt sick in my stomach with what she mentioned to me and wanted to expel the ugliness and harshness which was pure maliciousness, onto her face. Well, that wouldn't have proved anything, anyway.

World, help me out here. How can my illness have tainted me? Who gives anybody the right to judge that and question my abilities? Okay, World, there is no answer to the rhetoric, but that was a bit of a concern for me and I will let it pass. I will continue to be successful and carry on with what I have planned for my career and being the best that I can do and be. Ida taught me, and she is in heaven now, so I will be okay.

I read the parable that we are all given talents, are supposed to multiply those talents and not bury them in the ground, and say to the Master, "Here is your one talent, I buried it, and I'm giving it back to you". Human Resources sounded inaudible again today, and I had to strain to hear what they were on about. I think that they were mentioning the consideration of taking the disability insurance money or taking early retirement.

I cupped my hand behind my ear to make sure that the irregular sound waves reached my cranium for interpretation. Did you hear that too World? I wasn't sure if I had the correct understanding, but nevertheless, I point blankly refused. I want to contribute to society and not live off disability. I will fully recover, and that is my truth. And, as for retirement? I don't even know what that means. Isn't that for old people? So, are there "early" old-people? That doesn't make any sense: "early" old-people!

I think that we need to take the talents that we have and multiply those talents and not to live off benefit if we can help it. It means working with one's talents. "Working" is the active keyword. Actions to produce more than we currently have. Do you agree World? My auditory organs and temporal interpretation are being affected by all the gibberish at the office.'

CHAPTER 27

Hello World, impulse reactions

6 April 2012

'Hello, World. It's freezing today, but the sun is out which is pleasant. I hope that you don't mind the small talk in the mornings before I get into the seriousness for the day. I have to talk as I'm sitting in bed after my breakfast and starting to feel a bit sad. The reason that I'm sad is that it is the start of the Easter weekend and I'm contemplating getting through the weekend without much company, considering how I should fill my time. I'm sad to be alone today. I suppose it's okay and I should allow myself to feel sorry for myself because there is nobody to feel sorry for me is there? And I know it won't always be like this.

So, it's actually quite remarkable that my message for today is, "In the multitude of my thoughts within me, Thy comforts delight my soul[1]". I need to really pray hard to have my soul comforted,' Matilda laughs, 'because my soul needs to be comforted now. So yes, I will get on and do stuff, and it's okay for me to feel the way I'm feeling today because it is the Easter weekend.

I have had my breakfast and will start getting ready for church and take a slow drive to the Good Friday service. I'm going to feel uplifted and not discouraged today. I'm trying the American positive talk and affirmations again, to override the melancholy but don't know if that works.

My intention for today is to be comfortable within myself and to practice awareness, without judging. I will be okay with the mindlessness. I think it is mindless and not mindful. Okay, World. It all gets confusing when I watch the American YouTube videos, so I'm not sure if it is mindful or mindless.'

7 April 2012

'Hello, World. It's Easter Saturday today and I'm in a peaceful mood. My message for the day was about peace and maintaining sweet peace. So, my intention for today is to have a peaceful day.

I had an experience on Thursday at work which I have been pondering over and need your input. I was preparing a document for a project and went into reflex reaction that I needed to satisfy my colleague immediately. If I was to make those changes, I would have been in the office until seven at night, and I had already made dinner plans with Charlie for six o'clock, so I needed to be home to prepare the dinner. I was fully aware at that precise moment that I was in reactive mode. Repetitive thoughts recurring in my mind that the work had to be done and I was trying to dispel this voice in my head by saying, "I need to get this thought out of my head. Get this right out of my head. It is not even my responsibility to be doing this. I'm only helping this colleague out," when the next repetitive thought came without warning, "Oh, you have to do it". What does, "have to" mean World? I think that those two words were imprinted into my brain as my serious elder sister used those two words, "have to" very often. So, I just believe that "I have to".

How do I take control of my life as these subconscious programs will always be reactive? And, is the reaction meant to protect me from some kind of fear? What kind of fears do I have that caused the reaction? It's probably fear that I won't be accepted, or people won't regard me highly or have negative comments about me if I don't satisfy their needs. I am afraid that they may say, "Oh, what can you expect from a Coloured?" I need to tackle this as this will drive me crazy. Probably has been driving me crazy my whole life. Wow! How did all that come out so quickly?

World, yesterday the repetitive thoughts kept coming again like consecutive lightning strikes, "I will allocate time in the afternoon to complete this task. Oh, my goodness", the voice of reason in the head was sensible and said, "Matilda, it's Good Friday. Today is the day Jesus was crucified. You go to church in the morning and enjoy the rest of your day. Don't think of work that needs to be done that can wait until you are back in the office on Tuesday. Matilda, get a life". And even when I was trying to practice mindfulness or mindlessness and meditate, these breakthrough thoughts of, "have to", would persist, "Oh my gosh, I had better allocate time to complete the task as that would be a good reflection on me especially for using my Easter weekend for work".

'Come on Matilda,' pipes the reprimand and Matilda knows that she is talking to the voices in her head. 'World help me out here. I have gone into reaction with all these thoughts running a mock in my head. I don't have to complete this, this weekend. It can wait until Tuesday, so why are the thoughts in my head still focused on this task that needs to be done?

Oh, my goodness this is ever so difficult for me because I have always been in a reactive mode about things that need to be done. It stems from trying to please teachers at school or trying to please my brothers and sisters at home, or since I was trying to please my parents, and all I was doing, all my life is to please everybody. Is that what is going on here, World? It sounds to me like it is.

How do I stop these repetitive thoughts and reactions, hey World? At least I'm aware of it now. World, we can work on it together, like we did with the mindlessness and the Americans affirmations. Okay World, we will see how we get on.'

Matilda taking a peek inside of herself during meditation quietens her mind, feels her body and asks herself, 'What am I feeling at this moment?' Thoughts and feelings that she can observe and respond to instead of relying on reactions or reflex actions that cannot be directed.

8 April 2012

'Hello, World. It's Easter Sunday night. The first thing is that it is important for me to learn to cope on my own and do what is right for me. The second is that I have to accept that I don't need to rely on others to make me happy.

Today I realised that during loneliness, many feelings and emotions surface. I feel sad on most Sundays as I remember Ida's roast lunch after church. When I left home at the age of seventeen and I was at university, Sundays were the worst as I sat alone in my room after church picturing my four-by-four-metre dining room in my parents' home, with the Sunday roast chicken or roast leg of lamb, vegetables and gravy on the table. They would call me during lunch or afternoon tea on the phone, and I could hear the back-ground babble and felt homesick.

It was easier when I met Ed and his mum made roast on a Sunday, and Angelo always made a nice roast with parsnips and gravy, on a Sunday too, especially when the BPD was resting. With the break-up with Angelo, I have to come back to an empty house. So, Sunday's are my worst to be alone. Getting through the week is okay.

Okay, I have to embrace a new kind of Sunday on my own. I don't have a choice because even if I go to someone's house on a Sunday, I still feel lonely as I'm supposed to have roast lunch with my family. Today, being Easter Sunday made it a bit more difficult as it's a bigger roast lunch and celebration. Anyway, World, I have you to enjoy my roast with.'

CHAPTER 28

Hello World, the minds

9 April 2012

'Morning World. My message for the day is related to the way that the minds in one head have two different agendas. Does that sound sensible? "Watch and pray. The spirit is willing, but the flesh is weak[1]". In every person, there is a conflict between the subconscious and the conscious mind. World, how is it that there is only one brain in our heads, but we have many minds? I was trying to count the minds and ran out of numbers. It is like we have two hands, so we say, on the one hand, this and on the other hand, that. What if we had three hands? Would we say on the third hand, the other? I'm confused with the minds. Do they all exist in the one head or are the minds spread around the body?

I'm learning to cope with being on my own; to look within and replace or move away from any negative thoughts. I can't yet say that I'm doing well with accepting and coping with being on my own because some of the minds tell me one thing and then the other minds take over, which makes it hard to cope with it all, really. Okay World, I don't know anything that is going on.'

11 April 2012

Hello World. My thoughts really are in conflict, and there is that inward jarring as they contend with one another. I'm going to watch my thoughts to monitor how they are resisting one another. Where are they going? Do these minds stay in one place in the body? Or do they move around and most of the time, I noticed, is that they don't agree with each other. World, please explain this to me.

Each mind is consciously asserting their rights which cannot be maintained. I don't think so. The conscious part of the mind tries to be assertive and applies pressure on the rest of the body, but the rest of the body is also there, and so is the subconscious mind. It is awkward for the conscious mind to keep asserting itself and to maintain that level of assertiveness, so it caves in eventually to the other minds. It just doesn't stand a chance, and I then give up and go and make myself a cup of tea. At least I understand how to make a cup of tea.

I was watching my thoughts yesterday while using positive self-talk. You know World, I was trying to use the American affirmations again, so I said to myself, "I'm single, and I'm happy", throughout the day to cope with my feelings of loneliness. The Americans say that I should say this over and over until the one mind can be in control of the others. Like, you have to talk to the one mind constantly so that it can govern the rest of the minds.

So, I have to let only one mind think the thoughts that I want to think and not let the other minds take over, but that is hard work. I usually cave in like the rest of them and do what is in front of me. I think that is the best, instead of trying to have all these conversations that don't seem to be going anywhere.

It's no longer an issue, and I hope that I can maintain it. Well World, it helps to talk to you. There is no one else to talk to, so at least I can share what's going on in my minds. There are quite a few of these minds that we need to sort out, okay World?'

CHAPTER 29

Hello World, perfect imperfections

14 April 2012

'Hello, World. I'm in Wales spending a hiking weekend at Brecon Beacon with Charlie. My message for today is, "As having nothing, and yet possessing all things[1]". Sometimes we focus only on the gaps and the things that are missing.

World, I'm sure that you are okay with the small talk, so I'm going to let you know that it's been a lovely start to the weekend. The stone, country cottage is up in the hills and is full of character, simply gorgeous and provides a place of tranquillity for the weekend. To be full of character is important in England. It means that it's old, woody and may have some ancient stones, slate and rocks that they dug up from the earth to erect and decorate the house with. The British like their distinctive dwellings.

I'm in a quiet mood today and feeling peaceful, calm and content. I have so much to be happy about and to be content with. Today for me is a day of reflection on all of the goings on in my minds. It is a day of consideration of what I have learned from my life, plan for the future and enjoy the present. I think that is too much to do for one day.

Sometimes we feel that we are not deserving of happiness or not deserving of prosperity. We are deserving and should appreciate, enjoy and embrace every day. So, it is good when you are in that state where you can appreciate what is being offered. I'm not sure that Charlie is offering me anything, except passing the time with me, because he doesn't have anything else or anyone else at the moment.

Obviously, I don't know what will transpire in the future and have no idea how the next few weeks are going to develop. We can discuss this in a few weeks' time when these weeks have passed. Although my minds are anxious about the uncertainty, there are going to be ways forward for me, and I have to embrace and show appreciation for this glorious weekend.

It is what it is, and I have to accept it and be deserving of all the good things that happen in my life. I'm looking forward to a good weekend walking in the Welsh countryside, eating lots of good food, especially succulent local lamb, drinking good wine and having fun, consummating with Charlie. Okay World, I finished with a bit of small talk again which I know you don't mind.'

17 April 2012

'Hello, World. I had a really lovely long weekend at Brecon and did about eight hours of walking – five hours on Saturday and three hours on Sunday. I climbed over very steep beacons and hills as they don't have mountains there. I had to stop frequently along the way, but I did make it in the end, which was amazing! Charlie was ultra-patient with me, or perhaps he was pretending to be. I will never know, which is okay so that the minds don't need to contemplate that at all.

My legs were painful, but I had no ME symptoms, no ME fatigue and only normal tiredness and pain. I am certain that the ladybirds had taken the ME away when they flew off to another territory. That was reassuring to feel normal again. I know what ME is, and I know what normal is. We use the term "normal" because it feels like everyone else and we can blend in. When you have ME, you can't blend in, because your feelings are different, and your body responds in an unusual way. Anyway, World, where was I going with this? Oh yes, my legs felt normal.

Yesterday, I woke up in the morning with an ulcer on my lip. This is the first time that I have had this. It is what it is, and I can't do anything about it. I looked at myself in the mirror and dread going to work with a big sore on my lip. I can cover it up with lipstick but what the heck, such is life. It still looks atrocious. I think it was being out in the freezing cold with lots of rain and sleet.

I have to live with it now, and it should be gone in a week's time, slowly healing over the next few days. I think the sore came to express the emotions of rejection and disappointment that I am experiencing at the moment. It just reared itself so that I can stare at it in the mirror and wait for it to slowly heal and disappear. I know that it will go away because the last of the ladybirds in the annexe are also going to carry it away under their wings when they eventually leave.

My message is to have trust and have a peaceful day allowing tranquillity in everything that happens. This cold sore is irritating me, so I will try to ignore it and have a peaceful day and that is a good challenge. I know that to ignore it is impossible because every time I speak or lick my lips, I know that it is there. So much for the American's positive self-talk. I will try not to get upset about it. Okay World, I suppose that is it.'

18 April 2012

'Hello, World. My message today was also interesting as it was about having all the minds surrender. I'm not sure who they surrender to, which I think implies putting all of your cares and worries aside, and you get given guidance and direction. My intention today is to tell the minds to surrender and to try to have a clear comprehension of whatever is taking place. They can stop the chitter-chatter which gets confusing for me.

It is that level of awareness that I seem to have been losing a little of, as the minds wander about in the wilderness. They start to venture into their own world and tend to forget what is going on. The weather is not good, and it's windy, rainy and miserable outside, so I have to try to lift my mood as well. A lot to do today, okay World.'

20 April 2012

'Hello, World. Today I woke up feeling a bit dull. I don't know another word to describe this feeling. It is feeling dull and flat. I think it is because I really don't have much to focus on today. When the minds are quiet, I feel dull and bored. Today will be three weeks to my last day at work, which is not a pleasant time for me. I will keep my chin and confidence up, make the most of it while I can, and use the American's positive affirmations.

I was thinking while I was watching TV yesterday about the London debate and the coaching that would have gone into the debate for the election of the mayor. There would have been image consultants and verbal consultants, but I don't think that one of the candidates listens to any of these consultants looking at the state of him.

I can control my thoughts and I can let the thoughts I don't want to think about drift away. I am working through my emotional issues and I am interested in self-development. So, after listening to the debate yesterday, I did a search on image consultants and elocution lessons. I found a site where you can do elocution lessons online which would be good to rebuild my confidence. I'm going to try to focus on that and spend time reading aloud. I have a South African accent to accommodate for World, so I don't know how I am going to get on concentrating on twanging in Oxford English.

It is about perception and about how you present yourself. So, in preparation for my interviews for next week, I do have a lot of reading to do and will focus my attention on the manner that I communicate verbally. It is important to not go outside of my natural character and still be true to myself, with only a slight twang. I think that is okay.

So, I'm glad that I've overcome this feeling of being dull and flat this morning because the minds are active again. Trying to socialise this week with the cold sore made me feel self-conscious about it. I tell myself that it shouldn't affect the way I feel as I'm still the same person. The same person with an ugly abrasion on my lip line, which I am trying to cover up with lipstick, but that is not effective at all.

Okay World, I'm coping with being alone and coping with having a huge ulceration on my upper lip. I have been going to bed early and shutting off from the world. My message for today also helped me get through that dull and flat feeling. When you go through difficulty, the difficulty helps practice patience, and patience provides one with hope. I will live on the hope that this sore on my lip will disappear overnight. Okay, World.'

CHAPTER 30

Hello World, the virtue of patience

22 April 2012

'Hello, World. It's Sunday night, I'm in bed, and I sent Charlie a message asking how he feels about me. I hope that he doesn't take it up the wrong way, as I do value his friendship and enjoy spending time with him. Of course, he is going to take it up the wrong way World, but I am a person and also a woman that needs to know certain things. The big question is, am I wasting my precious time? The dominant minds think so. They think that I am a nice body with a lovely smile and a good nature for him to consummate with until he finds someone else to replace me. Is that true, World? I don't know anything.

He is going through his own issues and is not an easy time for him either while he is still trying to seek employment. I had to get that off my chest, World, so I sent the SMS message. I wanted to know how much I should invest in our relationship. I think when you spend enough time with someone, you sort of know and get an idea. So, he has to answer my question, I suppose. I suppose too that my minds already know the answer to the question. They said to me, "He is not that into you, Matilda!"

Anyway, World, I am asking you for guidance for my right home, employment and success for my future. I was thinking that when I was so ill, all I needed was one room to live in, and I lived in one room for many months. But things change, and the place I'm living in now feels too tiny for me. It had served its purpose when I returned to England. I'm well now, and my ego grew larger as I'm getting better, so I need more space for it. Perhaps a three-bedroom house for one person would be adequate. I think that will be big enough and there will be plenty of space for me, my ego and my minds to live in.

World, we will see what happens. I have interviews this week, so it's to stay peaceful, calm and have patience. I'm struggling with patience and getting frustrated with all the extra requests for the position I interviewed for in Cambridge.

I googled houses to rent in Knysna, and it looks nice. That's always an option if nothing comes of any of the job applications here; I can go and live in Knysna for a while and do some writing. I think I have been putting it off for too long, but I don't really have the inspiration to write. I don't even know why this topic about Knysna has come up. Six years ago, I went to live in Bali to write, but tore up the pages of my writing and threw them all away.

Oh World, now I know why this topic came up. I need a sense of purpose, I suppose. What is a sense of purpose? Is it having the motivation or drive for some purpose to get up and do things? Because I don't have any occupation or a project to endeavour towards, that affects my confidence and self-esteem, which then affects my motivation. I watched some of the American motivational videos to see if they had the answers, but it all seemed like a bit of hysteria to me. Why do they scream at us on the YouTube videos? I don't find that motivating at all, with all the shouting. I'm going to have a good night's sleep and get in the right frame of mind for these interviews. Okay, World.'

23 April 2012

'Hello, World. Today I have to prepare for my interview for this evening and for tomorrow, so that is going to be on my mind all the time. It's normal to feel a bit of nervousness as it helps with concentration, I think. I am going to be a bit calmer, peaceful and concentrate on what I know. It is also good to know your limitations, to prevent oneself from talking nonsense when we don't focus. My message is that no matter what happens or where-ever you find yourself, it is for the best.

Now, I am trying to understand the reason for spending this solo passé. I'm going to accept that I am in this life situation for a purpose. That was quite appropriately said. They preach that in church that everything is for a purpose, but I can't help getting extremely frustrated and irritable about why I have to spend so much time on my own, why I don't have a partner and am still recovering from my break-up with Angelo. The church's explanation about our purpose doesn't seem to be helping.

World, I have an interesting and challenging week, and I need to focus on getting through it in a calm, relaxed manner and be my true self. So, let's see how I do with your support. My intention for today is to prepare myself for both tonight and tomorrow's interviews. To focus on practising mindfulness and that I maintain sharp concentration and refrain from talking about things I don't know anything about, and then sounding stupid. Although they don't turn their eyes up in front of you, I know that they will mention that later to someone in the office. I can see them as they report on the interview, and then turn their eyes up to heaven, as if heaven will redeem them for their conduct in belittling someone else. The taxi will collect me at about four o'clock this afternoon, so I will have the whole day to prepare so that I don't make a fool out of myself. Okay, World.'

26 April 2012

'Oh, Hello World. Let's have a bit of small talk this morning while I drink my coffee. It's been pouring with rain the whole night which kept me awake. I don't have to go into work today so I will spend part of the day doing my reading to prepare for my interview for tomorrow afternoon, so that's all good.

I'm also waiting for feedback from my interview. My message is that "one day is as a thousand years, and a thousand years as one day[1]", which means that I have to practice being patient.

"I have done my best, and now God can take care of the rest". That is quite nice for me to say over and over as there is nothing more I can do. The Americans are right about the positive affirmations. We will see what comes of it. I also have a few things to sort out by the eleventh of May which is my last day at work. I thought of doing it today, but my intention is to practice patience and enjoy whatever every moment provides for me. Okay, to be honest, I can't be bothered doing some of the things today.

I'm going to do some meditation now, and that will put me in the right frame of mind. It frames my mind so that I can see and do what is in the frame. The clutter and chatter of the other minds can't defocus and sabotage me. Today will be a day of happy surprises so I look forward to all the happy surprises that I will have today. What else did I want to say to you World? The positive thing is that I am coping with being alone or my minds are not fretting about it today. It seems to be getting better and better.

I'm going to plan my trip today, and that will be nice to enjoy the good things about South Africa and to look forward to visiting the family. But, if I don't get to go, I will accept that too. I will make the most of what I'm doing now, focusing on what is in the frame of my mind. Okay, World.'

27 April 2012

'Hello, World. Yesterday I had to practice patience, and it was okay and got through the day in good spirits. Cooked a nice pot of beef stew and had that with Charlie. Went out for a walk and had an early night on my own watching a feel-good movie. I read an inspiring poem, "Appear I always what I am? And am I what I am pretending? And sound my word and thought the same?²"

When our words and thoughts are not aligned, it does come across as being insincere. So, my thoughts and words need to be congruent which is important for my interview later today. There is no complexity about that. I was wondering if I should try to impress the person that I'm going to talk to, but I will just focus on what's in the frame of my mind, be myself and speak in a sincere manner.

Anyway World, I haven't got any plans for this weekend, yet it is not daunting for me at all. Charlie is away this weekend, so I don't have any company planned so I will start to go through the material so that I can pass the "Life in the UK" test next week. I can then apply for my "Indefinite Leave to Remain in the UK" and have that sorted. I booked to go to Glasgow for the interview, so hopefully, that will all work out. Okay, World.'

CHAPTER 31

Hello World, another disappointment

28 April 2012

'Oh, Hello World. I had some news yesterday, and after going four times for various interviews, and meeting everybody, I didn't get the job. They felt that I am overqualified for the position. Be that as it may, it's all for a good reason. I woke up this morning and tried to plan what should be my next step.

My message for today is, "The Lord is thy keeper; the Lord is thy shade upon thy right hand[1]". Whether you are experiencing sunshine or a storm that, "All things work together for good to them that love God[2]". So, I went to bed early last night because I wanted a good solid night's sleep and I'm feeling quite rested. I have the "Life in the UK" test on Thursday next week and have the next few days to study for the test. All I can do is try, and I'm not going to let any obstacles come in my way now.

I am taking one day at a time and not looking too far into the future. Right now, the best is for me to carry on with my plans for taking a few weeks off visiting family in South

Africa, travelling around the country and enjoying my holiday. I will be like the ladybirds and stay just long enough until I can fly to another destination. After that, I can decide what the best option would be to move forward with my career. And anyway World, things work out in such a way that is it hard for us to understand. I did go through a trying year last year and when I reflect back on it, sixteen months have already passed. The time goes by so quickly. I'm really happy, content and satisfied with the progress of my health and I don't want anything to compromise that.

My intention for today is to study for this test, go out and do some shopping, eat healthily to keep up my stamina and exercise. I can also do the exciting part of preparing for my trip to South Africa. Okay World, I sound pensive and disappointed which I think is normal. That door is closed, and I have to wait for another portal to open, which it will.'

29 April 2012

'Morning World, it's been raining all night and after not having a good night's sleep agonising over the other job, I woke up this morning to a rainy day, when one's reserves are required. I hope you reminded me to fill my stash, World, so we will see if it lasts for the whole day.

My thoughts are oscillating and circling around the disappointment, what went wrong, what I could have done better, the what-ifs and regrets and now the minds have reached the conclusion that I have done my best. The minds are resting now after all the laborious discussion. Okay, World.'

21h00

'Hello, World. Had a lovely service today. The message was that even if you are not rewarded, you can still be righteous and feel fulfilled. The church tries really hard to help us cope with being alive, to cope with distress and encourages us to think good thoughts in the hope that the people coming to church are not going to organise any criminal misdemeanours. The church wouldn't serve its purpose otherwise.

I will book flights to South Africa and Mauritius and sort the accommodation for the holiday. Mae and her boyfriend are also coming to Mauritius. I hope all will work out for good and with only two weeks to go, I can't wait. I am so excited. Well, one part of me is excited and the other, I don't know, is all over the emotional planet.

I plan to go to Pretoria for two days to see Mae, drive down to Durban to see my dad and then collect Charlie from the airport in Johannesburg for the first part of our holiday, visiting the Kruger National Park. The intention is that from the Kruger, we drive to the Drakensberg mountains to do some hiking in the berg, and from there to Cape Town, and up the Garden Route to Knysna. Take an easy drive back to Johannesburg for our flight to Mauritius. Planning this trip has given the minds something to work on, so they don't have to worry me about starting work yet. They can enjoy a bit of freedom for a few weeks. All is looking fantastic. I am so, so happy. Okay, World at least I have you to chat to.'

30 April 2012

'Hello, World. I woke up feeling a bit anxious about my future remembering the news on Friday that killed the option for the research position in Cambridge. The minds were thinking thoughts of disappointment and were taking over. I couldn't stop them. I have been feeling a bit anxious for the past two nights, and I'm trying to calm the fretfulness. But when I woke up this morning, I was still in a frightened state, wondering if I was going to be homeless and then live on the streets scrounging the bins for provisions to survive. I know that this all sounds far-fetched, but that is what I thought.

I started reading my message and burst into joyful tears, "to move forward and not look back". To be sincere and not to be troubled or discouraged, "If he falls, he humbles himself but gets up at once, and goes on with renewed earnestness[3]". We have the tendency to move forward impatiently with everything that is happening in life, so that tomorrow I can have a job and a house and really, what is it all for.

Does it provide happiness? Does it secure contentment? It really doesn't matter, because as long as you are happy and content today, having peace of mind and joy, that's what life is about. So, this vigorousness of mine wanting to fast forward the chronometer and do all this senseless planning and using the crystal ball to see into the future is a waste of energy. Anyway, that message is loud and clear now, World. I need to move forward and not to look back.'

CHAPTER 32

Hello World, this chapter closes

1 May 2012

'Hello, World. Today I'm feeling a little anxious with knots in my stomach. Yesterday I received the termination contract and I am uncomfortable with some of the content which is coming out in knots in my stomach.

I have to work on releasing this feeling of being violated and let it go. To have cheerfulness and courage and the endeavour to realise my aspirations, trust the power and listen to my soul that has guided me so far and taught me so much. Okay, that is what I am hoping, but I have knots in my stomach which is one of the minds saying the opposite.

World, I need to know what my soul, the spirit part of my being is saying. The body is only this temporary conduit. I need to listen to my soul to hear what lies very deep inside of me, to guide me because the minds are not helping.

The soul says that the future will be worthy of the past, to clarify my principles and to do what I need to do to let it be. Okay, World, I'm not quite there yet, but through the course of the day, I will get there through deep meditative prayer. With your help, I will move away from the unease to a place of serenity.'

2 May 2012

'Hello, World. I did have a serious discussion with Charlie and wasn't thrilled with his response, so I have to accept that too. Okay, World. I knew that the minds knew what the response was going to be, but I still insisted on wanting to hear the sound waves penetrate audibly for precise interpretation by my brain, which worsened my state of confusion.'

4 May 2012

'Hello, World. I passed my "Life in the UK" test yesterday. They wanted to know if I understood that there were more sheep than people in Wales, that Northern Ireland was definitely a part of the United Kingdom and that the Queen was still in charge, which we know is not the case. I didn't understand why the bus drivers from the Caribbean and the Indian settlers had anything to do with allowing me to remain in the UK. I must have given the right responses about Colin Firth winning an Oscar, Andy Murray being a Scot, that the nation is proud of Rory McIlroy, Pancake Day being the day before Lent and England inventing cricket because I passed. Some of the people that couldn't speak English passed too. I tried to talk to them, but they mumbled some words that I didn't understand. So, I wasn't sure what it was all about.

I now have to complete the application to remain in the UK and take it with me to Glasgow. Okay World, I am trying to remain hopeful.'

5 May 2012

'Hello, World. Both employment submissions have come to a dead end, and I have to figure out how to cope with the disappointment, again, for the umpteenth time. I am sick of all this, and my minds agree with me. I had dinner with a couple of colleagues to say my goodbyes, which they attended politely, although I could see that they were awkward.

Oh, World, such is life, I suppose. I need to cope with the disappointment. It can't go on forever, it comes to an end and it's getting through it, that's the challenge. Anyway, I will go out this afternoon for a walk in the crisp Sussex countryside to give the minds some peace. At least I have a nice long holiday to look forward to. Always have a nice long holiday to look forward to when things become unbearable. Okay, World.'

8 May 2012

'Oh, Hello World. I am spending my last few days before my holiday to have fun. We went out for cocktails and dinner to Wabi, the Japanese restaurant in Horsham on Saturday night, stayed up till late, drank too many margaritas and suffered the consequences of that. It will take a while for the hangover to pass, as my liver is displeased with me again, after the last assault with the "dronk verdriet". I have to sort out my application for my visa today for immigration before I fly off to Glasgow tomorrow. Okay, World.'

10 May 2012

'Hello, World. I must tell you what has happened in the last couple of days. Firstly, I am so pleased that I now have my "Indefinite Leave to Remain in the UK". I had to get the early morning flight from Gatwick to Glasgow, so sleep was not a priority. Before I left in the morning, I read my message for the day, "The Lord gave, and the Lord hath taken away[1]". Well World, I was hoping that the Lord was going to give me my Indefinite Leave to Remain in the UK, to live in the UK without work restrictions, which He did.

Today I'm still feeling hungover from the late night and will need two days of full rest. Oh dear, I'm so tired and exhausted. I feel like Job, "Thou He slay me, yet will I trust in Him[2]". I think I'm coming out of difficulties now and will take time to enjoy myself.

Anyway World, I'm looking forward to seeing my dad, the rest of my family and can't wait to see Mae on Monday. I miss her so much. She is an adult and has to find her own path. I tried to encourage her to come and live here in the UK with me, but she doesn't like the grey clouds and having to wear a raincoat every day.'

CHAPTER 33

Hello World, I surrender

14 May 2012

Hello World. I'm in South Africa. The weekend before I left London was pleasant and unexpected. I went to stay with Charlie at his house, and he had chores to take care of as his parents were on holiday. He had to pick up all the horse dung, load it into a wheelbarrow and pile it on top of the dung heap. I was wearing high-heels and tried not to step in the horse poo. That must have been a sight. I didn't know I was going to walk in the paddock and wore high-heeled shoes, to look elegant in. I knew they were not practical when he asked me to keep him company while he did his chores. I couldn't refuse, so I went plonking around the paddock in my Kurt Geiger high-heels.

Dinner was nice though and had a glass of wine with the two of us sitting, listening to music and chatting. Was so chilled, relaxed and so easy. A nice evening and I felt contentment as if I was meant to be there or had been there before. You know World, it felt right and wonderful. I wasn't confused then, but I'm baffled again today. Life can get complicated. Okay, World.'

15 May 2012

'Good morning World. I'm in Pretoria, and the sun is shining. I have to get changed and ready soon for the long road trip ahead. Had a lovely message to prepare me for the day, "My Presence shall go with thee, and I will give thee rest[1]".

It's to find a wonderful place of repose within. And I think that I am doing pretty well with that. I see around me a lot of unhappiness, sadness and anxiety and somehow, it's as if I'm no longer affected by it and does not affect my sense of inner peace. It was payday today so got the pay-out. Reserved some money for the deposit for my house and that's going to be a good thing with enough to enjoy the rest of the holiday. Okay, World.'

24 May 2012

Hello World. Charlie and I are in the Drakensberg, appreciating the majestic views of the mountain. The last few days that we spent in the Kruger were humbling, under the magnitude of the laws of nature.

We spotted a huge herd of buffalo close to Berg-en-Dal and another on the way to the Crocodile Bridge rest camp. We photographed a large herd of elephant with their cute baby and teenage elephants. Hyenas were roaming around, looking left and right with their inferiority complexes, scrounging for opportunities to scoff.

Got amazing video footage of a huge pack of wild dogs who had just killed an impala which they were tearing apart in the road right in front of us. Okay, World, we were in the car, so they were not quite right in front of us. Hope that you can excuse the metaphor.

Anyway, the wild dogs were trying to grab some part of the meat and bones of the carcass which they devoured within just a few minutes. This was a once in a lifetime experience of wildlife in action. I don't know what the vegans would make of all the wild dogs consuming an impala to survive! We also spotted two young male lions sitting at the watering hole next to the sand track. They seemed depressed, as though they had been kicked out of the pride, spending their days wandering about the bush and waiting for the opportunity to take over some day.

We also spotted loads of white rhino with the game ranger explaining the difference between white and black rhino. All I understood was that the white is not really white and that the black is not really black as they are the same grey colour. Okay World that is confusing for me too.

The walk was also memorably mesmerising because we came pretty close to a small herd of elephant and a rhino that we were tracking. When we came within a few metres of the rhino, we had to hide behind a tree, in case it would charge towards us. You know, rhinos are almost blind, which helped, as I don't know if I would still be here talking to you if the rhino could see me and charged directly towards me, killing me. I was wondering if they would have a court case against the rhino if that was to have happened, but I guess not. That was really exciting and also learned all about the rhino bidden, or the toilets that the rhinos make in the wilderness. Imagine, they even know where to go to do their excretory business. This we were told was part of them signing the papers to claim their piece of land. I don't know if it would be legal if we signed on toilet paper. The rest of the other small and large animal dung was not as sensational. I wonder if Scott Ramsay, the photojournalist from inthewild.com that is traipsing all over Africa, understood about the bidden and all the dung that was lying about.

So, us two peas in a pod need to go and have breakfast. Okay World, I suppose the one thing that I wanted to say is that it was a really good idea to get away because I haven't had any of those feelings of despondency since I arrived in South Africa. Appreciating fauna and flora, smelling the wild odours and observing environmental splendour, places a new perspective on the subtleties of life, refraining from the interpretation of only the fragments of representation.

We travelled all day in the car from the Kruger to the Drakensberg yesterday. As we crossed back over Crocodile Bridge from Malelane Gate, we spotted hippopotamus, my favourite animal in the whole world. The hippos were out of the water, and we also tried to get video footage of the two fish eagles that were flying about.

So, we are in the Berg getting ready for breakfast, and a nice hike to the Blue Grotto planned for the day. The views from up there will be breathtaking. It will be too cold to swim in the Blue Grotto, but I will certainly put my feet in the fresh, icy water. Okay, World, I haven't spoken to you for a few days, but I will try to catch up with you later. Okay, it's time for a shower and then a cooked mountain breakfast. There you go World.'

25 May 2012

'Hello, World,' Matilda records while Charlie laughs at the crazy woman talking into her iPad. Matilda continues none-theless, 'What can I say today? It's a glorious day observing the Drakensberg mountains while having a cup of tea. We did a spectacular walk yesterday to the Blue Grotto, hiking for about five hours. Charlie needed a cold Castle Lager, the local beer, and I enjoyed a refreshing gin and tonic after and thought that life couldn't be better. Today we will do some more hiking then have a massage, read a book stretched out by the pool, and off to Cape Town tomorrow. Okay, World.'

30 May 2012

'Hello, World. I'm giggling with Charlie in bed as he thinks I'm silly saying "Hello World" into my iPad. What did we do in Cape Town? We drove along the mountainous Chapman's Peak drive, stopped in Kalk Bay for another seafood platter with crayfish, prawns, mussels and calamari and went to see the African penguins at Boulders Beach near Simonstown. We got back very tired, so we had an early night.

Yesterday was spent wine tasting in Stellenbosch. Bought some amazing wines which I'm sure we will start tasting and drinking today. We are now having coffee on the balcony of the Arabella Hotel and Spa in Kleinmond, near the coastal town of Hermanus. The stunning views overlook the golf course, which is rated number two in South Africa, stretching beyond the Bot River lagoon and surrounded by the picturesque Kogelberg mountain range.

I really need that spa session after the hiking and long drive. I need to detoxify the body, especially as I have to cope with the whining of my liver. We have booked the two-hour Rainforest Spa session that will be quite invigorating.

I still haven't driven Charlie crazy with all my quirks and morning rituals, or he is not showing any signs of irritability, as he doesn't have the BPD. So, now World, I am looking forward to the rest of the relaxing week here at Arabella, before driving up the Garden Route to Knysna. I have put on three kilograms which I'm going to agonise over to lose. Okay, World.'

4 June 2012

'Oh, Hello World. We are in Knysna, and the weather is lovely, with perfect sunshine like a summer's day. I'm so excited this morning as we are going to sea-kayak from

Plettenberg Bay beach to Robberg Island today to try to spot dolphins and seals.

It has been lovely weather since we arrived which made for a pleasant sightseeing trip to The Heads, the entrance to the vast expanse of the Knysna Lagoon shielded by two exaggerated east and west cliffs. We have been eating and drinking too much, which can't be helped as this is South Africa with all its flavourful extravagances and enchanting wines. We have been sitting on the patio outside our holiday apartment on the Knysna Quays, sipping champagne and eating world famous Knysna oysters, fresh from the lagoon for delicious consumption, while watching the small boats, catamarans and sailboats float by.

I think we bought too much wine in Stellenbosch, so will need to leave the remaining bottles with someone in Johannesburg before our flight to Mauritius. It would be impossible to drink all the wine, as my liver is delighted now after the spa detox, and I don't want to cope with any further moanings. I can feel its excitement in the right upper quadrant of my abdomen.

It was interesting this morning as I have woken up in a contemplative mood wondering what to do next and read the message for today which is about never giving up. Not to think that persistence is ever in vain, "Did you ever hear a man who had striven all his life faithfully and singly towards an object and in no measure obtained it²?" Nothing is in vain, and you have to go about life with the spirit to do right, and you will be recompensed.

Okay, World we have had our breakfast and now have to get ready to enjoy the sunshine, sea-kayaking. I'm really looking forward to being on the expanse of the ocean. Okay, World.'

CHAPTER 34

Hello World, dolphins

15 June 2012

'Hello, World. So, it's been a while. What's happened in eleven days. We are having a peaceful and relaxing time in Mauritius. Mae and her boyfriend are coming for our last week in Mauritius, and then I have to look for work. What else is there World? It was interesting as the other day I saw dodgem cars, and it brought back memories about the bumping cars and apartheid. What fun we had watching White kids bump into each other.

We are staying in a nice resort and eating lots of roti's, biryani poulet and biryani fish. Have been drinking good wine and Charlie is enjoying the local Phoenix beer while watching the sunset over Trou aux Biches beach, with its powdery white sand, calm waters and boats bobbing to the sway of the gentle waves. Hope we have a lovely sunset today. Well, another relaxing day for me from doing nothing, to doing nothing, to eating, to drinking and to doing nothing. Okay, World. I think Charlie may windsurf, kayak, wakeboard and do a few laps in the pool.'

22 June 2012

'Hello, World. We are in Mauritius having a good time, and I'm in a lot of pain with a hamstring injury after a water-ski accident. I will see if the affirmations and mindfulness help with the pain.'

30 June 2012

'Hello World, thank goodness, I have recovered from my hamstring injury. I'm laughing with Charlie this morning as I had a magical moment yesterday swimming with the playful dolphins. Being in the water with these mysterious, intelligent, aquatic creatures. Swimming below, above, alongside and in front of me, with their quizzical inquisitiveness, fascinated me, as they swam and played in the bay. This was life-changing, and I felt a renewal and reawakening, as they invited me on the adventure of life.

Watching the baby dolphins swimming under their parents then courageously swimming closer to gaze into my eyes, harmoniously delighted my senses. I felt a restorative energy that charmed my being. World, thank you for sending the dolphins, with their flirtatious smiles, as my spiritual ally, to heal and connect me with the limitless possibilities that I had forgotten about.

Well, the day has come, and we need to depart this tropical paradise with its lovely warm weather and astonishing sunsets. We fly back to Johannesburg, spend the last evening in Pretoria with Mae and her boyfriend, and then back to London. I feel the impressions of gracious balance as we leave this dreamy island.

Oh my gosh, it has all come to an end and what should I do? Anyway, I have made a special request to you World, and I'm still waiting for the response. Okay, World. Charlie is lying stretched out here on the bed contemplating getting up and going to eat more buffet "petit dejeuner", the French term for breakfast.'

CHAPTER 35

Hello World, back to solitude

22 July 2012

'Hello, World. What can I say, as all of it has reached a head. What do you think about the minds and what they tell me? The reason I'm asking is that I'm trying to cope with the loneliness again, living on my own since returning to the UK from our holiday in South Africa. The minds are taking over again, and I can't stop them. What do you think is going on?

Charlie said that I don't always concentrate when he is speaking, and I don't give him a chance to voice his opinion or give him my full attention. So, I have been practising mindfulness which the Americans say, is going to help me be in the present moment, and not have my mind wander too much, especially when people are trying to talk to me. So, today I will be on my own and practice mindfulness with being mindless. I have to make sure that the minds are not going to take over again and defocus me.

My message is, "But though your outer man perisheth, yet the inward man is renewed day by day[1]". Does that mean

World, that my ego should get some rest and the minds will follow suit? Is my inward man the soul? Because I can touch my body, I can listen to the voices in the head, when the minds are having their debacles, but I also need to hear my soul. Will you help me with finding out what needs to be renewed day by day?

It is not easy when you live alone, are unemployed, and your family live very far away, the minds get overwhelmed and start fretting. Why can't they stop? I will google again to see if I can find an answer and solution regarding this catastrophe. Okay World, we will see how I get on.'

31 July 2012

'Hello, World. Well, let's see how I got on with those over-whelming feelings of loneliness. I have learned to be on my own and enjoy solitude so that it does not become negative, but something that I am comfortable with. It doesn't mean that I don't feel lonely, but that lessens over time becoming pleasurable. I am coping a lot better because after spending the whole of last week on my own and the whole of the weekend, I could cope because the minds were behaving themselves.

Charlie and I went to watch the men's group gymnastics with China winning gold, Japan silver and team GB bronze. The final yesterday was absolutely gripping. The score came up with team GB for the silver medal, but the Japanese contested the score, and they ended up receiving the silver medals. It was all quite exciting for team GB and for me screaming and shouting support waving my Union Jack madly. I didn't feel like a Coloured or needed to Play-White, because now I am working on my pledge of allegiance to the Queen, which I can apply for in a year's time.

I even got to see my idol, Pixie Lot, perform before the final. I am looking forward to a nice day today, and I will adjust to a new country if I can secure employment in Switzerland. Everything is going okay and working out the way that it should. Okay World, all's good.'

19 August 2012

'Hello, World. It's Sunday and today is a beautiful sunshine day which is going to be utterly lovely. Today is a year since I was on my way to Australia. And the message I had for that day was, that all you need to do is take one step at a time. I am reading the poem, "Lead kindly light amid the encircling gloom, the night is dark, and I'm far from home, I do not ask to see the distant sea one step enough for me[2]".

On my journey to recovering my health, it was important for me to focus on taking one step at a time as it was such a slow and lengthy process. I still need to take one step at a time in everything that I do and completely surrender and move in whichever direction is necessary for me to go.

I have been building up my piano and organ repertoire again, you know, multiplying the talents as we are taught in church. I am practising really intensely and am excited about that, as it has given me a whole new sense of achievement and provides me with personal pleasure which is very satisfying. I won't bury them and give them back to the Master when He comes. I don't know when he is going to come, but I'm getting prepared to double my talents, anyway.

I'm going to have a joyful day going to church soon, practice on the organ after the service and come back home to a lovely Sunday roast. Okay, World it is also good that we don't only reflect but look to the future. Like my message for today to not look to the full distant future but what is ahead and that way, you don't stumble. I have an interview in Switzerland on Wednesday and see where that leads me. I will take one step at a time. That is enough for me. Okay, World?'

22 September 2012

'Oh, Hello World. Well, I have been taking one step at a time and coping with the aloneness and remembered what I said a month ago. I'm trying not to be busy which is okay. You know to quieten the voices in the head, I go and do the house-work, scrubbing and scraping and cleaning. So, now I'm just ignoring the chores and letting the inward man renew.

I did get the job. I know that I'm being productive and contributing, which has given me tremendous content-ment, doing what I am passionate about, working with professional colleagues and taking one step at a time. I'm back in the UK at the moment. I have been travelling for a few days each week to Zurich and staying in a lovely, com-fortable apartment when I'm there. When the time is right, everything happens the way that it should.

My message for today is to not just say and feel something but go out and do it. I remember the poem by Wordsworth, "To yield entire obedience to the law[3]", attracting all the good things into my life, giving thanks and surrendering. That conscience is the voice of Divine love in the depth of our being and to enjoy what you have and relish the inclina-tion for the inner life.

So, I'm taking one step at a time and focusing on where my feet are treading. Okay, World.'

7 October 2012

'Hello, World. The sun is shining so I will tell Mae that I don't have to wear a raincoat today. It is Thanksgiving Day in the UK. For the past few weeks, I have been complaining about my loneliness. I have been feeling uneasy and questioning why my life is like this at the moment.

The theme of all my messages for this whole week was thankful acceptance of everything and surrender. The poem that was written in 1604, "That I may murmur not, tho' bitter seem my lot[4]", resonates with this theme. And so, I arrived back on Thursday from Switzerland and managed somehow to stop complaining and be thankful knowing that there is something larger than me. World, I am going to have a good day trying to practice thankfulness and surrendering to what is. Okay, World.'

CHAPTER 36

Hello World, walking in spirit

6 November 2012

'Hello, World. Today is Tuesday, and I'm having my tea in bed. I am thinking about how one walks with God. I'm not sure if the Americans are right as they talk about The Universe. Isn't it all the same thing if I mention God? That was what they taught me in Sunday School, so I will just say God, if that is okay? It all means the same thing.

Where was I? Oh, yes. I was thinking: do I walk with God in the shop, in the office, in the house and in the street? When we are annoyed, can I still walk with God? Can I walk with God with a smile on my face and a smile in my heart, irrespective of who or what provoked my anger or caused me to feel disappointed and frustrated? I was wondering if it is okay if I can walk with God even if I feel disgruntled? I had a lovely few days, but they are always short-lived and not sustainable, that is why I was asking, as it is confusing when things change so dramatically from one moment to the next. And I think from that perspective, it makes me think through a lot of what I desire, especially when my needs are not being met.

I have a presentation later that does not cause me angst. I will do my best and walk with God by being true to what I can deliver. Why do some people in positions of power that can influence change and make decisions that affect our lives, think that they are high-class? I always remind myself that there is nothing to fear. Living during apartheid made me realise that equality is available to all, and I received a good message to confirm this today, "He will fulfil the desire of them that fear him[1]".

The next part of my message for today is, "delight thyself also in the Lord: and he shall give thee the desires of thine heart[2]". My desire is to reach my career aspiration. I will consider this every day with every breath I take, knowing that I will receive something greater and more glorious than I dared to consider.

I spent many months last year waiting for my body to heal. I had to nourish my body with the correct nutrition, supplements, rest, sleep, the correct level of exercise and pacing through a very slow therapeutic process. At the time, it was very difficult to focus on this on a daily basis, because the mind wants to wander and not stick with the plan, but somehow, we managed, and my body is now healed.

I think this was helped by the ladybirds who took the ME under their wings when they flew away. This was a miracle, but I also did my part by doing the body-scan meditation every day like the Americans taught me on YouTube. That trained me to acknowledge my physical pain and disability, without judging it and letting it be. I was able to gradually release the energy that had lodged in my musculoskeletal system and other parts of my body. I know that this sounds serious, but this was how I experienced it, okay?

I visualised the sun shining through the forest trees as I walked in the woodlands in West Sussex, feeling the crispness of being outdoors and being strong enough to actually walk. When I was finally capable of walking unaided, it was a miraculous moment experiencing what I had spent months visualising. Now, I'm able to do everything that I need to do. I think that I don't need to visualise what I have and can do. World, I think that it is time that I create new pictures as the old ones have been realised. Do you agree?'

13 November 2012

'Hello, World. Well, what can I say? Today is supposed to be sunny, but it's still raining, so the weatherman didn't confer with you.

World, you know that my body is healed, and you have been supporting me with the minds and now I know a bit more about how they operate. It was not an expedition that I had initially considered or prepared myself for as conceivable. Yes, I knew that the healing of my body was a path that I had to take, and it unfolded bit by bit.

The healing of my mind was not dissimilar. I wasn't really coping for a long time with being on my own, complaining about feeling lonely especially when the working day was finished, the evening began, and there was nobody to talk to. I resisted trying to use entertainment and tried to fill the space from within. I questioned why am I alone? I don't want to be alone, I want to share my life with somebody. I was then led to the book, "The Tao Te Ching[3]", which has very wise ancient teachings and I now understand how to surrender.

I entered a very deep presence within, where I can acknowledge my thoughts non-judgmentally, accept them as they are and create a cosmos for inner peace, inner joy, inner calmness, acceptance and surrender to my current situation.

I have learned to control my thoughts and attract to myself those things that make me feel good and that are good for me. The minds don't run amock anymore. My psychological structure and intuition have developed, and I would really like to help others appreciate and understand what it is that I have learned. I extended this to Mae and hope that I can spend time with her. Over the next few weeks, I will continue to explore the transformation of my mind as I am being taken to another pinnacle of understanding.

World, as you know, I wanted to move to a bigger place to live in. I was surprised when I placed an offer on the house that it didn't materialise and had to accept that it wasn't meant to be for me. When the agent came back with an issue, I didn't feel disappointment and didn't have the urge to influence the decision.

Within a matter of an hour, I found a suitable house that we could use for Christmas as this was my main concern. Mae and her boyfriend are coming for Christmas, and I don't have enough space for them to stay in my tiny annexe when they arrive. I found a holiday cottage close by, at a reasonable price and exactly what I was looking for, with a piano and a fireplace. This will be a fabulous Christmas.

I am learning how to still the mind when negative emotions surface, and become overwhelming by going deep within. When one has to cope with disappointment, the mind dwells on the disappointment, or the mind keeps dwelling on the harshness of someone's words or the mind dwells on the lack of certain things. I have to put that at ease, and go really deep inside myself and remain there until the emotion dissipates. The minds now don't stand a chance because I can observe them. They try, but they just stop their chatter and no longer are a source of confusion.

It doesn't take a long time. Sometimes a few seconds, sometimes a few minutes and sometimes I have to do this repeatedly until the negativity dissolves. I'm learning so much as I'm going through this process and so grateful, that I get overwhelmed with the profundity of what I am learning on a daily basis.

Now, my mind can recondition, which doesn't happen overnight and make sure that my soul sojourns with me on this journey. Okay, World!'

18 November 2012

Hello, World. It's Sunday, and I'm having my breakfast and listening to sacred music. As I mentioned before, I had worked on healing my body and in my prayer to heal my body this took an unusual path to the restoration of my mind. There was one prayer that I said every day and have been saying for more than a year now. It is a simple prayer, "Lord penetrate my body with your spirit, and let your spirit remain within me". I learned this prayer from the German faith healer, Bruno Groening. He died in 1959, and I am not even so sure how I stumbled across this prayer.

I can leave the mind behind when going deep into my soul and let the energy of my soul expand. I call it the soul, World, but the Americans have many other terms that they use. My soul then magnifies so that peace, love and kindness can emanate.

It is something we have heard all our life in church, and suddenly it makes sense at a deeper level. We try to put captions and definitions or try to categorise things, but there are no categories, no terminologies and no definitions when you are deeply rooted inside your soul. My message for today was so apt as I have read this many times before. I have known these words almost all of my life and for the first time today the light illuminated with the brightness of day. It is a peaceful Sunday morning which makes it significant for me.

The message is, "We dwell in Him, and He in us, because He hath given us of His spirit[4]". The tendency for us is to be driven by our thoughts, mental functioning, our egos and our intelligence. Yet the powerhouse is already there through the spirit within each one of us. I have been learning how to go within, "Learn Thy wandering senses gently to control; Thy dearest friend, dwells deep within thy soul[5]".

I am always reminded of these words, "Be aware of your own natural spirit and temper. Be patient under the sense of your own vanity and weakness, and patiently wait for God to do his own work, and in His own way[6]".

That is really my intention. To wait patiently. We don't know it all as we sometimes think that we do. It is not an easy thing to practice, the going within and being patient. Okay, World.'

CHAPTER 37

Hello World, being present

1 January 2013

'Hello, World. Today is the first day of 2013 and a day to look forward to a wonderful year ahead. I have just returned from seeing a delightful cottage in a hamlet outside of Horsham which is going to be perfect for me to move into. The house is newly built and modern and overlooks the fields and countryside. It has a large, modern farm-house kitchen and a wood burner in the living room. I have spent the day on my own but didn't feel lonely, stayed present deep within and felt certainty with being me.

I want to sort out the new house in the West Sussex countryside and look forward to a happy, peaceful, loving and kind year and one that will bring Prosperity. Bye World.'

5 January 2013

'Hello, World. I'm in one of the most picturesque locations I could have opened my eyes to. Words cannot describe the grandeur I observe. "How is this possible?" I ask myself, and the minds now know how to respond.

It was dark in Engelberg when I arrived last night and woke up this morning to the view of the majestic Mount Titlus from the balcony of my hotel room. I finally made it here and will have my first ski lesson today. I'm so excited and have to find out where I'm supposed to be meeting my ski instructor. I have never seen so much snow in my whole life. Oh, my goodness! This is overwhelming.

I am talking to you World, looking at this absolutely marvellous mountain covered in snow. This is a fairy tale, and I am in it. There is mist now, and I'm sure it will be sunny at the top of the mountain. I better get up and get prepared for my adventurous day.'

17 January 2013

'Hello, World. I have no one to talk to except you. I have to talk. Ah! Last night was an interesting evening as was my last night in the annexe as I was planning to move to the new house first thing this morning. Charlie and I had a heart-to-heart conversation and considered parting ways. So, a lot of pain of rejection resurfaced again, and I had to deal with that. I am over it now, acknowledging that it is so. I won't beat myself up about it and will try not to dwell on it. In a way, I'm happy that we spoke, and now I know where I stand with him. Although, the minds knew all along.

My message today is not to think too much about the things that try you, but to, "Rejoice in as much as you are[1]". You have to take every trouble, every disappointment and every pain you have as a true opportunity to die to self. Dying to self when the ego is hurt.

Yes, the thoughts will arise, but I then let them pass. Every day becomes one of prosperity. I know this, and it is resignation and complete surrender. My intention for today is to accept what has happened; accepting that I will feel some pain and I will accept that I have pain. This is an opportunity to die to self, to completely surrender and continue along the path of life.

World, I'm glad we had the chat and I will take your advice and won't dwell on thoughts of discontent. Okay, World.'

CHAPTER 38

Hello World, life goes on

18 January 2013

'Hello, World, what amusement and a turn of events from yesterday. To crown it all, it's snowing really hard this morning, and I have to move into the new house with the weather not being supportive. Charlie came back last night and said that we should stay together. He said that there is no other alternative. What exactly does that mean? I finally figured that he realised that he doesn't yet have anyone to consummate with.

Fancy that, World. So here I am: a means to pleasure. Anyway, some of the minds agree with him that I also don't have any other alternative and tell me to accept things as they are. He is helping me move, and at least that makes the move easier for me. One needs a man at times like these. Okay, World, thank you for sending him back to help me move because I was at a loss for how I was going to cope.'

8 February 2013

'Hello, World. It's been a whole year since I made the first
recording. It was my birthday last year, and I was snowed in
and had to dig very deep to get through the day cheerfully.
Remember that was a whole year ago, and I couldn't go
on the country walk with Charlie? Wow, it's a year later
and I'm a year older, but I still feel like I'm thirty. I'm in
Switzerland in my apartment today. It is snowing and a
fairyland outside.

My birthday wish is to enjoy a long-term relationship
with someone to share my life with on a daily basis. The
person who can see me for who I am and can still love
me no matter what happens, what I look like or am going
through. This is my intense desire. My message for the day
is to feel intense desire, have faith and believe that anything
is possible. Okay World, I can dream, can't I?'

10 February 2013

Hello World. It's Sunday today and looking at woody the
woodpecker outside and had a lovely birthday weekend with
Charlie and the Hart family. I enjoyed my birthday celebration dinner last night, was overindulged with presents, cards
and a surprise birthday cake that Charlie tried to decorate
with icing. There wasn't enough space on the birthday cake
for the "Happy Birthday, Matilda", which made us laugh as
it only had "Happy B Matil". The birthday cake really made
me very happy and reminded me of the time when I was
little, and we couldn't afford a birthday cake.

The important thing is realising that a whole year has
passed, and can reflect, knowing that the past year can't be
recovered. I can't rewind the clock.'

23 February 2013

'Hello, World. I'm in bed having my coffee and reading my message for today. I'm in San Antonio attending a medical congress. I'm jetlagged and its early morning. I had an interesting evening last night. During the latter part of the night, I couldn't sleep, and I was trying to use this time to feel and be at peace with myself. To be and not resist the fact that I couldn't sleep. The minute that resistance came up, I got anxious which worsened the insomnia. However, once I was able to step outside of myself, I could listen to my thoughts. Thoughts of the past stirred up certain emotions and thoughts about things that may or may not happen in the future surfaced. My mind focused on many possibilities.

As I could watch this happening with my thoughts, I kept bringing my thoughts back into the present, meditating in this light sleep state focusing on my breathing. I was able to acknowledge my thoughts and watch them for a few hours. This experience has given me relief, peace and a sense of being, accepting that everything that happens is meant to be.

I had a few thoughts that surfaced emotions that did not overwhelm me, as I could remain in a present state of peace. What bliss, as my understanding of emotional freedom develops. I knew that in San Antonio I was going to bump into some colleagues that had known about my illness and redundancy. It was interesting as all I was doing was being where I am and not allowing myself to go back and talk about the past. The past is history. It is of no relevance for where I am now, and for my future career. Okay, World.'

3 March 2013

'Hello, World. I'm listening to "Are we like sheep" from Handel's *Messiah*. Sheep are so trusting that they follow the goat to the slaughter. I am questioning, why are we encouraged in church to be like sheep? You think that it wouldn't be common sense to be like sheep.

Okay, World. I think that I am having a romantic relationship with myself and it feels so good. I made a fire, watching the logs burn, cooked a delicious meal and am drinking excellent wine. I have been listening to Handel's *Messiah* since I was six years old, and I'm going to listen to the whole of the recording today. I will wait for the answer regarding the sheep.

I am enjoying all that I have learned about my body, my heart, my mind and my soul and appreciating this peaceful and enjoyable Sunday afternoon with JoJo, my wooden tortoise, that the Hart family gave me as a house-warming present. That was so grand of them and surprised me with a potted herb garden for my yard. JoJo keeps me company when I'm having a glass of wine in front of the fire.

You spend your life waiting for something to happen, waiting for someone to come and rescue you. There is no one coming. When you realise that, you realise how happy you can be by being yourself with yourself, and that's what we have to do every day with no resistance. It is surrendering to whatever happens at that moment and being true to yourself. Okay, World I have you and JoJo. And, of course, Charlie in the background.'

CHAPTER 39

Hello World, It's goodbye

8 June 2013

'Hello, World. It is Saturday and a fine, warm day in the UK. The leaves are shaking in the breeze. Oh, what a fantastic day! I don't know why I am so upbeat today? Perhaps I'm using the American affirmations – that if I tell myself good things, then my minds don't have to get upset. I was woken up abruptly by my phone. I was so jetlagged after getting back from the long flight from Los Angeles. My sister in Australia called to find out how I am doing. She still worries that I will get ill with all the long hours I put into my work and the long-haul flights as I travel around the world.

This is what I was getting to, World. I had to deal with Charlie and me finally separating. Last weekend all he spoke about was his indifference, and it was back to the same old tale that I had been hearing for the past eighteen months. All of my pain surfaced, and yes, I felt sorry for myself because things are not going the way that I want them to go. Don't worry World, I didn't resort to the "dronk verdriet".

The positive thing is that I can practice coping with the challenge of being on my own again. Thoughts will pop up frequently that he is not there, and I can't reach out to him, but I intend to surrender and be content as good will come out of this.

It is a lovely day, and I intend to do small things; the small things that really matter. So, I will focus on doing the small things, doing chores around the house, giving someone a call and sending a few thank you notes. So, all's good, and I'm sure I know that I'm going to have a lovely day. I have to say that, or else I am going to cry again. Okay World, I surrender. It is what it is.'

14 June 2013

Hello, World. I got up early and I'm overwhelmed with my pain. I try to cope with the break-up and not having Charlie in my world anymore, and this has caused feelings of rejection. I feel hurt and as my pain surfaces, the initial reaction is to run away and be busy and not deal with the actual feeling.

You know World, I questioned why we do so much house-work and came to a conclusion while I was scrubbing the kitchen sink that didn't need scrubbing, when the voice in the head said, "Stop this Matilda, the scrubbing is not going to cure the pain". I realised that the house-cleaning wasn't going to freshen up how I felt inside. I have learned to allow that feeling to be there, observe the pain and the feeling of hurt that my world is different now, and the pain dissolves over time. The scrubbing of the sink doesn't work. Okay, World.'

21 June 2013

'Hello, World. It's Friday, and I'm here in West Sussex with Mae. We have a nice weekend planned, so all's good in the world. What do you want to say to the World, Mae? Say something, ask something and the World will give it to you. Mae says World, that she wants to be happy. I have encouraged her to use what the Americans taught me with their affirmations, "I am happy, my life is filled with happiness, I believe I'm happy". Okay, World.'

2 July 2013

'Hello, World. It's six o'clock in the morning, and I am in the US. It was hard to leave Mae as she is visiting me in the UK. We will have a few days together when I get back before she returns to South Africa.

My message is to take one moment and one day at a time, to take small steps and they eventually lead you along the path that you are meant to go. To let it be, let it go and surrender to the present moment. I feel a joy and an inner peace which I am happy about now. That is all I can be content with. Okay, World.'

CHAPTER 40

Hello World, coping again

16 July 2013

'Hello, World. I'm in Zurich and arrived late last night from one of my many travels. I feel wonderfully alive and energised and when I think of Charlie, I only think good, wonderful thoughts about the present and embrace the way that I feel.

When we think of love, we often mistake it for something that is physical, but it is not. Love lives in the soul. Having this love and showing this at work and in my daily activities to everyone around me, ensures that things work out well. I am enjoying being in the present moment, in this eternal feeling of love.

I have a whole day meeting today at work, and even though I arrived late last night, I had a restful sleep and feel quite refreshed this morning. I have some ME symptoms but nothing alarming. Only some tingling in my legs. I acknowledge that it is there to remind me to remain composed. Mae is doing well at university. All is good, and I am going to have a wonderful day, open to any possibilities while living in the eternal now. Okay, World.'

27 July 2013

'Hello, World. Hope I can start with a bit of small talk while I have my coffee. It's overcast today which is lovely and a bit cooler. It has been very warm lately. I arrived from Zurich last night and had a quiet evening of contemplation. What I can summarise is that looking at where I am in my life, I have found a place within where I can maintain the balance of my body, mind and soul.

I have been working on surrender and emotional freedom for the past two years. This opportunity provides me with another chance to practice. Gosh, World, it is so difficult, but the positive thing is that there is a slow and steady improvement and I have to keep moving in the direction of acceptance. And not go back to obsessive thoughts with no positive outcome. I surrender to whatever comes my way today, taking one thing at a time without resistance. Okay World, I am looking forward to a nice weekend.'

CHAPTER 41

Hello World, the one cell

3 August 2013

'Hello, World. It's Saturday afternoon. It's the summer, and the sky is blue with the late afternoon sun shining directly on my skin. I felt like a braai and there was only you to have the braai with. So, World, I went to the farm shop in the village, bought meat and salad, made the fire and braai'ed the home-made burgers, farm sausages and lamb chops. I can enjoy this with a salad made with cucumbers my neighbour brought for me.

I'm sitting here and enjoying being with Nature on my own and not feeling alone. Can I call you "Nature" too, World? There are so many terms in the English language that I get perplexed. I never thought this was possible as I had always depended on relationships, like everyone else. I am enjoying being with me and feel truly loved deep within my soul. I realised that I don't need to be with someone to feel truly loved on this beautiful day in England, with views of the green pastures. I have a loving relationship with myself, experiencing the miniature of infinite life and love that has no beginning and no end. I understand the essence behind who I truly am.

Okay World, I will enjoy the last of the glorious, late afternoon sun; feeling calm, content and letting go of the past because the future is filled with joy, love and kindness. I am glad to be here. I miss Charlie with good sentiments and feel completely content with being me on my own. I'm sitting here after the braai with the slow setting sun and have this lovely house in the Sussex countryside to relish. All's good, World.'

4 August 2013

'Oh, Hello World. Okay, I'm laughing at myself. I'm having a chuckle at the moment as I crossed my legs and crossed my arms to reprogram my mind like the Americans demonstrated on YouTube. I was saying, "I desire to be the best that I can be", practising the Americans affirmations again. It seems to be helping with the minds. I submerged into a deep meditation, remembering when I was five years old, and I wanted to be a doctor. And guess what, World? I became a doctor.

When I was five years old, I was living in four rooms with my parents, sibling's, extra cousins and an aunt in the house. I knew that I would be a doctor.

Okay World, when I was one cell, after my parents mated and the cell divided and develops into this whole person, that is me, Matilda. When I was one cell, my eldest sister was very serious. It was her personality to be very serious about everything. My second eldest sister was rebellious because she didn't know how to be serious like my eldest sister. And, at that time I was only one cell coming into this world.

I don't know what this world was going to be like, and this one cell was asking, "If I'm only one cell, what is happening out there?" The boy and girl twins were starting school, they knew everything and thought that they were very special. People would exclaim, "Wow, Oh, my goodness, you are twins. A boy and a girl!" Everyone was excited because they were twins which made them feel very special and important. They were the boy and girl twins.

When I was more than one cell. When I was a multicellular organism of four years old, they were sitting at the dining room table doing their homework. I was sitting there too listening to my eldest sister seriously saying, "Come on, everybody. We have to finish all of our homework". Note World, she used "have to". The second eldest was writing rebelliously, and the twins were grinning at each other.

I was only four years old, and I wrote a capital 'R' on a sheet of paper they had given to me to scrawl on. My brother exclaimed, "Oh my gosh, you wrote a capital 'R'. You are only four years old". I said, "Is that a capital, so this is the little 'r'", and I wrote a lower-case 'r', a straight line with a curve on the top of the line. I continued, "That is a little 'r'". He said, "You are not supposed to call it an 'arrr', you should call it a 'rrrrrrrrrr'." I knew that I was bright. I knew that I could learn things faster than others, absorbing everything that was happening around me. I was so privileged, as there they were sitting at the dining room table being very serious about their homework and here I was a multiple cell person, a sponge absorbing everything that was going on around me.

I knew that they would be impressed with my capital 'R'. I could do the capital 'R' quite a few weeks before, but I didn't write it. I held back with the capital 'R' and then I decided that day that I would write the capital 'R', and the little 'r'.

They then enquired, "Do you know how to do all the other letters of the alphabet?" I answered, "Of course, I do", and started writing, "This is a capital 'A' and that is a little 'a', this is a capital 'B', and that is a little 'b'", and I proceeded with all the letters of the alphabet. They all stopped, stunned looks on their faces with frozen pens in their hands, eyes wide open and in still silence. I looked at them and asked, "Why are you looking at me like that? I know how to do this. I don't need to go to school to learn. I have been learning from you all these years" and laughed.

Anyway, coming back to the main story. When I was crossing my legs and arms and doing this subconscious re-programming in deep meditation while saying to myself. "I desire to be the best that I can be", I realised that I'm going to write this book because this book has been living inside of me for years.

I had been relying on people to provide me with their encouragement, which is twaddle. Relying on others to tell me how much they love me and how much they care for me. So, that's why I'm laughing World, because it is so naive, to rely on other people to provide you with your creative ability that you know lives and stirs deep inside of you.

You don't need to hear that from anyone else except the one that knows you. The one who knows the essence of who you are. All you have to do is let it emanate from the depths of your soul. The Americans mention a lot about "manifesting", an English word, I'm sure I knew before I was one cell. So, I am going to bring to the fore what I know deep inside of me, the knowing within my nature.

We don't only have this physical body or physical realism, but we also have some other dimension to ourselves. When you are growing up, and you are only one cell or two cells, you know this other dimension. I couldn't see it, I couldn't feel it, but I knew that it exists. And it is as I know the World exists and say, "Hello World".

Okay, World I'm sorry for laughing, but I'm very happy that everything I desire, I receive at exactly the right time, exactly the right day and exactly the right moment. I have to ask for it and I receive abundantly. I had known this since I was one cell, or perhaps before I was one cell. I know that this book is inside of me and I need to get it out.

Okay, then there came the next set of twins who nobody fussed about, and shame, they were peculiar girls and had old fashioned names. Poor things, they didn't know where they fitted in because the one was not academic and the other was of poor temperament. Here were all these others at the dining table with books, writing and studying and they were wondering what the others were on about. What are they doing all this stuff for? We are not interested in all this. "What is a pen?" one of the twins questioned. I'm sure she said to herself, "I don't know what you are asking of me? I don't want to write words", and requested, "give me a crochet hook and wool, and let me speak the words". She can speak four different languages and is creative with her hands. The other twin wanted to be outdoors, running, jumping and doing acrobatics.

I remember I came home from school one day and they said that one of the twins was gone to get her stomach pumped out. What do you do to have your stomach pumped out? I was confused. She had taken too much of some medication that she found in my mum's medicine cabinet, and they had to rush her to the doctor to have her stomach pumped out. I don't know why she did that and it lived with me, because I thought that she was going to die, and I would be sad about that.

I pictured a big pump and that they pushed it on top of her stomach because I was so creative and small, what did I know about stomachs being pumped out. I thought that they put a vacuum cleaner down your throat and hoovered the stomach out. I didn't know what was going on. I really, really didn't know what was going on and didn't want her to die. Then she came home, and everything was normal again. Nobody mentioned the stomach pumping ever again. Then she started feeling better and grew a big heart of love and kindness.

I need to go to sleep now. I started thinking about the book, and indeed I will complete it. Okay, World.'

7 August 2013

'Hello, World. It's Wednesday morning and I can hear the birds chirping away. Last night, I took a walk to the pub to have a chinwag with some of the locals. This is West Sussex countryside in England, and I love it here.

Last night I had a minor disappointment and would have been easy for me to have entertained these negative thoughts. I'm really enjoying my solitude and can venture quite deeply within, knowing who I am. As I was observing my thoughts, dealing with this minor disappointment last night, my tendency would have previously been to respond in a way that made someone else responsible for the way that I was feeling. But this was not the case.

I am responsible for the way that I feel. If I want to feel happy, I must make myself feel happy. I can't expect some-one else to do that by sending an SMS or calling. Doing something that gives one short-term pleasure. I still have the feeling that things are taking an unusual course and the disappointment lingered a bit but not for very long.

My message is, "I will instruct you, and I will teach you in the way you should go[1]". Well, I wanted to go in a different direction World and was brought back to where I should be effective.

Okay World, I understand what that means, and shed tears of joy when I read, "If thou canst believe, all things are possible to him that believeth[2]". So, I looked up the word believe, and it means that you know it to be the truth. It means that you think about it so much that you know it to be the truth. I think it was like that when we were so poor and all I wanted and thought about was to be a doctor.

This part of my daily message really made me ponder, "Man can do everything with himself, but he must not attempt to do too much with others[3]". I was laughing, learning to be peaceful and loving with myself, and not to look outside for answers, considering, "The possibility of writing on the eternal skies the record of a heroic life[4]". Okay, World.'

CHAPTER 42

Hello World, dissolving the past

13 August 2013

'Hello, World. I'm having a giggle and a hearty laugh because I'm in Eglisau, this very quaint old town in Switzerland. It is on the Rhine River with the most charming ancient buildings and lush vegetation surrounding the town. I'm in the Hirschen Guesthouse which is probably sixteenth century and has been so well and lovingly renovated. This absolutely one of the quaintest places in the universe for me.

I can't question why I am in Eglisau of all places? I walked down to the river after receiving the keys for my apartment, and as I walked across the bridge with the vastness of the river flowing below, I felt as though I was in an enchanted realm. It was such a splendid day, not too warm with pleasant sunshine and blue skies. I walked across the bridge to the guest house as I don't have furniture in my apartment yet. I have to wait until tomorrow for the delivery of the bed and the couch.

I'm amused that I am actually in Eglisau, a place I had not even envisioned that I would be able to live in. My desire was to integrate into Swiss culture by living in the middle of a typical Swiss town. So, here I am.

It's not really a town so I don't know what you would call a place like this. But there is a good railway link, a good bus service and lovely country walks that I'm going to start exploring. The river will be fabulous for kayaking and swimming in the summer. I was thinking today, "Oh my word, I'm in Eglisau". My apartment is so gorgeous with so much space including a glass wood burner and indoor barbeque. I have not been thinking too much about missing Charlie and accepting that I can't question why it had to be this way. It is not up to me, and I have to get on with things.

This is a new beginning, and I can see that it will be a lovely place to live and will bring me as much happiness as the hamlet outside of Horsham does. Oh my, I have the best of both worlds. Wow, World, you do have a way of bringing miracles into my life. Okay, World, the world is mine!'

14 August 2013

'Hello, World. It is such a stunning morning. I am enjoying the views from this lovely hotel while I wait for the furniture to arrive. I'm looking forward to having things sorted. This morning, I looked up into the hills arrayed with green pasture and lush Swiss vineyards, opened my message book and read, "I will lift up mine eyes unto the hills, from whence cometh my help[1]". I had to laugh out loud with gladness for this message. Oh World, it is a glorious day today.'

3 September 2013

'Hello, World. I'm in New York for a meeting. I'm jet-lagged. It's in the morning and woke up early to prepare my mind. I spent a week in Switzerland swimming in the Rhine

River and picnicking at the lake in Zurich. All my furniture arrived, and the apartment is liveable now. I'm really, really pleased about that.

I was thinking that I was coping with the break-up, but I do miss Charlie. I miss doing things with him, and I miss all the fun times that we had. And then last week I found out that he has found someone to consummate with. A blow for me to cope with because I have to picture him with someone else, which is not that easy.

I knew that at some point he would want to go off and meet someone else. I knew it that weekend when he came and he was unresponsive. I think in a relationship that when someone wants to be with someone else, you have to let them go.

The phone is ringing. It's probably Mae telling me that she has the visa's which they were on their way to collect. I will need to call Mae now. Okay, World.'

23 September 2013

'Hello, World. Well, it's Monday morning, and I'm in the Dominican Republic having a holiday for a week with Mae and her boyfriend. We are staying in a lovely five-star resort, with huge rooms with spectacular views towards the ocean. I listened to my previous recording three weeks ago where I was still trying to deal with my break-up with Charlie. I am reading an article about dissolving the past, but as certain memories come flooding back, this causes the emotions to erupt like an active volcano spewing out hot lava. Okay, so World, I intend to dissolve the past in whatever way I can and not plan on doing any activity today. This will provide me with the space to be.

Yes, I am laughing at myself, World. It feels so nice laughing at myself because all of it is in my head and not based on any present reality. Mindset is the reality, isn't it, World? It's in my head, and some of the time I identify too much with what is going on in my head. I'm having a wonderful life right this minute and spending my time enjoying it. Okay, World, let's see how I get on. It's so amusing to have challenges like this. Off to another wonderful day in Punta Cana.'

5 October 2013

'Hello, World. It's almost midday on Saturday, and we are still having coffee. It's Mae and her boyfriend's last day as they leave for Johannesburg tonight. We were partying last night in Horsham, and now I'm all emotional about their departure. They were here for five weeks. It will be strange coming back tonight to an empty house. Such is the joy of life.

Mae got kicked out of the club for being wasted. That was so funny because she wasn't really wasted. She just had symptoms from her illness which caused her to be off balance which the bouncer mistook for inebriation. The taxis were lined up right outside Carfax waiting to take the drunk people home. We had fun last night and that's the most important thing. Okay, Mae has her calendar with a photo holding the stingray that was taken in Punta Cana. Bye, bye World.'

12 October 2013

'Hello, World. What can I say as it's another wonderful day? I'm back in the UK and had a lovely evening with my nephew who is visiting me from South Africa. I'm still lazing in bed. My message for today is, "Singing and making melody in your heart[2]". Just about having total resignation to the

Divine World. The good thing is that I don't get lonely and have learned that you don't need to depend on someone else to provide you with happiness. Happiness comes from inside of you. You can show happiness and demonstrate the love to everybody.

I have learned to be happy within myself, and this is such a wonderful gift that I have been able to enjoy about myself. I am a happy person. I have a busy work schedule ahead of me and can only do what I can. I will keep doing a great job.

Otherwise World, what can I say, I am laughing at all the commotion of dissolving the past. I'm so happy. The World is Mine!'

CHAPTER 43

Hello World, integrating the self

28 October 2013

'Hello, World. I'm still in this happy state. It's been an interesting week this week with many back-to-back meetings and presentations. I had plenty of opportunities to be anxious. But somehow, when I thought about my anxiety, it all stemmed from a negative thought that had crept in during early life for not feeling worthy of being part of something that is special. And I enjoy my job, and I am aware that these thoughts were coming into my mind. I worked hard to remain aware of them, and that dissipated the thoughts.

That you can grow up in poverty and so you may feel that you are inferior to other people that have grown up with privilege. This was a nice way for me to be aware of this and I also met up with an old friend I hadn't seen for ten years. It was as if ten years had not passed. It just goes to show how timeless things are.

I'm busy preparing mentally for a meeting that I will chair today. I'm content and happy and enjoying my work life. I have a good balance. I've had a good two weeks being on the road and now still in a hotel room. It is quite interesting that you say to yourself that everything goes well because you expect that it goes well.

Last night I spent a large part of the evening trying to integrate two parts of myself. Two divergent parts of my personality. I have always been aware of this discord within this particular aspect of my personality. I was quite aware of what those differences were. It is saying, on the one hand, I like this and on the other hand, I like that when the two likes are contrary to one other. Thank goodness, we don't have three hands, hey World?

Anyway World, I was trying to integrate these two parts of myself into one person. I'm having a bit of a chuckle that this conflicting dialogue in my mind is something that I have always been aware of. Now that I'm focused on it, I'm trying to finally complete the integration. I am sorting the minds out once and for all.

Subconsciously I didn't want to integrate them as I like both parts of these personalities. That was why I was having a giggle at myself, "You shall find that your condition is never opposed to your good, but really consistent with it[1]". That is what I was trying to accomplish to get consistency within these two. To converge these two parts of my personality will create more consistency and the less complexity you create into your personality, the easier it is for people to cope with you because there is less density. Okay, World, this is too serious, and I need to get on with my day.'

16 November 2013

'Hello, World. It's Saturday, and I'm in Pretoria on holiday and listening to all the African sounds around me. I went to the Kruger National Park with Mae and her boyfriend and got to see a leopard strolling on the track. During the bush walk, we came very close to rhino and had a good view of buffalo. Mae came on the walk and is still struggling with post-exertion fatigue and headaches. She is trying to get her body back into balance.

My intention for today is to be full of joy, peace and happiness and avoid anything negative. My message is, "If Thou dost perceive such feelings arising, turn gently away from them²". Okay, World that was a lovely message for me and I have to make a decision now about the rest of my holiday which I am looking forward to.

A holiday is a feeling inside of you, of being at peace, relaxed and enjoying yourself. Although I was on holiday this last week, I didn't have that feeling, and only now I am enjoying having that holiday feeling. I found solace from this simple, wonderful message, to not let anything disturb my joy, peace and happiness. I was able to do that for a long time and then got derailed. I'm back on track now. Okay, World.'

25 November 2013

'Hello, World. I have woken up on this Monday morning, and I'm still sitting in a cosy bed drinking a cup of coffee. I'm at the Arabella Spa, the same one that Charlie and I were at more than a year ago. I'm here on my own after spending time with Mae in Pretoria. I'm reading Emotional Freedom by Judith Orloff and working through the chapter on fears. I looked at that word fear, and the negative emotions that I was feeling had something to do with fear. She says to identify your fears, and my first reaction was that I don't have any fears. I went to sleep and woke up knowing exactly what those fears were. She encourages to examine where those fears come from and what the triggers are, and to overcome these fears.

The fear of my heart being broken again causes me a lot of emotional distress, just thinking about the pain of a broken heart. I didn't realise I had that fear. Now I can see that this fear is keeping me far-removed from any potential danger of having my heart broken again and of suffering feelings of rejection.

Oh, World, the fear of getting old and frail. Old, frail and wrinkly. Okay, so I'm laughing about this one picturing myself old and wrinkly.

My message for today is to, "Go face the fire at sea, or the cholera in your friend's house, or the burglar in your own[3]". Fancy that World that the message for today from the book bought so long ago at Winchester Cathedral is based on how I am to overcome fear.

To face the fear is to replace the fear with love. Loving myself first. It was wonderful being in the Kruger and doing the walk and getting that close to rhino and buffalo, and then you understand fear. You are alert and understand that, that's real fear. The psychological fears and more difficult to deal with as these fears have been programmed into me and now I have to deprogram the fears. Okay, World, it's been a lesson learned, and I'm going to go forward and "face the fire at sea".

I will watch a few of the American videos again and see if they help with "facing the fire at sea"! Okay, World.'

CHAPTER 44

Hello World, a New Year

5 January 2014

'Oh, Hello, World. I have enjoyed the Christmas with Mae and her boyfriend, and they are gone back to South Africa now, and I'm going to book ski lessons. I'm enjoying the snowshoeing too. I didn't know that it could be such fun. It doesn't cost a penny, and you make your own tracks and it's so lovely to be outdoors and energised in the fresh mountain air and snow.

Okay World, what can I say? I'm really happy and at peace and looking forward to a prosperous New Year. I know that Mae is doing well and is being well taken care of having the love of her boyfriend which I'm grateful for. I started to think of some objectives for this year for me. To do the best that I can do at work, building up my piano and organ repertoire and learning some German phrases to use. I can only do what I can see in front of me.

Okay, World it's me and JoJo, my wooden tortoise. He is a good pet; he doesn't consume much of my energy, and he listens to me like you do. Okay World.'

15 January 2014

Hello World. I had terrible flu last week and now the post-viral symptoms are returning. Some of the ME symptoms have come to have a bit of fun in my body. I'm sitting here by the fire because I'm tired of lying in bed. I can only use one arm as I over-used my right arm yesterday and now the joint pain in my wrist and muscle pain in my arm is severe. I can't do much with my right arm. My legs are in excruciating, burning pain as if I have run a marathon. Yesterday, I did a lot of work with my right arm, picking up wood and chopping vegetables and now my right hand complains to the rest of the body, "I have had enough. You can't do this to me anymore". It is now on-strike and doesn't want to function, so I have placed it in a sling to keep it comfortable until it decides that it is part of the rest of my body again. So now I can only say, on the one hand, this, as the other hand can't contribute to the opposing side of the argument. Okay World, I am trying to have fun as these ME symptoms are causing havoc again.

I called Mae to try to get her to come and look after me, so I will let that one go. I have been on my own for two weeks, either stuck in bed or laying on the floor in front of the fireplace. I'm going to do everything I can to recover from this ME relapse. Where are the ladybirds? I will imagine that they will take this with them to distant realms. I have all the dietary supplements, my diet of fruit and vegetables, no processed foods and am drinking lots of water. When I was ill before I got through each day, so I have to get through each day now. Being ill and all on your own requires a lot of inner strength. I am strong and at least have Miranda Hart to keep me going with her comedy show.

Okay, World, onward and upward to good vibrant health and to hiking in the Swiss Alps. Although I'm house-bound,

I can visualise lucidly being in perfect health and climbing up mountains. I can only climb one mountain at a time and this one I have started climbing. Okay, World!'

9 June 2014

'Hello, World. I'm laughing as I listened to my recording of the middle of January after I had the flu and post-viral symptoms. At the time, I was feeling sorry for myself and in a lot of pain. And now I'm in full vibrant health. A lot has happened in the past five months, and we need to catch-up.

Since the post-viral symptoms relapse, I needed to alter the thoughts that were controlling my mind. The emotion I dealt with was guilt. I had been harbouring guilt as a result of a negative influence, and once I acknowledged and observed the guilt that I was suffering, it dissolved. I could enjoy a sense of freedom and my body healed naturally.

I improved my fitness level and have completed a few challenging mountain hikes. In the middle of January, I still felt that my heart was broken and that was a painful emotion, and now I feel completely healed and opened myself again to have another relationship. I fell in love, and although it's not reciprocated, my heart is healed. The truth is how I feel and not that it needs to be reciprocated and can enjoy that in-love feeling which is sufficient.

I received a special message a few weeks ago which made me think. The context was that it doesn't matter how much you give and even if you give everything, have faith to move mountains, but if you don't have love, then you were nothing. I thought about that as one of the things that I needed was to fill myself with love. Love for myself, everything and the whole world.

I attended the Munich Pentecost service yesterday which was a very uplifting experience and one that I wanted to mention as I had been wondering about giving to others. The message for Pentecost was that "it is more blessed to give than to receive[1]". It is better to give and if you give, give with love and give love. So, I feel in such a good place because my life is filled with love. I am able to give more love, and I'm able to receive love. And I have love all around me. World, I know that I am on my own, but I do not feel alone.

To think correctly helps you create the correct actions and the correct actions lead to a great way of living your life with love. Love for yourself and love for everyone else with happy, joyful and thankful thoughts. Workwise, this is a period of uncertainty, but I don't regard this as a period of uncertainty as everything is certain. I have an interview tonight, and that as well is no uncertainty, and I can go calmly and relaxed to meet my future boss.

I am visualising writing the book. I have the picture in my mind now, and it's going to happen. I am grateful that I'm able to spend so much time in silence and solitude. I think it is a privilege. In the beginning, I thought of it as loneliness which was a negative observation. It is not loneliness. The World can only talk to you in silence, and you have to go deep within your soul and listen in that space of silence. In solitude, all the answers that you want are given. All the peace, joy, happiness and harmoniousness convey my sense of purpose.

And I had another experience which is related to being prejudged because of my age. What is age discrimination? I don't feel age I feel myself, and I almost responded nega-tively but got around to see it for the truth that it was. That age for me is an illusion. It doesn't exist, and I'm happy to be who I am irrespective of how many years I have lived on this planet and how many years that I'm still going to live on this planet. So, they still whisper behind my back, "Do you know how old Matilda is?" It's the same as when they whispered behind my back, "I wonder if she is a Coloured". It's the same thing really. The malice of discrimination.

So, it's time now to get ready for the airport for my trip to London. Hope that I have a really good evening meeting my new boss. Well, World, it's been five months, but we have caught up.'

14 September 2014

'Hello, World. I spent Sunday lunch and afternoon on my own. When I first started spending Sunday's on my own, I missed my mums roast lunch and being with the family. I would always read the message for that Sunday. Another period of my life when I moved to England and I would spend Sunday lunch and Sunday afternoons on my own, it was just the same. I missed my mum's roast and during those long, long years of spending Sunday lunch and afternoons on my own, I would still read the message and listen to beautiful music.

Today I find myself in a splendid country with views of the Swiss Alps. I am enjoying my Sunday roast lunch and drinking a lovely wine from the Valais. I was asking the question regarding the lesson to be learned from this opportunity of spending Sunday lunch and the afternoon on my own, when the choir sang for the baptism this morning, "Who dwells in the secret place of the most High, shall abide under the shadow of the Almighty[2]".

I feel at peace and divinely happy to be given this privilege of spending a Sunday on my own. So many would go home now. There would be much commotion, plenty of activity and not much time to reflect on the message that was shared in the Sunday service. I feel so privileged and so honoured to be in this amazing body to enjoy life with.

I have realised the purpose of the many Sundays on my own, and I am at complete and utter peace with myself. Okay, World.'

CHAPTER 45

Hello World, The World is Mine!

27 February 2015 00:20

Okay, World, it's in the middle of the night, and I want to tell this story. When I write it, it should be a charming story. When I was so ill and lying in bed in a darkened room in Sydney, for the whole day, I had plenty of time to talk to The World. I had loads of time to talk to the World. So, I would say "Buongiorno Dio, lo sai ce chi sono aquio", which is Italian for, "Hello God, I know that you know that I am here". I used to call God, World, acknowledging the vastness of the Universe. I would say, "Hello World, you know I'm here".

I was alone in that dark, quiet room and what was I supposed to do? There was no one to talk to because I had to lie still with eyeshades covering my eyes and earplugs in my ears. There was only The World to communicate with. I then thought about the words, "Love your neighbour as yourself[1]", and started to deliberate on that. So, I had to learn that I needed to love myself and that I should love everybody and everything in the whole wide world as much as I loved myself. I travelled on the harmonious journey of love.

On this journey, I realised that I was in conflict with myself. A deep-seated, passionate conflict with myself and this uneasiness would not go away and remained with me. A feeling deep in my body as if my solar plexus was on fire, burning, moving frivolously and rumbling like thunder. And I asked The World, what should I do about this disquiet? The reply was, "to have joy and peace". And so, I had to remove this conflict, desire and craving which was causing turmoil inside of me and to travel in the direction of joy and peace.

It was a blissful journey because I started to understand what craving meant. I truly began to understand for the first time what craving meant. It meant a passionate desire for something that you think is going to give you pleasure. Not, is going to give you pleasure. I only imagined that it was going to give me pleasure because the potential gratification of the desire was in the future. You don't actually have a craving at the time that the craving is being satiated.

Craving is the belief that the imagined fulfilment of the desire is going to be a source of pleasure in the future. There is inner conflict as one part of you wants one thing, and the other part of you wants another. And the two are having a joyous debate inside of you. How do you resolve intense craving? So, I went on the journey to reach joy and peace.

This journey ended with passionate desire. I could feel the desire but no longer experienced the craving of the imagination's promise of pleasure. What was the conflict inside of me? Why was I fighting with myself? Why was I trying to sabotage myself? It completely resolved, and the way that it happened was surreal. I was laying up in the loft in my apartment. It was very quiet, and I was feeling very peaceful and drifted into a deep state of introspection.

As soon as all the thoughts in my mind were resting, I became overwhelmed with the realisation of what I truly wanted. What I honestly wanted was not an imagined source of future short-term pleasure, and I felt this deeply and completely. There was no more conflict, and I knew precisely what I desired. Not only did I know what I wanted, I knew that I was going to get it. I believed it. I truly experienced faith, trust and belief and could completely surrender. This was not the striving for temporary pleasure but the achievement of long-term joy and peace. Okay, World. I'm signing off now and want to thank you from the bottom of my heart for being my Navigator, my Captain, the Consoler of my soul and my dearest Friend.'

Matilda, at that stage, was sincerely in love with herself and The World. She received this confirmation during the next summer while pouncing around the delightful, colourful English gardens surrounding the Glyndebourne Opera House, dressed in a ballroom gown, sipping champagne with all those magical, golden bubbles, before the performance of Gaetano Donizetti's comic opera, Don Pasquale. Happy and radiant, Matilda accompanied by Mae enjoyed a traditional English summer picnic on the lawn on a sunny day, during the long interval typical of the Glyndebourne summer festival.

Matilda had fallen in love with herself, her body, her heart, her mind and her soul, three years after returning from Sydney and smiled to herself knowingly considering, "The World is Mine!"

Part Three

CHAPTER 46

Smiling at the trepidation

Matilda, unemployed for the fourth time in five years and facing the loss of her plush apartment in Eglisau, waits and watches her mind to see what fears surface.

Sitting on the balcony of her apartment on a warm summer's day in 2017, Matilda gazed at the deep green vineyards in their sloping array along the banks of the Rhine River. Matilda sat and waited for the voice in the head to send thoughts of dread, but nothing came. Matilda thought to herself, 'Come on! Are you afraid of having no money to pay the bills? Are you afraid of running out of your savings and becoming homeless?' Matilda pondered for a moment. 'No, I don't think so,' said the voice in the head. 'I've been there before, and it wasn't so bad. I have to start off a new base and continue to be content no matter what life throws my way.'

Matilda was at the peak of her career contributing to substantial research that contributed to a positive economic outcome when she was informed that her executive position would not be located in Switzerland. Matilda smiled and thought, 'This is a disappointment after working tirelessly. The World surely must have a better plan for me.' Matilda professionally accepted her fate and ensured that the transition progressed smoothly, knowing that she would need to adjust to the change.

Sitting on the balcony that afternoon, Matilda gazed in the opposite direction to that of the vineyards and looked at the far-reaching views to the south, where only the snow-capped tips of the Swiss Alps were visible. The gentle breeze blew cool air on her face and cooled her body down on that warm summer's day. Matilda remembered the interviews that she had many years ago when she needed employment for the first time.

Matilda remembered that phase of her life like it was the day before. Those memories never fade. Mae was only a few months old, and Ed and Matilda had just bought a house in the southern suburbs of Johannesburg. Within a few months of the property purchase, mortgage interest rates skyrocketed. Matilda and Ed, faced with this financial dilemma and trying to care for a baby, decided that Matilda would need to interrupt her studies and seek employment. Matilda often interacted with medical representatives from various pharmaceutical companies, while doing her training at the University Hospital. She supposed that, that would be a suitable form of employment. A good basic salary, a company car and extra commission that would certainly save the dire financial situation that they were enduring.

Matilda prepared her resume and began the hunt for a position as a medical representative. She had noticed that all the medical representatives were White but was not concerned as she had the papers to show that she was classified as White. Some of the apartheid laws were in the process of being repealed, and this provided her with further encouragement. Applications were made and the process began.

Matilda's first interview for a medical representative position was confirmed. They had called Matilda on the phone and with her highly-polished White, English-twang she impressed the hiring manager with her knowledge and determination. The well-groomed, smartly-dressed Matilda regarded her reflection in the mirror, certain that she would do well in the interview. She was well-presented and had good verbal communication skills. She arrived at the reception of the big pharmaceutical company ready to present herself for the interview. The White receptionist looked sceptically at Matilda and said, 'Are you certain that you are here for the medical representative position?' Matilda replied in perfectly articulated English, 'I am certain that I am here for an interview with Mr Solomon for the southern suburbs representative job.' When the receptionist repeated the question in disbelief, Matilda knew that there was something amiss.

Matilda was escorted to Mr Solomon's office, and his face dropped onto the floor when he saw that Matilda was not White. Matilda sensed this immediately, and after the pleasantries of introductions, no further questioning was being proposed. He sat up from his chair behind his desk and said, 'Thank you very much for coming and was nice to meet you,' while showing Matilda the door. Matilda regained her composure and with repose, breathed in deeply, slowly exhaled, smiled and made her way out of the building past the watchful sneer of the receptionist. She thought about the Song of Solomon[1], "I am black and beautiful. Do not gaze at me, because I am dark", which cheered her up.

Matilda would not let this deter her and with determination continued submitting applications. One of the recruiters who gave Matilda the same look as she had now become accustomed to, after over twenty interviews said, 'I am really sorry girl,' the use of the word, "girl", was said in a derogatory manner. He continued, 'You will need to sell motor-car parts first before you can even attempt to be a medical representative in the pharmaceutical industry.' Matilda smiled gently at the man, thinking to herself, 'I go to my success, and this is only your opinion.'

Matilda had by then counted a total of forty-three interviews, most lasting only five minutes and some about fifteen minutes long, before the hiring manager would show her the exit. The longest was a twenty-minute interview with a gentle, soft-spoken man. Matilda felt pity for him as he was just going through the formalities. He was too embarrassed to let her go earlier, as that would have been too obvious, and he was trying to save face. He certainly was not going to give Matilda a chance, or even consider her for the shortlist. Nevertheless, he was trying to be polite, and Matilda endured his discomfort. Matilda thought to herself, 'He has never had a Coloured or a Black woman in his office, unless she was bringing him his cup of tea or cleaning his office,' and smiled inwardly.

Another appointment that she had made didn't even get her past the reception desk. The recruitment consultant made a call directly to the company saying, 'I have a European with good qualifications. Are you prepared to interview her?' Well, the loaded word, "European" was their secret code for "Play-White". Matilda knew that she was not a European, and thought, 'I think that they assume that I am stupid,' as she had never even been overseas, and although received a B grade in geography, knew that Europe was far away from southern Africa. Matilda understood the innuendo and straightened her posture even further when she exited in her professional dress and high-heels, standing tall and refusing to feel humiliated by this exchange.

Matilda enthusiastically looked at herself in the mirror prior to each interview and before leaving home and knew that she would make the same effort with her appearance and would present herself with impeccable professionalism.

Months had passed, and the family's financial situation reached critical levels. With resolve, Matilda pressed on with further applications until she found herself in an office in Sandton, facing a recruiter that had her origins in Israel. The sincere smile that she gave Matilda was the first warm response that Matilda had received for the past few months. After interviewing Matilda for over an hour, the recruiter said quite directly, 'Matilda, I know what you are facing. Don't worry, I will find you a liberal company that will consider you for employment. I will find you something suitable,' which she did.

Matilda found herself in a research position with a pharmaceutical company after being interviewed by an open-minded hiring manager and a tall, eloquent Black man who was head of Human Resources. What a change and she had a higher salary than that of a medical representative. Matilda was offered a BMW as her first company car and her career which spanned decades had been launched. A portal opened and Matilda, although working her butt off to prove herself, felt as though she had glided in.

Three decades later, Matilda was faced with losing her fourth job in five years. With the same determination, Matilda thought, 'I go to my success,' and smiled to herself on that warm afternoon, sipping champagne while lounging on the balcony of the apartment in Eglisau that she was being coerced to vacate by her neighbours.

Neighbours, whose dissidence for the cheerful and joyful Matilda showed intolerance to her ethnic disparity. Intimidation, bullying and subtle discrimination that was unbearable and Matilda would need to seek a new abode.

CHAPTER 47

Strength in distress

Matilda wondered what fears had allowed this current turn of events, all culminating simultaneously and remembered a time a few years before.

Matilda was ravaged by various fears that she did not admit to. One morning, Matilda sat bolt upright in bed, eyes wide open and counted on her right hand her fears. 'Oh, my goodness!' Matilda exclaimed to herself out loud, 'I count five fears and now have to admit these to myself. How did this happen?' thought Matilda, 'I went to bed last night thinking that I had no fears.'

Matilda considered that she had a lot of courage so could not admit to any fears. She had been reading Dr Judith Orloff's book, *Emotional Freedom*, and Dr Orloff suggested to admit five fears to yourself. Well, Matilda told herself, 'I don't have any fears, so I will keep reading the book.' Until that morning when the infinite blue sky perpetually opened and Matilda admitted, 'I can identify five fears. Five fears that I have been carrying around with me for a very, very long time, too many years to count.'

'Okay', thought Matilda and took a writing pad and a pen and started writing down in neat handwriting, her five fears. Matilda put the pen down a few times considering, 'This is harder than I thought,' while resting her chin on the back of her right hand.

There was no way of smiling through this. This would take all her courage to admit to herself. 'Ouch,' Matilda squealed, 'I have the fear of getting old. Okay, one out in the open now and still four more to go!' Matilda had no idea how she was going to tackle each of these fears, but nevertheless she persisted through to the next fear.

'But, before I get there,' thought Matilda, 'this does explain a few things especially over the past few years.' No wonder Matilda acted and dressed as though she was thirty. Her last two relationships were with partners that were more than a decade younger than she was. She still went dancing in nightclubs and bars, imagining that she was thirty-something. 'Oh, my goodness!' Matilda exclaimed surreptitiously, 'And that is only the first of the five fears. Well, at least I am getting somewhere with this.' Matilda breathed a sigh of relief that she was brave enough to admit this fear. The fear of getting old. Gerascophobia was a real thing, and Matilda knew that she could not keep her head in the sand about the fact that she was getting older.

Why do we dread ageing? Why are we so scared of it? Is it not a joy that wisdom and experience can support us in the future? Matilda was sure that she would deal with this fear and thought, 'I haven't resorted to Botox or any other chemical or surgical intervention yet. Would I or would I not go down that path to look younger?' Matilda questioned herself. Matilda satisfied with the knowledge that this was a perfectly natural fear and had not experienced it intensely as yet, having travelled many times to California where it is in its extreme. She knew that she had time to face this fear and embrace wisdom and experience and retain her beauty that radiated from within.

'Okay', thought Matilda, 'Now own up to the second fear.' Matilda remembered the words from Dr Orloff's book, "You are going to track down what scares you, then use courage to transform it". Matilda asked herself, 'Matilda, what scares you?' Matilda laughed to herself, 'I am afraid of getting fat.' Now almost in tears laughing so much, Matilda admitted, 'I am scared of getting fat. I am petrified of getting fat.' Matilda was a slim UK size 8 and fluctuated between a size 8 and a size 10 all her life. So why would she be afraid of being fat when she ate healthily and counted calories. Matilda climbed on a scale each morning to weigh herself and exercised regularly. Procescophobia, the fear of putting on weight, Matilda knew was irrational and was the fear that had caused her to determine her self-worth by her body weight and muscle tone.

She was terrified that if she ate anything she wanted, she would not be able to stop eating and blow up like a balloon. Matilda, after acknowledging this ludicrous notion to herself could face the fear and put these terrifying feelings into perspective. She was in reality never fat, never overweight and with a normal body mass index all her life, struggled in private with this fear. Matilda would need to work towards creating a new reality of feeling healthy. She would diminish the fear and anxiety that went with having this fear that had rooted itself so deeply within her psyche, that she would need to consistently talk herself through these preconceived perceptions. 'This is going to take effort,' thought Matilda. 'And there are another three fears for me to work through too. Oh dear!' Matilda sighed.

The next fear Matilda acknowledged to herself and was the feeling of being restrained by an invisible force, in whatever she had committed herself to accomplish. This was the fear of failure. That lingering doubt and lack of confidence in her abilities. Matilda thought about where this fear could have originated and remembered being ridiculed in a demeaning manner, 'Who do you think you are? You are just a poor Coloured kid from Wentworth.' Someone also said to her as a teenager, 'So you are also just going to work in the check-out counter at the supermarket like all the other girls from your township,' and another phrase that she heard often, 'Nothing good ever comes out of Wentworth.' Matilda would feel diminished, and the fear of failure continued to grow and directed negative self-talk which Matilda even after admitting to this fear, would have to catch her thoughts in their tracks.

A story Matilda reminds herself of is related to the fear of failure. As a senior executive, she had to present in New York City at a public event. Matilda had a good night's rest, woke up to prepare for her presentation and started getting dressed for the day ahead. Matilda was immaculately dressed and professionally presented when she opened the door to exit her hotel room and realised that a demeaning thought had popped into her head.

The voice in the head ridiculed, 'Who do you think you are Matilda? Who do you think you are going to fool today? You are just a poor, ignorant kid from Wentworth. What do you think you are doing at the Yale Club Hotel here in New York City?'

Matilda with shock could not believe that these thoughts were still haunting her at this critical time before the presentation. Matilda took a deep breath in and re-entered her hotel room while exhaling slowly. She sat on the edge of the bed and stared at her reflection in the mirrored wardrobe opposite the bed. 'Well now Matilda,' she thought to herself, 'You cannot go out of this room until you have cleared these sabotaging thoughts from your mind. Look at yourself, you are beautiful, elegant and you have had much success so far in your career,' the kind, loving voice pepped her up.

Matilda lay back on the bed and gazed at the ceiling and started her breathing meditation to clear her mind. She then slowly lifted her hands in the air and prayed, 'I know that you know that I am here.' She took another deep breath in and out, and a confident, cheerful Matilda left the room, to a successful presentation with flawless responses to the challenging questions that were thrown at her by the attendees.

Matilda knew that she had to continue to monitor her thoughts and control any disrupting feelings that would take root in her mind impacting her behaviour, performance and achievements.

Now came the "people-pleasing" fear that worsened Matilda's self-esteem, caused a lot of unnecessary anxiety and contributed to extreme melancholy. This deep human fear caused Matilda to imagine that everyone critically regarded her and therefore had to do whatever was necessary to please. No wonder she worked incessantly to please everybody and remained in an emotionally volatile relationship for so long with Angelo. All, driven by the fear of rejection and criticism, the fifth of Matilda's fears.

By this stage, Matilda was laughing at herself so loudly and so much that the tears were freely rolling down her cheeks. She laughed even louder and thought about the appearance of her face if she couldn't stop crying with laughter and the tears cut grooves into her cheeks. 'Okay,' thought Matilda, 'now that, that is in the open, I need to re-educate my body and my mind to have courage.'

Matilda talked to the voice in the head. Matilda reached for her pen and on a clean sheet of paper started to draw a picture. She drew a long suspension bridge over a river.

On the one side of the river were her fears and her worries which were thoughts about negative outcomes, and on the other side of the river was emotional freedom and positive outcomes. Matilda named the bridge, "Courage" and knew that she would need a great deal of courage to take the first step over the bridge, let alone walk the entire distance to the other side.

Matilda doubted, 'What if the bridge cannot support me and suddenly collapses as I walk across it?' Matilda would need faith and trust to propel her body to the middle of the suspension bridge. Trust that the suspension bridge was built securely, and exercise faith that it would support the weight of her body, her mind and her soul. She would need to cross the bridge, to reach a state of freedom, joy and peace, free from her fears. She would use her imagination to visualise and capture exactly what it would feel like when she reached the other side.

Matilda lifted her imaginary leg and started the journey taking her first step across the bridge of "Courage", with faith to freedom. Matilda knew that this would be a life-long journey with the fast-flowing river beneath, touching her life as she traipsed cautiously across the bridge.

CHAPTER 48

Logarithmic decline

The following week Matilda had invited a few friends to her apartment in Eglisau for a dinner party. Matilda wanted to know all about Peter and his fiancé, Tracy's recent golfing holiday when the conversation took an unexpected turn.

Peter was saying, 'Just as we landed the flight into Zurich from Dubai, one of the other business-class Swiss passenger's erupted with a loud voice swearing and saying that Dubai was rubbish and now that we are back on Swiss soil, he can do whatever he wants.' 'That's not the point,' thought Matilda, 'I wonder if this negative energy gains momentum?'

Peter continued his story. He mentioned how angry he was with this loud-mouth on the plane and couldn't wait to alight from the aircraft. 'Oh dear,' thought Matilda, 'I hope this has a good ending,' without expecting that this was going to be the case.

'Well, can you imagine how angry I was,' and Peter continued, 'To top it all, when we arrived to collect our luggage, my prized golf clubs, myyyyyyy golf clubs were completely destroyed,' Peter's pitch and the volume of his voice was now raised, 'and now had to take time to fill in forms to lodge the complaint.' Matilda thought to herself without saying a word, 'Peter has absorbed the negative energy, and this can only get worse. His anger had certainly boiled over into his life, and he was walking with it out of Zurich Airport and taking it home with him.' Matilda could see the blood rushing to Peters red blotchy face as he was relating the story.

On the way in the taxi, they had an accident with another vehicle that they were trying to overtake, and the worst of all was Peters brand-new Audi's winter tires were stolen from the parking in the basement of their apartment building.

At this point of the story being told, Matilda raised both her hands up in the air crying, 'Stop, stop, did you neutralise this negative energy?' There was a moment of deep stillness at the dinner table, and Matilda said a silent prayer. With that everyone began to laugh heartily, and the rest of the dinner progressed with pleasantries.

Peter wasn't letting up on continuing his story. He needed to pass a test the following day and sounded anxious. Matilda hoped that he had neutralised the negative energy, as this could certainly spill over into his test the following day.

When they met for coffee on the Monday morning, Peter was quite upset and said, 'I had adequately prepared for the test, but I was still feeling a bit edgy.' He certainly was still harbouring negative energy, and Matilda wondered how this story would end. It turned out that Peter's negative emotions overwhelmed and engulfed him for the first part of the test. He said, 'During the test, the situation got out of control.' There was too much energy to dispose of, and there was no time for him to think about anything and he reacted, thankfully, with a positive outcome but just on the verge of the limits for a pass.

Matilda threw up both of her hands again and said, 'You have to neutralise this negative energy, Peter. You have been carrying this around since the incident on the plane when it landed at Zurich Airport,' and Peter nodded in agreement. 'But how Matilda? How? Every time I think of that guy I am disgusted about the things he was saying, and I can't get this out of my head. And now with all the other things that have happened, I must go and buy new winter tires for my car and new golf clubs, just a waste of my time and energy when I am so busy.'

Matilda sighed, and said very slowly articulating every syllable, 'Peter, you need to be a neutral observer of the way you feel right now. Can you do that?' and Peter stared blankly into Matilda's face. 'There is a technique that I use called mindful awareness. You should try it out, and I can send you some material to help you silence the voice in your head which will free you from those negative thoughts that are amplifying your emotions. You know,' Matilda said to Peter, 'negative energy declines logarithmically.'

Matilda remembered a time a year before when Peter came over for a visit one evening. He had emotional pain that was referred to his hip. He hobbled around Matilda's apartment obviously in physical pain talking for about four hours about his recent break-up with his girlfriend at the time.

The following morning, Matilda woke up to prepare for a long hike along the Rhine River from Schaffhausen old town, along the river passing the Rhine Falls to finally end at the Abbey in Rheinau, an ancient Benedictine monastery. While preparing for her hike, she put her right foot in front of her while bending to pick up her backpack and felt a tweak in her left hip. The same left hip pain of her dear friend.

'How is this possible?' Matilda thought, knowing that she had absorbed Peter's pain in an attempt to give him relief and now had to focus on providing herself with relief.

It is a good human gesture to show empathy and Matilda was pleased that this experience helped her to understand that she was highly sensitive to sharing others' energy. Her desire to provide relief meant that she needed to be aware of density and heaviness when interacting with others. Using this knowledge, Matilda could expel the negative energy from her mind and body by expressively shaking it off and laughed to herself.

Her morning ritual was to shake her body vigorously for a brief period, shaking off the past, followed by the conviction, 'I renounce all negative thoughts and surrender.' Every morning became a new basis for constructive focus.

CHAPTER 49

"La vie en Rosa"

Matilda was sitting on the sofa in her apartment in Eglisau one evening in early spring of 2016. It was pitch dark outside as all the street lights had already been switched off and most people had retired for the evening. Sipping on a glass of Merlot while listening to Andrea Bocelli singing, "A Mano, A Mano", "Little by Little". She felt the peace and tranquillity of that moment when suddenly this was disturbed by the beep of her mobile phone. A message appeared on the screen, 'Hello, it's me.' Another message followed shortly after, 'Can I call you?'

Matilda recognised who the messages were from and thought, 'I wonder if this is Dr Jekyll or Mr Hyde?' and replied, 'Certainly. You can call me.' Matilda's voice of reason was seriously complaining, 'What? Really, Matilda?' but she quietened the voice of reprimand. She was still in a state of delusion when it came to Angelo.

The last she had heard from Angelo was when she had left him eight months before. They had arrived at Heathrow Terminal Five from a holiday on the Greek island of Corfu. Matilda, Mae and her boyfriend were continuing on another

British Airways flight to Zurich and Angelo was remaining in the United Kingdom. The luxury European holiday that ended with Angelo's psychotic BPD drama. The emotional roller-coaster that reached a peak one of the evenings and got derailed leaving a mess that nobody knew how to clean.

Matilda hadn't realised that Mae and her boyfriend who were in the adjoining room, had heard his BPD ranting and raving, 'I don't believe it, blah, blah blah, f'ing blah, blah.' Matilda's wasn't listening to anything that Mr Hyde was saying and practiced focusing on her breathing and smiled gently. There was no reasoning with this monstrous assault.

He called Matilda deplorable names and went on and on in an insane, psychotic stupor. When he finally ran out into the middle of the gardens in front of the hotel room and shouted for all the residents of the resort to hear, 'I am Angelo f'ing Banks,' multiple times, while banging both fists against his chest like Tarzan, wailing out to the jungle, the two in the adjoining room came running out to investigate the commotion.

By this stage, Matilda was laughing out loud. How can one take this behaviour seriously? He looked as though he had accomplished a great achievement and stood there beating on his chest until he got tired of that and came back to sit on the patio. Well, they were all going back home the following day, and that was that.

Matilda looked at the messages on her phone and thought, 'I wonder what he wants to talk to me about now?' and FaceTime started beeping on her iPhone. Matilda answered the phone and stared directly into a tear-streaked, bedraggled looking Angelo sitting up in a bed. Matilda could see that he was high on something and answered, 'Hi, what's going on? Where are you?' She couldn't help herself asking these questions which were of no concern of hers. Matilda, while still looking at the FaceTime face of Angelo on the screen of her mobile phone, remembered that awful night in Corfu.

While Angelo was screaming abuse at her, she remained still and silent, not paying any attention to the words he was using while smiling and breathing, and said 'Angelo, I love you,' which was all that she could console his pain with. Matilda remembered calming Mae down that night and told her, 'It's okay. Go to bed now.' Matilda went to bed with a numb feeling that night, a numbness that she had experienced many times over the years that she had lived with Angelo. This senseless feeling engulfed her as she drifted off to sleep that night.

Matilda had a strange dream that night in Corfu. As she was trying to run away from danger, her left leg was dragging behind her while she was trying to run. Her left leg was not functioning properly, and as much as she tried to run, she felt that she was being constrained by a force that she couldn't see. The force was strong enough to slow her down, and the harder and faster she tried to run, her speed was being dictated by this resistant force. She was being held back and unable to push forward against her will.

As she entered her second sleep cycle that evening, she had another dream. Matilda and her sister were waiting with a few other people to be executed. As they lay on the benches, they waited a very long time for the executioners to arrive, Matilda turned to her sister and said, 'Why don't we just leave as they are taking so long to arrive and look around there is nothing stopping us from leaving.'

Matilda recalled during that dream that, as she waited for her execution, she felt as though there was still so much for her to do with her life. There was still so much to be done. She turned to her sister in dread and said, 'Come with me, and we can leave together undetected. They won't even know that we have left here.' Matilda was still thoughtful about her two dreams when the four of them had their final breakfast in Corfu.

Matilda focusing back in the present, asked Angelo while observing the dread in his face, 'What's going on? Where are you?' Angelo was trying to speak, but he sounded stifled, and Matilda simultaneously said, 'Slow down, Slow down. I can't hear you. What are you saying? What has happened?' Matilda thought, while Angelo continued to cry, 'She has left me. She hates me. I don't know what to do!'

Matilda asked, 'What do you mean?' although Matilda knew exactly what that meant. Matilda in the calmest voice she could muster under these circumstances said to the sobbing Angelo, 'I love you.' The words were out of Matilda's mouth before the voice of reason could stop her. She was still viewing Angelo through rose-tinted glasses and even after all these years, had in her fancy a hopefulness that somehow, they would have a nice detached family home in Horsham, and they would live happily ever after.

Matilda still living on this hope that the fairy tale in her mind was possible, asked again, 'Where are you? I see you are sitting on a bed,' and then 'Oh, you are in an apartment in Horsham.' Matilda said, 'Angelo, I love you. We can figure this out together.' Angelo then told Matilda, 'I need to be with someone who loves me, truly loves me.' Matilda ended the conversation confirming for him, 'Angelo, I love you.'

CHAPTER 50

Inner conflict

Matilda was reading one of Goethe's poems:
"You are aware of only one unrest,
Oh, never learn to know the other!
Two souls, alas, are dwelling in my breast,
And now one is striving to forsake its brother"
Matilda thought, 'Knowledge is one thing, and common sense is another,' but still agreed for Angelo to come visit her in Switzerland. Waiting at the arrivals hall at Zurich Airport, Matilda heard the voice in the head saying, 'Matilda, what the flip do you think you are doing?' Matilda responded, 'Waiting here for Angelo to arrive.' The other half of Matilda objected, 'Shush, I'm not thinking about the past now,' and quietens the voice of reason, as she sees the love of her life walking into the arrivals hall to the awaiting Matilda, with his tog bag slung across his shoulder, dark shoulder-length hair and a broad grin on his face.

Matilda knew that she certainly had "two souls dwelling in her breast" and consoled herself with the words by Goethe, "Love and desire are the spirit's wings to great deeds".

'So, Matilda. What psychotic behaviour is going to end the relationship, this time?' questions the other voice. Matilda gives Angelo a big kiss and a warm hug and puts her hand into his as they walk out of the airport to the parking garage where her Range Rover was parked for the drive to Eglisau.

Matilda could see everything in Angelo's eyes. When he had that distant faraway look, those were the feelings of emptiness. Those eyes contrasted with the eyes glowing like fireballs during a bout of intense rage. Then came the loving, smiling eyes, the calm lake following the storm and the playful crinkly eyes of mischief, like a naughty child playing a prank, the playful colour of dance.

The "I hate you, don't leave me", eyes were like a glass filled with tears that welled up but could not find an escape. And finally, the extreme closeness and tender, intimate eyes, the bottle-green colour of a clear and deep ocean.

The eyes of paranoia were jittery, darting from one object to another as if trying to find the culprit responsible for the conspiracy. The grey, observant eyes were those of Angelo observing himself from outside of his body. Sometimes piercing darts were shot from the eyes that bounced off the surfaces that they were being stared at.

The worst were the eyes of psychosis, those out of touch with reality eyes, and Matilda breathed deeply as she would need to keep very still and quiet and remain at a safe distance, run into the bathroom, lock the door and pray, 'Dear Lord. Please have mercy on me. Please help me, dear God.'

The psychotic eyes Matilda had first experienced only a few months into their relationship, almost a decade before. Angelo was watching the television in the lounge and Matilda was already upstairs in bed reading a book. Matilda jumped with fright and held her breath as she heard, "stomp, stomp, stomp", as Mr Hyde plodded his way heavily up the stairs.

Matilda will never forget the look in his eyes when he turned the corner and entered the bedroom.

His raging face was a few centimetres from Matilda's, and he bellowed in a loud, low-toned voice. He was shouting, but Matilda only heard the words, 'Blah, blah, blah. F'ing blah, blah blah.' Matilda had no idea what was going on, couldn't hear a word he was saying and thought to herself, 'He is crazy. He is certainly crazy,' while wondering what was coming next. She said to herself, 'How did a crazy person get into my house? Who let this crazy person into your house, Matilda?' Matilda gazing into his left eye then the right eye saw the madness, and the voice in the head was still enquiring, 'How did a crazy person get in.' Eyes adrift in their sockets not knowing which way to turn, shot from left to right in quick succession, swirling in a mist of confusion. Matilda will never forget those eyes.

Matilda realised as they walked hand in hand that there is no end to love. That love has no beginning and no end. Love is a bottomless pit and at the same time penetrates into the osmosis of the universe. Like Rumi says in one of his poems, "Love makes bitter sweet, Has foolishness ever brought you so high".

Matilda had reached the peak of the mountain of foolishness a few months later. The two souls dwelling in Matilda's breast would have to confront each other.

Matilda was lounging next to the pool of the villa they had rented in Ubud in Bali. Matilda thought when she booked the opulent and luxurious villa, that it would be the perfect holiday with Angelo.

Angelo remained attached to his mobile phone, SnapChatting, Twittering, WhatsApping, and Facebooking without any interval for conversation. He had not had any dialogue with Matilda for a few days, so she was forced to face the voice in the head. The two souls had plenty of time to rival with each other. 'They both want to be right,' Matilda as the moderator said to the two souls, 'but there is no right or no wrong, is there?' Matilda continued to moderate the conversation in her head, 'It is as it is,' knowing that she could not sway events. She was caught up in the suspension of time, a deferment that she had to confess to. A deliberate delayed decision.

Matilda thought, 'I can't stand this any longer,' and lifted herself off the sun-lounger, took a refreshing swim in the pool, towel dried her body and went to get her iPad. She would book a flight for herself out of this ridiculous situation, and get back to her apartment in Eglisau. She was going to leave him here in Bali for the rest of the holiday. Matilda had reunited her two souls, 'Enough is enough,' and booked a business-class ticket on Qatar Airways via Doha to Zurich for the following day.

Rumi's poem resonated with Matilda, "Never tell when you leave; there are those waiting to know of these things; that they might take advantage of you". Matilda kept silent about her intended departure for the next day. While packing the following morning, like a mantra, Matilda recited, 'Keep moving Matilda, keep moving forward and don't look back.' Matilda recited this until her taxi arrived and she said, 'Goodbye Angelo, I love you,' as she sashayed out of the villa and into the abyss of anticipation for the future.

Matilda was smiling to herself thinking of the glass of champagne that would be waiting for her as she boarded the plane. Sipping on the glass of indulgent bubbles popping in her mouth, Matilda felt like the world had been lifted off her shoulders as she gazed out of the window of the plane. She remembered the taxi ride with the hustle and bustle of the cars, buses, scooters and pedestrians and was at peace knowing what had been done, has been done.

Accepting the unacceptable after ten years, while her two souls were reunited.

CHAPTER 51

Mae's visit

The following summer, Matilda lay awake at night thinking about Mae's visit. Matilda had adjusted to being on her own and was looking forward to spending time with her daughter. Matilda thought, 'She would be sleeping on the plane now,' as they were in the same time zone. Mae was in first-class on the Airbus A380, British Airways flight from Johannesburg to London. 'Mae would certainly be enjoying the experience,' Matilda had known when she used her miles to secure the seat on the flight for Mae.

Mae was coming to spend the next two weeks with Matilda in Switzerland as a kind of retreat. Mae said to Matilda a few weeks earlier, 'I want to give up smoking. I want to eat healthily. I want you to show me how to be happy.' Mae had always been sceptical about Matilda's transcendent practice and over the previous five years had seen and experienced first-hand the miracles that occurred in Matilda's life. Mae was now finally prepared to learn more and was having an open mind about what she had previously regarded as, "mumbo jumbo". Matilda considered her daily practice and thought, 'I hope that she will restore the balance of her mind, her body and her soul.' Two weeks are not enough, but at least will be a start for Mae to begin the journey.

Matilda cast her mind to that tragic few days fifteen years before. The thirteen-year-old Mae had woken up one morning with loss of vision in her right eye and loss of sensation and numbness in her left arm. The radiologist was showing Matilda the MRI scan on the screen. Matilda thought, 'There must be a mistake. This is not happening. This cannot be the MRI scan of Mae's brain.' Matilda could see the bright spots where the contrast media had highlighted inflammation in the occipital and parietal regions of the white matter of Mae's brain. The radiologist was talking to Matilda, ' . . . demyelinating lesions in the occipital and parietal regions of the white matter . . .' The echo of the term "demyelinating lesions" reverberated throughout Matilda's body piercing her heart. Matilda and the radiologist could not bring themselves to mention the diagnosis that they both knew was evident from the MRI scan and they both left it as such, "demyelinating lesions".

'She was only thirteen-years-old,' thought Matilda. Mae at a young age was a talented and aspiring cellist. She idolised Jacqueline Duprey, the famous British cellist. Mae had all Jacqueline Duprey's CD's and watched the movie of the two Duprey sisters many times. Mae listened to the many recordings of sonatas performed with her husband Daniel Barenboim, but Mae's favourite recording was of Jacqueline with the Royal Philharmonic Orchestra performing Edward Elgar's 'Cello Concerto'. Mae always said, 'Jacqueline has ruined it for me. I can't listen to any other cellist perform this in the same way again.'

Matilda had driven Mae home after the MRI scan and told her to go and rest in bed while Matilda called the consultant who said it out loud. Mae had Multiple Sclerosis, MS, and should come immediately to the hospital for her first intravenous infusion of high dose corticosteroids. The treatment would take five days with twice daily infusions, and Mae would need to stay in the hospital for this period.

Matilda put the phone down and went to lie in a spoon position behind her daughter. Matilda whispered into Mae's ear, 'You have multiple sclerosis, Mae.' Mae immediately turned on her side to gaze deeply into her mother's eyes and said, 'That is what Jacqueline Duprey died from.' Mae had watched the movie so many times and knew how the life of Jacqueline Duprey had ended. Matilda with a voice of conviction said to Mae, 'We won't think about that now. You will get the best treatment, and you will live a full life.' Matilda held onto this belief using her will to influence Mae's thinking. They were going to get through life, 'having faith and living life to the fullest,' Mae's own words.

Matilda knew the side effects of the high doses of corticosteroids that Mae would suffer after the treatment and focused on making sure that Mae was comfortable in the hospital bed. Matilda thought, 'How quickly life can change.' Mae was then placed onto a subcutaneous injection given three times per week.

This was the screaming match played by the two parents and Mae each evening before her injection was due to be given. Ed would hold Mae down, Mae would scream, 'I'm not ready yet, I'm not ready yet,' while Matilda took the injection and injected the screaming Mae in the subcutaneous tissue of her buttocks. Mae's "bum ditches" as they jokingly referred to the scarring that left dents in the tissue that looked like a panty-line across Mae's buttocks.

By the time Mae was eighteen years old, she had mobility problems, unable to walk further than one hundred metres without the use of a wheelchair. The invisible symptoms of MS that others do not see: severe headaches, insomnia, depression, extremely painful muscle spasms, incontinence, poor bowel function, poor cognitive skills and many more that fluctuate without warning.

Matilda thought about Mae in her first-class seat on that British Airways flight, 'I hope that Mae has worn an incontinence panty before going to sleep on the plane. I will see when she arrives how she is coping with her depression, anxiety and her severe hypertension. Well, at least she allows me two weeks to help her get her balance back,' Matilda knew that the interconnectedness of body, mind and spirit were essential to a full, healthy and joyful life.

CHAPTER 52

I am here

Matilda, still thinking about being unemployed and having to vacate her apartment in Eglisau, received a message that made her feel as though she was tumbling into a boundless hollow with no end in sight. She took her iPad out to book a flight.

Trier, the ancient German city, known for its well preserved Roman and medieval buildings, is home to the High Cathedral of Saint Peter, the oldest cathedral in Germany, where the skull of St Helena, the mother of Emperor Constantine, the first Roman Emperor to convert to Christianity, is displayed. Matilda was fascinated when she went to visit the cathedral many years before, and now she was on a trip that she had to take to see Angelo for the last time.

As Matilda left The Promised Land with its unlimited supply of milk that tastes like honey, she gazed out of the window as the plane took off into the mist from Zurich Airport. Focusing on the raindrops of condensation still in its purest form on the outer window of the aircraft, Matilda asked the voice in the head, 'Where are you going, Matilda?' The voice of reason and the voice of intuition were her spiritual navigation and in harmony and congruent for the first time. Matilda knew what her expectation was, she knew where she was heading.

Matilda studied the information displayed on the monitor in front of her detailing the data of the flight when there was extreme turbulence, and an announcement from the cockpit was made. She was still caught up in her thoughts when the captain in a calm voice announced, 'This is your captain speaking. We are expecting severe turbulence for the next few minutes. We will make one approach to land, and then we have to consider diverting to another airport. I will provide you with further news later.' With that, the aircraft began shaking with extreme turbulence and sudden decreases in altitude that caused Matilda's tummy to lift and shriek. Passengers started crying and shouting as thunderstorms carrying rain and hail caused the plane to vibrate. Cabin attendants provided assurance with anxious voices and fear, noticeable on their pale faces.

Frantic and sweating passengers knocked liquids onto themselves. The galley floor was a mess as items of food, drink and broken glass lay about as the galley was not properly secured. The captain decided to do a go-around and remained in the hold for about ten minutes when another announcement from the cockpit was made, 'This is your captain again. I have to, unfortunately, inform you that it is not safe for us to land at Luxembourg Airport. We will now need to divert to Hahn Airport. The ground handling staff will take care that you reach your final destination.' The plane altered its course to land at Hahn Airport, which Matilda knew was only an hours' bus ride into Trier. She hoped that she would get there in time.

As the plane touched down at Hahn Airport, Matilda turned her mobile phone's flight mode off to find a message. A message that she was dreading. Matilda read the message off the screen of her mobile phone, 'Matilda, he is gone. Matilda, he is gone. We have lost him. We have lost him.'

Matilda turned her head towards the passenger sitting beside her and with astonishment noticed that sitting beside her was a man with the face, hair and handsome looks, dressed like Angelo who smiled at her with that same honky smile that she fell in love with ten years ago. The stranger remained looking and smiling at Matilda as though they had known each other all their lives. Matilda's heart skipped a few beats and saw her life reflected back in the eyes of the stranger sitting beside her. 'Hi,' he said. 'You have been pre-occupied throughout this flight. My name is Andrew, they call me Andy for short.' Matilda half-smiled back at him as she had not acknowledged the stranger with the same name as St Andrew, whose sandal, an important relic, still remains in the cathedral in Trier.

Once Matilda arrived in Trier, she walked towards the Porta Nigra, the large Roman city gate whose name reflects the darkened colour of its stones. The Black Portal, reconstructed on the orders of Napoleon who was exiled on St Helena island – a link that Matilda has with her ancestors, who were from St Helena. 'This is no coincidence,' Matilda thought, and the stranger named Andy was still beside her looking at the Porta Nigra and then back at the attractive women next to him.

Matilda had to get to Einsiedeln to pray before the Black Madonna and now walking out of the Einsiedeln Abbey she recited Rumi's poem, "Solitude":

"Spiritual joys come only from solitude
So the wise choose the bottom of the well
For the darkness down there beats
The darkness up here
He who follows at the heels of this world
Never saves his head".

'I saw the light of solitude when I was born into the calm and loving arms of Ida and now can also see the light of life,' Matilda thought to herself. Matilda spoke to the voice in the head, 'Enough is enough. No one is here to help me, so I need to help myself.' The voice in the head replied, 'But you will suffer.' Matilda finally reckoned that she was to suffer. No more running away from pain and suffering. She was going to get to the other side of this journey as she mourned the death of Angelo. The journey of the mind navigating through the unknown, under the tutelage of her spirit.

Matilda knew that she would need to turn herself inside out, journey along the hard route not wanting to die without at least taking the first step. 'It's me against me,' Matilda acknowledged, 'Suffering is the true test of life, the test of belief and faith.'

It was very quiet and dark, and Matilda asked herself the question, 'Why am I here?' The answer was prompt, 'To live Matilda, to live life to the fullest,' the deep knowing consoled Matilda. This is, "the Law of the Spirit of Life". Matilda said one final prayer as she walked out of the Einsiedeln Abbey, 'Lo sono qui e Dio. I am here.' Matilda strode confidently into the abyss that was her life.

Prologue

L ife is about living and feeling the excitement of being here. There is no more pain and suffering when you accept that pain and suffering are a part of living. The two cannot be separated. The realisation of this brings joy and happiness, as the pain and suffering are dissolved. This is freedom and you are set free from the transgression of Divine Law. You are set free from the Law of Death.

NOTES

Introduction

1. Röckelein, Der Kult des heiligen Florinus in Essen, p. 84.

Chapter 1

1. "Bakkie" is a South African word for van.

Chapter 3

1. Story created from the wow.gamepedia.com/Dark_Portal.
2. Alice in Wonderland: 1865 novel written by Lewis Carroll.
3. www.christs-hospital.org.uk/about-ch/history-of-the-school/
4. Song by Edith Piaf.

Chapter 4

1. http://www.sahistory.org.za/article/apartheid-legislation-1850s-1970s

Chapter 6

1. Song by Louis Armstrong.
2. Braai- barbeque; Mieliepap - a South African staple dish made from softly grounded maize; Boerewors – A traditional South African beef sausage.
3. CODESA: The negotiations to end apartheid in South Africa.

Chapter 7

1.   Amandla - Zulu and Xhosa word meaning "power."
2.   Awethu - Zulu and Xhosa word meaning "It is ours."

Chapter 8

1.   Soweto: South Western Townships/
2.   Wits: abbreviation for "Witwatersrand."

Chapter 9

1.   The Highland Clans, book by Alastair Moffat.

Chapter 14

1.   The Strange Case of Dr Jekyll and Mr Hyde, book by Robert Louis Stevenson.

Chapter 17

1.   Spanish phrase meaning "Merry Christmas".

Chapter 18

1.   He leadeth me beside the still waters: Psalm 23:2.
2.   War Horse: a movie based on the English novel by Michael Morpurgo.

Chapter 19

1.   "Lay aside this ardour of mind that exhausts the body and leads you to commit errors.": Fenelon.
2.   Thou shalt love thy neighbour as thyself: Mathew 22:39.

Chapter 22

1.   Don Giovanni: Opera by Wolfgang Amadeus Mozart.
2.   They live in blest eternity: Henry More.
3.   In quietness and in confidence will be your strength: Isaiah 30:15.

Chapter 24

1.   Lord I know not what I ought to ask of Thee; Fenelon.
2.   Thou only knowest what we need, Thou lovest me better than I know to love myself. Oh, Father give to thy child

that which he himself knows not how to ask. I dare not ask even for crosses or consolations; I simply present myself before Thee. I open my heart to Thee, behold of my needs that I know not myself; Smite, or heal, I adore all Thy purposes without knowing them; Teach me to pray. Pray Thyself in me: Fenelon.

Chapter 25
1. There shall no evil befall thee: Psalm 91:10.

Chapter 26
1. Surely goodness and mercy shall follow me all the days of my life: Psalm 23:6.
2. Thou shalt guide me with thy counsel, and afterward receive me to glory: Psalm 73:24.

Chapter 27
1. In the multitude of my thoughts within me thy comforts delight my soul: Psalm 94:19.

Chapter 28
1. Watch and pray: the spirit is willing, but the flesh is weak: Mathew 26:41.

Chapter 29
1. As having nothing, and yet possessing all things: 2 Corinthians 6:10.

Chapter 30
1. One day is as a thousand years, and a thousand years as one day: 2 Peter 3:8.
2. Appear I always what I am? And am I what I am pretending? And sound my word and thought the same? Anonymous.

Chapter 31
1. The Lord is thy keeper; the Lord is thy shade upon thy right hand: Psalm 121:5.
2. All things work together for good to them that love God: Romans 8:28.
3. If he falls, he humbles himself, but gets up at once, and goes on with renewed earnestness: Jean Nicolas Grou.

Chapter 32
1. The Lord gave, and the Lord hath taketh away: Job 1:21.
2. Though He slays me, yet will I trust in Him: Job 13:15.

Chapter 33
1. My Presence shall go with thee, and I will give thee rest: Exodus 33:14.
2. Did you ever hear of man who had striven all his life faithfully and singly towards an object and in no measure obtained it? H, D, Thoreau.

Chapter 35
1. But, though our outward man perish, yet the inward man is renewed day by day: 2 Corinthians 4:16.
2. Lead kindly light amid the encircling gloom, the night is dark, and I'm far from home, I do not ask to see the distant sea one step enough for me: Wordsworth.
3. To yield entire obedience to the law.
4. That I may murmur not, tho' bitter seem my lot: Rutilius, 1604.

Chapter 36
1. He will fulfil the desire of them that fear him: Psalm 145:19.
2. Delight thyself also in the Lord and he shall give thee the desires of thine heart: Psalm 37:4.
3. The Tao Te Ching: Chinese classic text, 6BC, Loazi.

4. We dwell in Him, and He in us, because He hath given us of His Spirit: 1 John 4:13.
5. Learn Thy wandering senses gently to control; Thy dearest friend, dwells deep within thy soul: G Tersteegen.
6. Be aware of your own natural spirit and temper. Be patient under the sense of your own vanity and weakness; and patiently wait for God to do his own work, and in His own way: WM Law.

Chapter 37
1. Rejoice in as much as you are: 1 Peter 4:13.

Chapter 41
1. I will instruct you and teach you in the way you should go: Psalm 32:8.
2. If thou canst believe, all things are possible to him that believeth: Mark 9:23.
3. A man can do everything with himself; but he must not attempt to do too much with others: WM von Humbolt.
4. The possibility of writing on the eternal skies the record of a heroic life: T Carlyle.

Chapter 42
1. I will lift up mine eyes unto the hills, from whence cometh my help: Psalm 121:1.
2. Singing and making melody in your heart: Ephesians 5:19.

Chapter 43
1. You shall find that your condition is never opposed to your good, but really consistent with it: H Bushnell.
2. If Thou dost perceive such feelings arising, turn gently away from them: G Tersteegen.
3. Go face the fire at sea, or the cholera in your friend's house, or the burglar in your own: R. W. Emerson.

Chapter 44

1. It is more blessed to give than to receive: Acts 20:35.
2. Who dwells in the secret place of the most High, shall abide under the shadow of the Almighty: Psalm 91:1.

Chapter 45

1. Love your neighbour as yourself: Mark 12:31.

Chapter 46

1. The Song of Solomon 1:5,6.